I'M WAITING

for **YOU**

and *Other Stories*

KIM BO-YOUNG

HARPER Voyager

An Imprint of HarperCollinsPublishers

Translated by Sophie Bowman and Sung Ryu.

This is a work of fiction. Names, characters, places, and incidents are products of the author's imagination or are used fictitiously and are not to be construed as real. Any resemblance to actual events, locales, organizations, or persons, living or dead, is entirely coincidental.

Originally published in the Republic of Korea as three separate books: 당신을 기다리고 있어 (*Dangsineul gidarigo isseo*) in 2015 by Miracle Books, 저 이승의 선지자 (*Jeo iseungui seonjija*) in 2017 by Arzak, and 당신에게 가고 있어 (*Dangsinege gago isseo*) in 2020 by Paran Media. The publication/translation of this book was supported by The Daesan Foundation and the Literature Translation Institute of Korea.

FIRST EDITION

Designed by Angela Boutin

Background image on title page and chapter openers © P-fotography/ shutterstock.com

Library of Congress Cataloging-in-Publication Data has been applied for.

ISBN 978-0-06-295146-5

21 22 23 24 25 LSC 10 9 8 7 6 5 4 3 2 1

FOR TWO AND ALL LOVERS

The way I see it,
loving one person means loving the universe.
When you do something for the sake of one person,
you do something for the whole universe.
A gift for one is a gift to all.

CONTENTS

I'M
WAITING
for YOU

I'M WAITING FOR YOU

Translated by Sophie Bowman

HIS FIRST LETTER

One day into the voyage,
one day in Earth time

I SAID GOODBYE TO THE GUYS, AS THEY WON'T BE SEEING ME until the wedding. In four years and six months, to be precise. They all said they'd come. We took photos and I gave each of them a small leather frame on a lanyard to hold the pictures. The wedding venue gave them to me for free when I paid the deposit on our booking. I told them to come to the ceremony wearing the photos around their necks so I won't have to go around asking each of them who they are. They made fun of me too. "It must be great to be getting married. Leaving your pesky friends behind, huh?" "You interstellar marrying types are all traitors."

I told them it wouldn't be an easy time for me either. I almost got punched when I added it was going to take me a whole eight weeks to get to our wedding day. A month to get up to the speed of light, and a month to slow down enough to make a safe landing. That's how it works. And that's even with the newest engine and latest gravity controller. It's always at least two months, however fancy the ship.

I REMEMBER HOW worried you were before leaving for Alpha Centauri with your family four and a half years ago.

"Are you sure you'll be all right?" you asked me. "It'll be only four months for me, but over four and a half years for you.

And that's assuming you'll take a space journey to cut your waiting time by half. It won't be easy, you know."

"I'll be fine," I said, our foreheads touching. I tried to make you laugh: "You really got lucky, didn't you! When we meet again I'll be two years older than you, instead of the other way around." Finally, you gave a goofy smile.

"You know what they say," my friends teased, "people really mellow out after an interstellar journey. Either that or go crazy. Must be something to do with spending months on end doing nothing."

I told them I wouldn't have time to loaf about. I'd have two months' worth of work with me. Different ledgers to sort out, accounts analysis, research on my firm's competitors, sales figures. To be honest, it'll all be outdated in four and a half years, but as they said at the office, they don't really expect much. They'll just be looking to see if I made the effort.

I MET SOME other grooms-to-be on the ship and we all decided to share a cabin. Every night we stay up chatting, joke around and boast about our fiancées. You won't believe how cheesy these guys are; the big romantics made the place look like a wedding cake. They hung ribbons and paper flowers around the cabin, and the ship attendants had to chase them around attaching everything to the walls with Velcro. One of the attendants explained that if the acceleration stops, we'll lose gravity, and the room would be chaos.

Speaking of hopeless romantics, I bought something for you at the flea market on board. The seller called it a "music ring" and said she could put whatever songs I wanted in it. I thought of a few for you and got her to put them in. If you press the jewel it plays one of the songs. I hope you'll give them a listen.

THE SHIP'S LIKE a small city. It's got that flea market and cafés as well. Sure, the company I work for makes parts for space vessels, but I only ever saw the parts, never all the parts put together. I get a kick out of reading the user instructions for the different parts printed on stickers around the ship. I was the one who edited them. I've even taken some photos to show my friends how my work's being used.

It's getting really dull after almost a day on board, though. I thought in space I'd get to see loads of stars, but I couldn't see a single one when I got a chance to look out a window. You know how you can't see anything when you're in a brightly lit house and it's dark outside? Well, it's always nighttime in space. Whatever, it's fine. It's only two months.

The people on board call this route the "Orbit of Waiting." It draws a helix around the sun and then returns to the place it departed from.

Everyone on the ship is emigrating to a different time, not a different place. Trying to get to the future faster, for whatever reason. Some people are traveling to the year their pension plan matures, others hope real estate taxes will come down while they're away. There are artists too, who believe they were born in the wrong era. I even met a high school student who's waiting for the new university entrance exam that's supposed to be implemented soon. And there are other dopes like me, of course, traveling to arrive back on Earth at the same time as our fiancées flying in from other stellar systems.

The year we all end up arriving in will be better than the one we left. Discrimination against people coming back from other stellar systems shouldn't be so bad, and welfare and state pensions will have improved too. The busy hive of people on Earth will rush around putting things together, taking things apart, then fixing them, right in time for us to benefit. Though I guess that's the kind of attitude people scorn with the saying "blowing your nose into someone else's hands."

It might sound over-the-top, but when I think about our wedding I'm too excited to sleep. I toss and turn in bed like a little kid, hug my pillow tight, and hum myself to sleep. When I open my eyes in the morning, I picture you lying next to me. Even just imagining us like that makes me so happy. Sometimes I hide under the blankets and dream about what it'd be like to be a dad. I even imagine a baby wriggling on the bed between us. I don't know how I'll manage to wait two more months. Another day is hard enough to bear. I wish I could be with you right now.

I love you.

HIS SECOND LETTER

One month into the voyage,
about four years and four months later in Earth time

I ONLY GOT YOUR MESSAGE WHEN WE REACHED LIGHT SPEED. So you'll be arriving on Earth two months later than planned. No, three months later in Earth time . . .

It's all right. There's nothing you could have done when your ship received an SOS signal with no other vessels around to take the call. One of the attendants here said, "It's not common, but it's not that rare either." What does that even mean? I guess he must have meant that, although the universe is boundless, the travel routes are on fixed coordinates, so things like that just happen sometimes.

I asked if they could extend our journey a little so I won't have to wait the whole three months on Earth, but they said that wasn't possible. The ship's schedule is fixed, and there's no other option, I'll just have to wait out the three months after we land.

I was looking out the window, feeling depressed, when I saw a merchant ship anchored to ours. Boxes of snacks and sacks of parcels were coming and going between them. I just stared out at the ship for a while, but then suddenly came to my senses. I asked where it was going and someone explained it was a ship that goes between passenger liners selling stuff. I asked what day it was set to arrive back on Earth, and would you believe it, it was exactly three months later! I'd hit the jackpot.

I caused a bit of a scene when I said I was going to transfer onto the other ship. I couldn't see what the problem was. "Why can't I just change ships?" I asked. "It's right there."

"That ship may appear stationary," the ship's captain bellowed back at me, "but we're currently moving at 293,000 kilometers a second. Typhoons that destroy apartment blocks are only tens of kilometers per second at most." He was so tall he towered over me and he looked like a ruthless warrior. I wish I could show you his face. He'd fit right in on some Manchurian plain beheading people from atop a galloping horse . . . if only he'd been born in the right era.

I asked why people couldn't go back and forth when objects could. He said that they just couldn't. I asked why not and he said, "Because it's never been done."

I refused to let it go and carried on. "Earth moves around the sun at thirty kilometers per second, and the sun moves around the galaxy at two hundred and twenty kilometers per second. Our galaxy is flying toward the Virgo cluster at six hundred kilometers per second. But that doesn't demolish apartment blocks on Earth, does it?"

Despite my best efforts, he kept insisting, saying there was no mention of it in the regulations.

I never dreamed I'd have to live another three months without you. I explained to the captain that I'm a groom on my way to meet my bride, and that if I had to wait an extra three months I'd probably shrivel up and die. I told him, if the waiting kills me, I'll become a vengeful bachelor spirit, wandering the universe eternally unsatisfied, and haunt his dreams every night. Luckily, he didn't seem to understand a word.

It was only after I changed ships that I wondered whether I might have made a mistake. Our wedding venue was already booked for that date, and I'd paid a big deposit. Who knows whether the message that we need to postpone for three months will get through? What can we do if they won't return our deposit?

I'm worried about the tenants I rented my apartment to as well. The agreement was that they'd live there for four and a half years and then clear out. But what if they go behind my back and claim property rights because I didn't return when I said I would? I'll have to rush straight home as soon as I land at the port.

IN THIS SHIP you don't get the feeling that you're moving. There's no wind and no noise. The stars all lean to one side, streaks across the window. All the stars in the universe shimmering in one place. On here the whole universe, Earth, my home, my friends all pass me by at the speed of light, and it feels like I'm standing perfectly still. So time is standing still for me too.

Someone once said that space and time are actually the same thing.

That would mean going to a different time is the same as going to a different place.

My dad lived his whole life in his hometown, but around the time he passed away it was like he'd traveled the entire world. In fact, he really did. By the time he passed away our hometown was a completely different place from where he was born. Buildings had been put up and roads laid, mountains flattened, and the courses of rivers diverted. Time moved him to somewhere completely different. Who could possibly say that he lived in one place his whole life?

The elderly captain of the merchant ship questioned me, so I told him about you. He asked how I could possibly still be in love after waiting so long. I explained to him that I'd been waiting for all the twenty-five years of my life before I met you.

The more I think about it, the more amazing it feels; it won't be long now. I know you'll be just like I remember you. You won't have changed a bit.

"They've got no regrets, the guys that take these ships," the captain said as he poured me another drink. It was all right up to that point, but when he went on with, "They've got no friends, no family, or even if they do, they don't like them very much . . ." I just left and came back to my cabin.

HIS THIRD LETTER

*One month and three days into the voyage,
four years and eight months later in Earth time*

I'M SORRY, SWEETHEART.

So sorry. I really didn't know things would turn out like this.

The captain said he'd made a mistake and gotten the time and acceleration calculations wrong. Someone asked how much longer it would take, and he said that for us it would only be a few minutes. Then he added that our arrival on Earth would be three years later. He went back inside his cabin with a totally bland expression, like some aircraft pilot who's just announced a delay of ten minutes due to bad weather. Merchants in Arab- and Indian-style clothes started getting up one by one and going back to their cabins without even a frown. They looked as though they were thinking, *Three years, huh? That's not so bad, I thought it'd be five at least.*

A little while later a stewardess came around handing out letter paper and told us to write to our families or close friends. When I asked, "Don't you use quantum mail or something?" she explained that the only parts of the ship made in the twenty-first century were the hull and the engine. "Even the solar wind warning system runs like a wind-up alarm clock." She added, "When it comes to machines, simple ones last the longest."

I asked how my letter would be sent, and she said it would

be converted into Morse code or something, and then transmitted out into the universe. Ships passing nearby would pick up the signals, amplify them, and send them out again. The ships that received the amplified signals would send them out again, passing on the message. *Wow,* I thought, *what a surefire way of getting through! Why didn't the postal service ever think of hurling letters from one speeding truck to another?*

I told the stewardess that I'd booked a wedding venue, that my bride was already on her way, flying 4.37 light-years to be there. How the hell can a groom be three years late for his own wedding? The attendant made a "poor you" face but didn't seem to care. She patted my shoulder and said, "If you have an important appointment it's best to take a ship run by a big corporation with comprehensive insurance."

I woke up ten times in the night. What if my letter doesn't get through? What if you get it and turn back in anger? What if you get mad and turn back but don't bother to write? What if you write a reply but I don't get it?

Every time I fell asleep again I dreamed the same dream: I disembark on Earth to find you coming toward me with one of my friends and a baby in your arms. Then you say, "A letter? I didn't get any letter," and start to laugh. Then I'm at some bar with my friends. They're all chatting away and I'm sitting in the corner alone, downing glasses of soju.

Don't laugh. I mean it. What could be more pathetic than that?

I'm begging you, sweetheart.

Wait for me.

Just three years. Please. Just three years. I promise I'll be good for the rest of our life together. What do you say, huh?

HIS FOURTH LETTER

One month and twenty-five days into the voyage,
seven years, eight months, and twenty-five days
later in Earth time

I GOT YOUR LETTER.

So mine got through after all. It was a real surprise. To be honest, it's even more surprising that your reply reached me, here on this old ship. We were both lucky, huh? Though it sounds stupid to say in these circumstances.

I'VE NO IDEA what processes your message went through, but I got it as a voicemail. It was pretty weird listening to your words spoken in a man's voice. It sounded like he didn't understand the content of what he was reading, like he was just looking at phonetic symbols and sounding them out. It was hard to decipher, so I listened to it over and over. Then, once I'd gotten the meaning, I listened to it some more.

I understand. It's all because of me. None of this was your fault. You did the right thing in changing ships. I changed ships because I couldn't bear waiting another three months to see you, but for you it would have been three years.

You said that almost as soon as you disembarked on Earth you got on the next departing ship. That you were in such a hurry you took the first ticket you could get out of there, and boarded a research vessel going prospecting instead of an Orbit of Waiting space liner. Those research ships are so old now, many of them are kept running long after they should have been sold for scrap.

Thank god you were able to take shelter after the accident, even if the facility is a long way from the usual routes.

DON'T CRY, LOVE. Every so often in the letter there was a weird "huk-huk-huk" sound, and I wondered for ages what it was. Somewhere along the line a machine must have transcribed your crying that way.

ELEVEN YEARS, THOUGH!
I listen to your letter again. This is what I can hear.

I'M FINE. JUST *a few scratches. But one of the crew died fixing the ship. Still, they're saying if it hadn't been for that crew member we wouldn't have gotten this far.*

The ship's captain says that it's only freight carriers or research vessels that pass by this space stop. And they can only take a certain number of people, so we had to draw lots. My number came out with two options. I could wait here for two more months and then board a Light Voyager back to Alpha Centauri, or else take a hibernation-type freight carrier to Earth that will arrive here next month.

I asked when the freight carrier would arrive on Earth. They said eleven years from now.

The captain told me to take the Light Voyager and go back to my family in Alpha Centauri. That Earth eleven years from now isn't a place where anyone would want to live. That it'll be uninhabitable, even for people who have been there all their lives, let alone those returning from years on other planets.

I said I had to go to Earth anyway. The other passengers all laughed when I explained that my fiancé would be waiting for me. According to them, there isn't a single man alive who would wait around for eleven years to get married.

I know it might sound strange . . . but I'm not only going there because I think you'll be waiting for me.

By the time you get this letter I'll already be in deep sleep. Write back. I'll be able to read anything you send when I wake up. Whatever you decide to do, I'll try not to be hurt. I've made my decision, you will have made yours.

Huk-huk-huk

No. It's not true.

No words could describe how much I'm hoping you'll wait for me. It's so much that I can't even bear to wish for it. So I'm going to sleep. That way the painful thoughts will stop.

Will you come out to meet me all the same? Whatever you decide. Whatever state you're in, I don't mind. I think I'll be pretty sad if there's no one waiting when I arrive. If you're not there at the port, I'll go to the wedding venue. Even if I'm on my own I can go and play make-believe.

AND THEN IT ends with a dry voice, saying, "Huk-hu-gu-huk-hu-huk."

I'M SORRY. MY sweetheart, I'm so sorry. But I can't wait eleven years.

We're already three years late. Seven and a half years have gone by on Earth. Even if I go back now, there's no guarantee my apartment or my job will still be there. Once someone's been out of contact for three years they're worth less than if they were dead. If my uncles have emptied out my bank account and shared the money out to my nieces and nephews, I can't make them give it back. If my tenant claims my apartment belongs to them, there's nothing I can say. It wouldn't be strange if my employers had gone under, considering how the economy was going when I left. And if the company's been bought up, why would they bother taking back an old employee like me?

Eleven years, no, eighteen years! In eighteen years all my friends will be ancient, and I'll have no one to hang out with. And where the hell can I use knowledge that's eighteen years out of date? Everything I know will be completely useless. There's no guessing whether ordinary workers at parts supply companies will still be able to make a living. After eighteen years of not knowing what's happening in the world, what could I do to get by?

I'm sorry. I want to go home. This isn't right. Sure, we can meet eleven years from now, but what use is a wedding if the groom is a homeless, penniless bum? I guess we just weren't meant to be. I don't know what went wrong, or when it all started, but everything's a mess.

You have to stay healthy. Take care of yourself. They say hibernation travel takes a toll on the body. When you get to Earth I'll treat you to lots of good food. I'll be there to meet you. I can promise that much. I'll be there, I won't forget. I promise. I love you.

HIS FIFTH LETTER

Two months into the voyage,
seven years and nine months later in Earth time

How've you been?

You haven't seen the last letter yet, right?

Yeah, of course you haven't. It'll take a few more years. But you will have read that letter by the time you read this one.

I . . . well . . . I came back home. Actually, just to the port on Earth. I couldn't go home. Well, I couldn't go to the port either. I was stuck on the ship for a week, unable to put my feet on the ground. They put us through all kinds of tests. Fumigation, vaccinations, even a mental health screening. I filled out twenty pages of forms, and I had to do it three times over. When I said, "I've filled these out already," I got shouted at. There seemed to be thirty different departments working on processing arrivals. The TV on the ship only showed the news, and only one channel at that. All the internet portals had gone down too, so I couldn't access my emails.

After a week of our being stuck on the ship in the port, some plucky kid still wet behind the ears stormed in with a trail of recruits behind him and started mouthing off. He had a real temper, like he had a stomachache. He went on and on about how it's all because of the old generation, people like us; it was our laziness and inaction that got the country into such a mess. That was a bit much, I thought. It'd only been seven years.

According to this guy, a terrorist group had taken over Seoul. But the city was still safe. I couldn't understand what that was supposed to mean. The brave national forces would put the insurrection down soon enough, he said, but we couldn't be processed properly if we entered the port, so we should leave and come back later. There was a big commotion with people clamoring to get off and go home, but the grumpy kid and his entourage just left.

A little later a woman from the Red Cross or Lawyers for Democracy or somewhere came in and told us that there had been a military coup. The party that had lost the election had proclaimed martial law and seized control of congress, but citizens were fighting back. When someone asked what the UN was doing, she explained that America had filed for bankruptcy the year before, and the whole world was in economic collapse in the aftermath. So the overall situation wasn't great.

She said that if we came back in about ten years' time the global economy should be in a better state, and things would be much more stable. She told us to get a move on. That this was our last chance to escape, while the country was still relatively safe. If we waited much longer and a declaration was made restricting port traffic, then we really would be stranded.

I managed to get the aid worker's attention and explained that I'd booked a wedding venue. I asked her to look into whether I could get my deposit back, but she just blinked at me a few times and left.

Ha, you know what?

As we took off from the port there was only one thing I was wishing for.

That the last letter I sent to you wouldn't get through!

I should have waited a few days before sending it, gotten back to Earth and scoped out the situation first. What was so urgent that I had to reply straightaway? You won't get it for a good few years anyway.

It would have been great if I hadn't sent it. I would've had an excuse to get off the hook every time I came home late from after-work drinks. "Oho, what's a couple of hours every now and then? Have you already forgotten that I waited for you for eleven whole years?"

Daydreams like that make me feel better. But then I remember that ship has already sailed, my letter was sent, and I get depressed again.

I was wondering about whether I could somehow blackmail the captain of your ship into destroying the letter. But then I heard it's artificial intelligence. How do you go about blackmailing a computer? Maybe I could try sweet-talking it instead, with the promise of new memory chips.

You know, sweetheart, wouldn't it be really funny if we both disembarked in the port at the same time? The moment I see you I'll hug you tight, tell you I love you, and beg for your forgiveness. And to mark the occasion, let's make a bonfire and send every trace of our letters up into the sky as smoke.

HIS SIXTH LETTER

Four months into the voyage,
thirteen years and nine months later in Earth time

It's been a while.

Wait, you wouldn't know that, would you. I heard you didn't get my last letter. A message came back saying the recipient was in deep sleep. That any letters would be collected and given to you all in one go when you wake. That captain of yours really gets things done. You're in good hands.

I returned to Earth.

A bit earlier than the planned ten years. The whole ship was in uproar; supplies were short after leaving in such a hurry last time. The loudest complainer by far was a lady who said her skin would be ruined if she couldn't stock up on her favorite moisturizer. Someone was threatening to sue the ship's insurance company and some man kept going on about how he was friends with a third-term congressman. When people protested, I went and shouted along with the mob. I was worried about all sorts of things, of course: my apartment, my bank account, and my job. I'd prepared so many documents, it was hard work just sorting through them all. Proof of identity, proof of residence, litigation invoices for unpaid rent from my tenant. I'd also prepared papers for reclaiming my assets in case anyone had made off with them.

The captain was in no hurry. In fact, he looked like he

wasn't interested in going back at all. Thinking about it now, the crew had probably gotten word somehow.

In the end, we returned to port six years later, though it was only a couple of months for us.

As we got closer to Earth, something felt odd. I couldn't see Korea. It took a while before I realized the reason. There were no lights. At night the Korean peninsula always glimmered, like it'd been sprinkled with gold dust. But it was dark. As if no one had turned on the lights. As if no one was there at all.

As we landed I was thrown around by the ship shaking violently. When the passengers, already on edge, complained, the captain said the runway was a mess. People disembarked, muttering things like "What a load of nonsense," but it really was a mess. Weeds grew lush in patches of soil between the churned-up strips of tarmac. The completely rusted sign at the port had buckled over.

We waited beside the ship, but no bus arrived. People started walking to the waiting room, but the ground was thick with sticky mud. Someone mouthed off about the shoddy maintenance of the port.

The waiting room was empty. Inside, everything was covered with a layer of brown dust and the caved-in floor was flooded. Water weeds grew in the big puddle, with insects hatching and swarming about. The lady who'd been shouting about where to find the duty-free shop stood with her mouth open.

My mind flashed back to the thought that passing through time is no different than passing through space. That was when it hit me. I can't go home. The home I set out from is gone, left behind in some past time. There's no way I can go back.

Everyone was standing there in a daze holding their luggage when someone right beside me crumpled to the floor. I couldn't understand why they'd fallen over like that when there was nothing to trip on. Everyone just looked, like me. Until the puddle started to turn red. Until the second person fell.

In the midst of all the screams and struggle, time dragged in slow motion and then at certain instants it flew by so fast I couldn't catch a thing. I ran and hid. I shoved and kicked people aside. Even after I came to my senses, I hadn't really. For a long time, I stayed still, long after it grew silent. When I finally crawled out of my hiding spot, there were bodies strewn everywhere.

A voice ordered those who weren't injured to help those who were. I was swept around like a ghost. The lady who'd been looking for moisturizer moaned and groaned as I changed her bandages. Then she fell quiet and I realized she was dead.

Like the time before, people with guns rounded us up and some man gave a speech. Apparently if they hadn't come to our rescue we'd have all been killed. Well, fair enough. The man got all angry, saying people from the past were clueless. The group called themselves a civil militia, and they told us not to come back because there were gangs of thieves who roamed the port preying on unsuspecting travelers.

The man told us we were lucky. But I couldn't see how. Apparently, they were the only ones looking out for the chumps arriving from the past. And with that, they raided our bags and the whole ship, taking everything. They really might have been good guys, though. They left behind the things people begged them not to take. I barely managed to hold on to the music ring I got for you. I explained to the guy going through my bag that the jewel wasn't real, that it was just a toy. I pressed it to play a song and the line "My dear, how I love you so . . ." rang out. He snorted, threw it in my face, and moved on.

I went after him. I couldn't bring myself to ask about the wedding venue, but I stammered that a freight ship would be arriving in five years' time and asked him to look out for it. He glanced back at me and said it wouldn't come. All ships that had gotten news were rerouted. My fiancée won't know that, I said, because she's asleep. "Why's she sleeping?" he asked. Then he walked away before I could speak.

FOR A LONG time we all wandered around like elderly employees laid off in a reorganization. A few people just left, saying they were going home. Their battered cases clunked along behind them.

We fixed the radio in the ship and listened to the news. It was the kind of radio where you have to put up an antenna and set the frequency, a model I'd only ever seen in museums. Still, in such a situation, it was the only thing that worked.

We heard that there'd been an explosion at a nuclear facility in the south. The martial law command had executed a bunch of nuclear technicians and the next day there was a huge accident. The media was shut down for a month in the wake of it and all the other specialists went into hiding. With twenty-two more nuclear power stations in the country and everyone who looked after them long gone, they said that another one might blow up at any moment. The Korean peninsula was proclaimed a disaster zone and other countries passed decrees banning travel to the entire region.

THE CAPTAIN AND his crew announced they were going to another solar system. I told them that I had to come back to this port in five years, that my bride was on her way. Of course, I mentioned the venue booking too. That I'd already handed out the party favors to my friends.

I guess the captain thought I looked pathetic. He produced a small spacecraft from out of the ship and said I could have it. It looked like it was made around the twentieth century. "Simple means durable," the old captain said.

The ship was about the size of a small room and looked all right for one person to live in. The captain said, "You won't be able to hold out very long in this thing, so go a fair way and then settle down somewhere." I said I'd be fine; back when I was jobless I'd stayed locked up in my room for a couple of months playing computer games. And so, without a word, the captain put his hand on my shoulder and sat me down.

He opened a notepad and started drawing diagrams and explaining what I had to do.

With this tiny ship, I couldn't go to another star system. He said, "It'd be like trying to cross the Pacific in a canoe." But I didn't have to go to another star system, I protested. I got as far as "My wife-to-be is on her way . . ." He cut me off with "Whatever you say, son." The ship accelerated using solar wind and a solar battery, he explained. He told me to ride the orbit of Jupiter, because the gravitational force would help with propulsion. Then he worked out how much propulsion it would give me.

He also calculated the amount of acceleration the ship, not to mention my body, could withstand. All things considered, the maximum propulsion would be gravitational acceleration.

I couldn't remember what "gravitational acceleration" meant. About ten meters per second, the captain said, with the speed of light around 300,000 kilometers per second. I still sat there completely blank. He explained that to get up to light speed in my ship I would have to accelerate for a year. To go forward five years, or by however many years, it would take two years, taking into account both the acceleration and deceleration times.

The captain was adamant I wouldn't be able to do it. That there was no way to load two years' worth of food into the ship. Even if it could all be packed in, it would go bad before the time was up. The ship wouldn't get off the ground loaded with two years' worth of food anyway.

HIS SEVENTH LETTER

One year and one month into the voyage,
fourteen years and six months later in Earth time

Sorry it's taken me so long to write.

Honestly, it's taken me long enough to work out how to send a letter at all. It seemed absurd to start with, but then once I understood the principles of it, I think it'd probably be possible to send a letter even if the whole of human civilization were gone.

I set off without a second thought at first. Then when my food supplies were half gone I came back. I rifled through abandoned stores and collected up canned foods, then went back into space. I did that a few times.

Believe me, though, with the state I was in then, that was the best I could manage.

I tried going to another country too, just on the off chance. A woman I met there said that the fact my ship hadn't been shot down by pirates was the kind of good fortune that couldn't come around more than once a century. "What do you mean?" I said. "It hasn't even been a century since interstellar travel first took off." She said it must be because my ship was so small, they probably don't even realize it's a ship at all. What a thing to say.

Still, thanks to that encounter I gained a feed maker. The way it works is a bit like a 3D printer. It's technology that didn't exist even a decade ago. Whatever you put in it, dirt or stones or whatever, gets dismantled at the molecular level and then recombined. When it's ready, something edible, a bit like dog food, comes out.

As she gave me the feed maker, the woman said I was the kind of lucky person that only appears once or twice a millennium. And she added that if that wasn't the case I'd surely die in my next voyage. She asked me, "What on earth were you thinking getting into a tiny ship like that and traveling around in space?" When I responded that I hadn't thought anything at all, she said she'd guessed as much.

THE THIRD TIME I came back I found a car and drove to my old workplace. The streets were quiet but I felt like I was being attacked. The road was full of dark gaping potholes, and shopfront windows like empty eye sockets seemed to glare at me. Packs of dogs prowled around the streets, acting like they'd never been tamed. They growled ferociously, as if to prove that dogs could never have behaved another way.

I needed a device for collecting space matter. There's hydrogen, oxygen, calcium, sodium, water, and organic material out there. Just in incredibly small amounts. But if it's collected at the speed of light, it builds up. I should be passing through space fast enough. I figured I could think of it like making a giant vacuum cleaner. I went to the workshop to get the parts I needed, double-checking all the names, and set the machines running with the emergency generator. I don't know about anything else, but the factory manual was still saved under my old password. I had to make the device as simple as possible. So I could fix it on my own.

While I was working, out of the window in the distance, I saw a skyscraper start to slant.

At first I thought it was my body leaning over, then dust swirled up and the huge building crumpled without a sound.

Like a sandcastle in the incoming tide, like a dead, dried-out tree.

"Would you look at that," I murmured as I watched it. Back when it was being built, people said that building wouldn't last more than ten years.

I thought of that time we visited the house in the country-side that your family had left empty for a few years. In such a short time that house had become a complete eyesore. The toilet was blocked and the drainpipes and boiler had cracked and exploded. The places where the sun shone in were dried up and crumbly, while the places it didn't reach were soggy with mold.

It seemed like the house had been aged to a rotting crust by loneliness. Like it was saying: *What's the use in carrying on when life is this lonely?* As though in the space of a couple of years it had lived two decades alone.

"I told you, if there's no one living in a home it gets like this in no time," you said as you stroked the discolored doorframe. "I should have been here for it."

It felt to me like you were smoothing my hair, not stroking the doorframe. Like you were speaking to a past me, so lonely before I met you. To that me who was always alone.

AND NOW THREE months have passed since I last set out.

It's taken three months for me to come to my senses. Now I've come to my senses I'm starting to realize what a crazy thing it is I've done.

I told you, didn't I, that I once spent a few months alone in my room without stepping outside once.

I think I know now. That wasn't actually living alone. I have never once really lived alone. Someone cleared away the trash I left out for collection, and emptied out the septic tank. They ran the power stations and connected up power lines, in-spected the gas valves and replaced the water in the cooler and cleaned out the drains. In another place they boiled noodles and put them in a dish and delivered them, then came back to collect the empties, cleaned them and used them again. I had never lived alone, not once. How would really living alone even be possible?

Back then, just the fact of living meant I wasn't alone.

Every time I wake I think: *This can't be happening. I'm going to die. If I don't die today, then it'll be tomorrow.*

I can't keep the feed down anymore. I throw everything up whenever I try to eat. I thump the walls, shouting, "I've got to go back! Someone save me!" but even if I want to go back now, I still have to spend as much time as I've been out here already decelerating.

It's all right.

It's all right. It's only two years.

Because of me, because I did something stupid, you're coming to this dangerous era, not knowing what you'll find. What if you come, not knowing what to expect, and then have something terrible happen to you like what happened to me?

HIS EIGHTH LETTER

Three years, two months, and three days into the voyage,
nineteen years, two months, and three days later in Earth time

I WENT TO THE PORT IN TIME FOR THE DAY YOU WERE SUPPOSED to arrive.

I thought that if a team of bandits or vigilantes showed up I'd be killed in an instant. But no one came.

In the meantime, there must have been a flood or something, because the port was covered in soil and had become a wild plain. On the soil there was mugwort and horseweed growing lush and green. I was reminded of the time I went to the district office to complain about how they hadn't come to do repair work fast enough after a flood in my old village.

I hadn't realized before that there was a small stream running right through the middle of the port. I guess the water had been rerouted to the sea with a pump or something until then. The waiting room was covered with creeping vines and looked like a small mound. The windows had all been broken or blown out and were just empty frames. But, despite all that, there were still biscuit wrappers littered around and traces of where we'd made meals there five years ago. I had to laugh.

You didn't come.

I waited all through the night and all of the next day but you didn't come.

I lay in the field and watched the stars come out and then

fade again. I watched the sea of stars floating past the Earth. I imagined that I was on a gigantic boat. Which was kind of true. *It's all right,* I thought. *If it's a journey that takes about an hour, it wouldn't be strange to be ten minutes late. With a ten-year journey it'd be normal enough to be a year late.*

I didn't wait a whole year. But I did wait four months and three days. I slept in the ship and made meals out of soil with the electric cookpot.

You didn't come.

But for some reason I wasn't sad. Well, I wasn't happy either.

Just serene. It felt like a completely inevitable and natural turn of events. If you had appeared from between the tall reeds, I probably would have said something like, "Wow. Who knew such a preposterous thing could really happen? It's too weird. You'll have to go back and come out again a bit later."

After that I took off.

There was no real reason for me to leave. Because I no longer had any reason to go to the future. But I couldn't work out what to do if I stayed either. At least if I went to the future the pollution would have eased up and there would be a more livable environment. I didn't think any further ahead than that. I didn't have the nerve to think at all, really.

I thought anywhere but here would be fine. A place where I wouldn't be reminded of any of this. You included.

HIS NINTH LETTER

Five years and two months into the voyage,
(maybe around) seventy-four years later in Earth time

Sorry it's been so long since I last wrote. But, you know, when I sent the last letter I was in a bad way. I didn't want to think about you. I guess it'd be more precise to say I didn't have the energy to think at all. Sometimes, I felt so betrayed in the midst of my own imaginings that I gnashed my teeth, and other times there were flights of fancy that made me sob.

I thought that maybe you weren't able to send letters. Or you could still be writing emails to my old Hanmail address. The next moment I got angry at the fact that you hadn't sent any word. I also thought, maybe you hadn't received a single one of my letters. The next moment I was angry again, thinking that must be impossible. And after that I would start sobbing again.

I'll confess. For a long time I was just surviving.

I went through my things one day and came across all those documents I'd prepared before, like the account book I wrote and the legal papers I'd put together. It must have set something off inside me. I ripped them all to shreds then bawled my eyes out. I must have lost consciousness after that.

One day I pissed onto the walls of the ship. I left the drops of urine in the air, floating around, as they went into my nose and mouth and seeped into all the gaps in the machinery. I was completely powerless, like a cancer patient in their final days.

Then I got really sick. Whatever passed my lips came shooting straight out again one way or another. I couldn't handle it. It felt like all of me was spilling out and I would soon disappear. I barely managed to breathe, but every time I inhaled it was urine-laced air. It was only when drops of it started to build up in my nose and block my airways that I came to my senses. I fumbled on the dashboard and started the accelerator. When gravity kicked in, the urine fell down like rain. Everything that'd been floating about came down to the floor and I passed out in a heap.

I don't know why I lived. But thinking about it, I also don't know why I was trying to die. Well, that's kind of what death is, when a person does nothing at all; like that deserted city. You have to be doing something, anything, to be alive. You need to have some kind of will, and not give in.

I SUFFERED A terrible fever, and only when I started to recover did I remember that I was traveling at the speed of light. How long was I knocked out for? An hour? A day? A month? A year? How much time went by outside? The surroundings didn't tell me anything. I shook the clock the old captain had given me, but the coil hadn't been wound up right and the stupid thing had stopped working. There was no way of knowing.

I SLOWED THE ship down, and when Earth came into view the bad feeling I had turned into horror. Earth looked like the moon. Dark and bumpy, like life had never once existed there.

IT WAS ONLY after I went in closer that I realized the gloomy, rough-looking surface was actually dark clouds. The whole of Earth was shrouded. There was no way to tell where I should land. It was just a big swirling of black cloud.

It was only a while later that I realized I was screaming. After that I rested my head on the dashboard and wept. When I was little I witnessed a landslide come down near the back of our house. Another house was completely swept away by the soil. Luckily there was no one inside at the time, but I screamed as I watched it happen. Mom said she had to hold me tight in her arms for about an hour before I calmed down. I would always scream in the face of things disappearing. Faced with things being ruined, breaking apart, aging, becoming obsolete, decomposing, dying, and collapsing. I mourned things that were lost in one monstrous stroke and could never be brought back.

The thought occurred to me that it must have been a war. Some terrible bomb from a research lab had sent ash up into the stratosphere, and then the ash that had gotten up there stayed blanketing the Earth. Or else an asteroid or some big foreign object might have hit. I heard somewhere that would have a similar effect. Or else . . .

Why am I here? Why am I able to see something like this?

I want to go home. I tried imagining that I'd gotten into a time machine and come to get a look at the future. I could just say to myself, "Aha, so this is what the future's like," and then return to my time and brag about it to my friends. "You'll never guess what! I went and saw the future." "What? Damn. The lottery! Did you check the lottery numbers?" "Oh shit, I forgot to look them up." "How stupid can you get?"

But I can't go back in time. How could I get back? If I were to go home, would I have anything to do anyway?

I had a wedding venue booked. We were planning to get married. What would we have to do to coincide?

I WENT DOWN to the port. When I broke through the atmosphere and descended I could see the lay of the land. I did think of just leaving again without landing, but I'd imagined so many different terrible scenarios, I thought it would be better to see what had really happened.

It was daytime, but it was no different from the middle of the night. The port was buried in snow and a blizzard was swirling like a white sandstorm, so I couldn't make out a thing. Ice had formed along the coastline, so it was impossible to identify the old topography. Worried that my engine would freeze in the cold, I thought about taking off again.

And then I stopped.

There were traces of a ship having landed. A patch of snow was melted in the shape of a ship. Less melted, more compacted, in a shape like a huge bowl had been pressed into the ice. The raging wind and snow were covering it up fast. It must have been here not long ago. A few weeks at most, maybe a few days, or else just now.

I ran over, my feet sinking deep into the snow with every step, and dug around inside the hole. As though if I dug deep enough I would find the ship. Digging around I saw more traces. It seemed like the same ship had come some time before. And many other times before that.

I battled my way through the snow like a madman trying to get somewhere. My feet sank, I was blocked by snow and fell over. I screamed out your name with all my might, but the raging snowstorm swallowed my voice. Beyond the dim fog there was a line of skyscrapers, like a crowd of ghosts.

There's no guarantee it was your ship. But there's also no guarantee that it wasn't.

I've just hurried up into my ship to write this letter. I'll come back to the port this time ten years from now. If you look at the place and time this letter is from you should be able to work the timing out. If you get this letter please come to the port.

I'll be waiting.

HIS TENTH LETTER

Seven years and two months into the voyage,
(I guess around) eighty-four years later in Earth time

You didn't come.

I was met instead by a ship I had forgotten all about. Seems they came after getting my letters. You know the first ship I took? That I said was just like a small city. The ship with cafés and a flea market.

I was able to recognize it, but it was somehow different. Time had formed a strange crust on the ship like moss or mold. It was more yellowing, decayed, and stinky than when I had passed through.

When I saw the people on board I remembered what my friends had said to me right before I first set out. You know, that people who go interstellar traveling get either really calm or really crazy. I think those people would come under the crazy category. Not that I'm any better.

Even before I got out of my ship the people were already angry.

I guess no one could ever have imagined that someone could ride such a small ship, and alone at that, all the way here. By here I don't mean this place but this time. I'm certain they were all convinced they'd meet a ship like a hypermart, filled with instant noodles, frozen meat, and supplies.

The people dragged me out of my ship and tipped it over. They ripped out the parts, yanked out the wires, and forced off the gauges, the drawers, everything, then threw it all into the snow. When I tried to stop them, they clobbered me. Every time I tried to stop them I got hit, so later on I just stood there. But that didn't mean they didn't hit me anymore. Once they'd rifled through everything and turned the ship inside out, they seemed to be twice as angry. The whole ship just stank of urine and there was nothing in there that was edible.

In their worst-case scenario they probably expected a huge battleship and were ready to fight, but the only thing they had to beat was me, so it seemed like they were three times angrier. I was sure I was going to die, but perhaps they thought it was a waste to kill me. If I died they wouldn't be able to beat me anymore. Or else it was no fun beating me once I'd passed out and didn't respond, so they left me be.

I was put in a cell in the big ship, where I met the captain again. You know, that guy I said looked as though he were living in the wrong era. Seems as though he found his perfect time. He looked like an old lion that's survived right in the middle of the savannah. He was slick and lean and full to bursting with a self-assurance that made me wince. His eyes gave away that he had invested his survival with something like divine providence.

Seems he read all my letters. He read right through every single one of them, with me there, my body throbbing so hard I couldn't move. As he was reading he kept sniggering. He explained that because he hadn't been able to watch any television dramas these days, listening to my letters was a rare source of joy. He asked me to write a few more. I shuddered with the overwhelming thought that I had to wipe this bastard out once and for all. In my head I was making up comic-book lines like: "He has uncovered my deepest indignity. I must destroy him," you know the kind of thing.

He asked me how I got this far on my own, and when I didn't answer he started to strangle me. And then he loosened his grip, as though satisfied that a person's life or death was in his hands. His expression was unbearable.

When I asked why they hadn't gone to another star system when they had such a big ship, he told me they were going home. When I responded that home wasn't there anymore he said that it didn't matter, they were still going back. That everyone else on the ship, all of them wanted to go back home. But I knew there was no way someone who held people's ultimate fate, other people's life or death in their hands, could ever really know what another person wanted.

He let me out of the cell to take a look around the ship. I'm sure letting me go gave him just as much pleasure as he would have gotten from killing me, since he'd exercised his power. I stayed on board with the thought that once my wounds had healed I had to leave again. When I went to the on-board doctor and asked her to bandage my wounds, she found it absurd, but still helped me out anyhow. I knew she would help me. Because the people on the ship hadn't beaten me because there was anything to gain from it. If I had been on that ship too, who knows what I might have done to some lone traveler.

I thought about how lucky it was that you didn't show up.

And it dawned on me that now I would never be able to meet you.

I realized that if you were to have made it this far you'd need to be on a really big ship. And that if you were on a big ship you wouldn't be able to have it go wherever you pleased. A vessel of this size wouldn't turn its course just to let you meet with one man, especially not one in such a beggar-like state.

You can't come to meet me.

We're like people praying that we'll bump into each other by chance as we're rushed along in an infinitely wide river surging in one direction. The river has no end and there's no way of traveling upstream.

A scientist who lived back in the twentieth century once said that there surely must be aliens out there but we cannot meet them. That it isn't a problem of not being able to cross space, it's because the time it would take to travel blocks the distance between star and star. The way they explained it was funny; that although Earth has been around for 4.5 billion years, humanity was only born a mere two million years ago, and it's only been twenty thousand years since we began sitting around to eat meals and have meaningful conversations, so even for an alien to come and meet with us for a cup of tea, they'd have to travel such a vast distance and arrive at the meeting point inside such a short window of time.

WHILE THE PASSENGERS from the big ship went back and forth to the seashore in a line like penguins, casting nets and bringing in their catch, I went back to my beat-up ship. I gathered up all the things that had been flung about and started putting it together again. Fortunately the sun came out, otherwise the scraps would all have frozen in place and turned into fossils.

As time went on I developed an audience. They even brought me parts that I didn't have enough of. When I needed a component, I spoke the name of the material. They even took things out of kids' toys and buttons from clothing for me to work with. Among those people there were some who had beaten me till I passed out. We didn't say anything to each other. Who knows, if the roles were reversed, I might have joined in with the beating. And I probably would have gone in with all my might, trying to make a good impression.

When they'd filled up their food store I got into my ship too. As I closed the hatch I thought I heard you saying to me, "You should go with them. You'll be able to live a little longer."

I felt you taking hold of my hand as it closed the hatch. "No matter how far you carry on, we can't meet. You should do what you can to stay alive."

I snapped back that the captain had intercepted all my letters. For that reason there was no way I could go with them.

HIS ELEVENTH LETTER

Eight years and eight months into the voyage,
145 years later in Earth time (at a rough guess)

WHEN I CAME BACK, EARTH WAS FROZEN OVER, LEAVING JUST the area around the equator. The clouds had cleared, but I figure it was caused by the cloud cover.

I once heard that Earth is actually close to being an ice planet. That humanity is pretty much like plants that have a one-day life span: flourishing during a very short summer. I heard that an ice age can be brought on by a very slightly long winter. If a little more snow falls than the year before, and the permafrost grows just a little, the slightly increased snow cools the Earth down a fraction, and the next year a little more snow falls than the year before, and it all repeats.

Those dark clouds would have blocked off the sun for a year. That would be plenty to bring on an ice age.

The coastline would lower and glaciers would form. The map of the Earth we once knew would be totally transformed. The tidal currents would change and the changed currents would carve away at the land in different ways. The new glaciers would push down on the land and grow the topography, so it would be irreversibly transformed forever. The slow creeping of the glaciers would crush all traces of human life to powder, with their bodies of ice weighing hundreds of millions of tons. The pathetic vestiges that had just about managed to hang on between the water weeds and reeds would all be ground to dust.

I slowed down just enough to confirm this from a distance and then accelerated again. I thought, let's come back when the world has warmed up a bit.

It won't take that long anyway.

HIS TWELFTH LETTER

Nine years and two months into the voyage,
170 years later in Earth time (at a rough guess)

I'M WAITING FOR YOU.

Even if you're already nowhere to be found. Even if you settled down years ago, on some distant star, met a good guy, had ten kids, and lived out your days surrounded by an adoring family. Or else, you're traveling along on some distant trajectory of light, waiting for Earth to recover. Even if, somehow or other, you're just stepping out of a ship off in a distant star system, remembering me like some quaint memory from your youth. "Ah, yes, I had a man like that once. But he must have died a long time ago, in some other time stream."

IT TAKES A whole day's work to survive another day.

If I let things go, even for just a few hours, time expands endlessly. I have this premonition: the moment I can no longer control the endlessly expanding time, that's when I'll be done for.

I set an alarm clock to go off at regular intervals. Regardless of what time it may be outside, I sleep at the same time and wake up at the same time. I exercise at the same time every day and eat the same amount of food at the same time too. After all, there's no one to fix my body for me if it breaks down.

The ship keeps creaking from somewhere. I'm pretty sure the moisture from when I pissed everywhere is still causing problems with the machinery. If I start trying to fix something a whole day goes by. I study the ship's instruction manual daily. After all, no one's going to know it on my behalf.

I STARTED GROWING vegetables in the ship. With just one seed, a few months later you get hundreds of times more. I need the natural oxygen they make. In the beginning most of them died, but now they all seem to have adjusted a fair bit. Which means recently I've been able to eat something besides the feed made by that dirt-transformer machine.

ONE DAY I awoke feeling like I couldn't breathe. I thought, *I've got to open a window.* I had to open a window and let in some air. It was night outside. I just assumed I must have slept in real late. Then I realized, *Oh crap, today's the wedding. I've got loads to prepare.* I went to open the window. It wouldn't open. What kind of stupid window doesn't have a handle? So I got out the wrench I keep in my pocket. I thought, *I'll have to smash it open.* I was sure I'd die if I had to endure another minute with that damn window closed. How long had it been since the ship was aired out? The place reeked of stale sweat and urine. I was about to smash the window when my other hand grabbed the hand brandishing the wrench. I stayed huddled up, clutching that trembling hand, until I came to my senses.

I heard you say, "I'm here. I'm waiting for you."

I WOULDN'T HAVE been able to gain back control if I hadn't had that thought.

So you saved my life. Whatever age you're in now, whether you're dead already, or still alive somewhere, traveling among infinite clusters of stars.

HIS THIRTEENTH LETTER

Nine years and seven months into the voyage,
(could be) 223 years later in Earth time

WHEN I WAS SLEEPING, THE SHIP STARTED VIBRATING. It seemed like it wasn't just my ship but the whole solar system that was being shaken hard. I looked out the window and saw a huge meteor colliding with Earth. It must have been crashing at a dreadful speed, but it was so huge it seemed to be going in slow motion. Even this far away, I could see the oceans surging upward with the impact. The water that exploded out spread to the surroundings and in an instant had boiled up into a hot red wind engulfing the land. But the Earth looked so tiny I couldn't feel a thing.

Back when that planet was full of people, they would have been able to do something about it.

While I was staring straight at it, Earth became a ball of fire. At that rate the entire atmosphere would have been burned up. And the oceans would all have boiled away. There would be nothing left alive . . .

Then I woke up.

But once I was awake I couldn't tell where the dream began and ended. When I had a dream that felt too real, I used to think about which side was completely implausible, and then I'd think, ah, that's right, the side that isn't plausible must be the dream, but these days there's no telling between the two.

Music was flowing out of the ring I'd left on the table. *The ring is singing. This must be the dream,* I thought. When I looked around me, the grooms in waiting who'd boarded the same ship were snoring away, all tangled together on the floor. There were flowers and ribbons hung from the walls, and banners with the words ABOUT TO GET HITCHED were stuck up here and there.

I went out of the room to look around the inside of the passenger ship like a small city. People were walking around dressed up as though they were going for a summer picnic. They all looked excited and happy. *Aha!* I thought, *it was all a dream, thank goodness it was only a dream.* On the high ceiling of the ship, along with the captain's face looking down on us, there was a glowing neon sign that read WE'RE GOING HOME. So of course I thought, *Wait a second, that's impossible.*

I found you sitting among a group of people, looking just the way you did when you left. No, just as you looked when we first met. Just as you were when I accidentally smeared ice cream on your newly bought clothes while working my part-time job.

It was I who burst into tears then, scared that I'd have to give up my whole paycheck in compensation. And it was you who took me into the bathroom, saying, "Don't worry, we can hide the whole incident from your manager." We worked together to get out that chocolate stain that seemed like it would never budge.

"Oh, goodness me! Look at that man over there."

The people who were sitting with you got a shock when they saw me.

"The groom looks so much older. Oh, what can she do! It's just embarrassing."

Not knowing how to react, you bowed your head. With bloodied bandages wrapped around her stomach, the woman who'd been looking for moisturizer whispered in your ear.

"That young man you fell for is gone now. Even if you do meet him, he's not the same person. Time is a brutal thing, you know."

I pushed my way through between the people, grabbed your hand and pulled you up. "You have to get out of here. Out from among these clowns. These people are nailed into the past. They haven't grown or aged a day."

I've gotten older. Each day a day older. Each month a month older. Each year a year. I've lived with time mounting inside my body. And that means I'm just right for you. I've become someone more suited to you than I was ten years ago. I've become a more all right person than hundreds of years ago. Tomorrow I'll become someone a day more suited to you. Next year, I'll become that much more again.

And when I opened my eyes I was inside my ship. I was afloat along with everything else in there. Only the ring playing a song was the same as it had been in the dream.

I closed my eyes and opened them again. When I opened my eyes you were here with me. You were lying on top of me. Well, depending on how you look at it you could say that I was the one on top too.

You spoke to me. "Let's have a baby here."

"Here?" I laughed.

"In this world, flowing by at the speed of light. In a world where time doesn't pass. The child won't think that it's weird at all. This time stream will be their home, it'll be all they know." You whispered in my ear, "Instead they'll think the other timelines that flow slowly are unnatural. They won't get scared or feel out of place, like us, every time they reach a new timeline. Just like you didn't find it weird going from being twenty to twenty-one, they'll think that passing a thousand or two thousand years of time is completely natural. They won't get sad about time that has passed by. They won't cry when they see things disappearing. They'll think of it as natural and inevitable.

"Our child won't keep having to feel their way like we do. They won't wander around tied down by gravity either. They'll fly out to the ends of infinity. They'll come to see all the things that we can't."

Yeah, that'd be amazing.

If only we manage to meet.

HIS FOURTEENTH LETTER

Ten years and two months into the voyage,
no idea about Earth time

I was outside trying to fix the sail when an alarm started going off. It meant that a solar wind was approaching. Even having heard the alarm, I was looking out to space. I was just looking at a star cluster raining down.

"All right, all right," I said to the alarm. I wasn't intending to die. I knew that I had five minutes to spare and I could easily take shelter in that time. No, I'm not sure. I was just simply staring at the stars. I thought of the countless glowing lives over there on the far side of time.

I came back into the ship four minutes later. I got inside the shelter capsule within one minute and fell straight to sleep. I don't know what happened after that, but when I tried to get out the door was locked.

I didn't cry. I just thought, *It'd be pretty shitty to die stuck in here*. Remembering all the times before now when I could have died, I thought I would have been better off if I'd died then. But I don't think it would've been easy however it happened. Then I fell asleep again.

As soon as I fell asleep you were there. When I greeted you with "You're here!" you suddenly started telling me off. You said, "I went to the church on the day we arranged. Where have you been? What the hell have you been doing all this time?

There's never been anyone who would humiliate their bride like this." I used up all my energy trying to console you.

When I came to, I really came to my senses. When I came to my senses, you also became calm.

"You stuck your tool pouch to your leg, remember?" you said. "You stuck it on there with Velcro."

"Oh yeah, I'm really not in my right mind."

When I reached my hand down, you said, "Don't drop it. You won't be able to find it again in here."

With a screwdriver, I picked at the gap in the door and found the latch that had dropped into place on the other side.

Just like when you and I tried to wash out that chocolate ice cream stain, we put our heads together and sweated profusely.

"The latch is really stuck. What if the screwdriver breaks first?"

"That's possible," I said. "But I want to think about that after it's happened. If we worry about that in advance we're needlessly thinking twice as much."

That was when I realized I was repeating exactly what you'd said that day word for word. I also remembered how I stared blankly at you when you said that. And how, at that very moment, I fell in love with you.

"It's funny," I said.

"What is?" you asked.

"Even though we're apart like this, I'm becoming more like you."

"We're not apart," you responded, looking at the latch through the gap in the door. "We're living in the same time stream; even if we're not together, we're alive at the same time. We're aging together, and we're growing old together."

I gave an empty smile.

"Just like when we lived on that spaceship called Earth. On that massive spaceship, with galaxies flowing past, we ate and slept and grew and got older."

"That's not true," I mumbled.

"We traveled together even before we met each other. It was just that the ship was a bit big."

"That's not true!" I yelled. "You're not here. Even if you are you've got no intention of meeting me. If that wasn't the case you'd have left me some kind of sign, some way or another. Written a phone number or something in piles of stones somewhere at the port so I could see it from the sky. Or else gotten onto a radio broadcast and made a missing person appeal . . ."

It seemed as though you were sealing your mouth shut and you disappeared from before my eyes. And with that the latch snapped open.

I escaped, soaked in sweat.

I had the thought that, from now on, I wouldn't be able to see you again, not even in my imagination. As soon as I thought that, I started to lose all will to live. I tried to fight the feeling, to deny it. The hope of meeting you was all that had kept me going.

It's over.

I just knew it. I was finished.

Let's go home, I thought.

I didn't think I'd be able to live any longer. I was too lonely, and too alone. I'd become a ruin like that countryside house of yours. I even thought, *Let's end it now.* But then I thought, if I was going to end it all, I might as well go home and do it there.

When I had that thought, somewhere came to mind. It seemed like it would be appropriate as a last place.

HIS FIFTEENTH LETTER

THERE WAS NOTHING LEFT THAT YOU COULD CALL A PORT. I just got there by calculating the latitude and longitude. There was a lush forest of fir trees laid out along the coast. It was the first time I'd ever seen such a big, beautiful forest.

Even if you tried to come, I don't think you'd be able to find it now.

Even now, I still have thoughts like that.

IN THE END I made an emergency landing. The lay of the land had changed too much. The coastline was in a strange place and the land was too high. I turned the helm toward the sea to soften the impact, but the sea level was much shallower than I'd expected. If I hadn't hurried into the capsule I would have been crushed along with the ship. And if the locking mechanism on the capsule hadn't smashed in the fall, I would have been trapped in there again and died like that.

I went up onto the beach, retched for a long time, and then threw up loads of seawater. I watched as my ship sank below the water.

It's all right, I thought.

Yeah, it's all right. It made it this far. That's more than enough.

Sand clung to my wet shoes, making it hard to walk. I chucked off my shoes and started walking barefoot.

White fog billowed around the forest floor and sunbeams shot through the fog, rich and full. Drops of dew formed in beads at the ends of my fingers. From between the branches a flock of blue birds flew up with a collective flapping of wings, and shocked by the sound, a large herd of roe deer bolted off, leaping through the thicket. They were all vigorous and brightly colored and full of life. It looked as though they had never once been pestered by humans their whole lives. As if to say, "Who would we ever need to hide from?" they were all brightly colored like peacocks.

In my head I rubbed out the forest of firs and brought back the empty plain that had once been there. That field of weeds that couldn't put down proper roots because of the asphalt still hanging on beneath. The plain that was filled with giant daisies and foxgloves. I rubbed that out too, and thought of the waiting room. I pulled off the tangled vines that twisted all over the walls and lifted the fallen balcony up to where it used to be. I repainted the walls where the paint was all cracked, and scrubbed the water from the floor that had been a huge puddle. And I brought back the people. I thought of people approaching, chatting noisily. And people waiting.

I thought of me, waiting.

My legs gave way and I collapsed. After staying in a heap like that for a long time, I got up and walked again. When I could go no more I would pass out by the trunk of a tree and sleep. When the sun rose, I slept, and at night, I walked. Because doing that was better for maintaining my body heat.

As I went inland, debris of the city began to show itself little by little. It was all thick with water weeds, but there were still traces of it remaining.

One by one, I put the decayed and crumpled buildings back up. I fitted windows where they had exploded out, polished and painted them again, and turned on the lights. I started the engines in the cars that had been abandoned lined up in the road. I set straight the skewed traffic signals, stuck the numbers back up on a bus, and turned on the headlights. I thought of the people piling out of the bus at the bus stop.

I thought of myself, waiting at the stop.

I saw you getting off the bus with your face buried in a book. I saw you trying to work out where you were, having been totally caught up in reading, looking around and then seeing me. You approached with an expression of delight.

I passed a theme park where a mascot statue stood without any eyes in its head. Water had gathered in the Viking ship swing ride and shoots of water weeds poured down from the sides of the hanging boat. I walked along the train tracks where red blooms had grown tall. I passed through a subway tunnel half flooded with water. A subway train approached, ploughing through the water, and from inside passengers, completely soaked, walked out wringing muddy water from their clothes.

You walk off the train too, lost in your own thoughts. Worried that you might have gotten off at the wrong station, you scan your surroundings, until I go over to you, in my old oil-stained clothes, and poke your cheek.

THE GUESTS DROVE in a car covered with flowering vines. They get out of the car, batting off grass and cockleburs from their clothes. They pick the flowers, carrying them instead of envelopes of congratulatory cash, and enter the building that is blanketed with moss and ivy and morning glories.

You're there, standing in the doorway. Hopping from one leg to the other, saying, "How am I supposed to move in this dress!" As soon as you notice me approaching from among the guests, you give me a telling-off.

"You're late."

"Yeah, true," I say, brushing the sand from my bare feet. "I guess I was nervous, because it's my first time."

I FROZE ON the spot.

The church we had arranged to get married in was standing there before my eyes.

I was so taken aback, all I could do was gaze at the surroundings. The church was the only building still standing, alone, in the middle of a city of ruins. As if to say that all those hundreds of years of time were nothing; as though laughing off all those typhoons, the rains and snow and wars, as though they were no match for it. As though that one building had ridden a completely different stream of time. It was shabby and worn down, and one corner of the roof had caved in, but it stood steadfast.

I went up the stairs and stroked the doorframe that was darkened with age. I had to touch it because I thought I might still be fantasizing. It was just then I thought of you as you had stroked the doorframe of the house in the countryside. I thought of what you had said.

Buildings people go in and out of stay standing.

Homes where someone opens and closes the doors and airs the place out, where they unfold bedding and lie down to sleep and wake up, where they light the stove and cook a meal, where they sweep the dust and wipe up the water.

Only then did I recall your letter.

I listened to it over and over at least fifty times. How could I not have thought of it until now? What was it that you had said at the end . . .

If you're not there at the port—

SOME CARD-TYPE THINGS dropped from the doorpost. It seemed they were so old that the fabric cords they were pinned up by had snapped. I picked them up. They were old and mildewed, but I could tell what they were. They were the leather frames on lanyards that I'd given to my friends. With trembling hands, I took out the photographs inside. Behind the first photo I took that day, there was a photo that looked as though it'd been taken at the church on what was supposed to be our wedding day.

It looked as though they'd kept coming even after that too. There were still more photos, taken with their lovers or children. There was also a photograph of an old man lying on a bed, making a victory sign at the camera with his fingers. Written on the back was: *I'm off first, punk.*

"If you're not there at the port," you whisper in my ear, "I'll go to the wedding venue. Even if I'm on my own, I can go and play make-believe."

The rotting carpet creaked beneath my bare feet like compacted snow. Every time I took a step white dust billowed up like incense smoke. The chairs were rusted and worn out, but they were all lined up in rows.

Layers and layers of faded bits of paper stuck up on the wall behind the altar caught my eye. It looked like they might once have been colored paper, but they were all gray. There, in inky handwriting, similar things were written over and over again.

I'm waiting
I'll wait
I'll come back
I'm still here
I dropped by again
Don't forget me

I lost my footing.

I got myself back up and went over. The paper turned to dust between my fingers. Each bit seemed to have been stuck up at a different time. There were ones from hundreds of years ago and others from decades ago. It looked as though there was a time when whoever it was had been every few years.

I walked along the wall and grabbed on to the curtain that hung there. It tumbled down in one gust. Behind it, the papers and ribbons stuck to the wall were all shredded as though someone had slashed them in a fury. On top of that, someone had spray-painted: *What the hell are you doing. He's gone. He must have died a million years ago.*

I stood before it for a long time. The words cut out my heart so blood couldn't run through it. I sank to the floor and sat like that for a long time.

I mumbled that it was for the best. Inside I said something different, of course. But still, my words were that it was for the best. It was for the best that you'd given up.

I stayed there for what must have been hours, then, as I was about to get up, I caught sight of a scrap of paper stuck to the fallen curtain. It caught my eye because it was yellow.

It was yellow.

The fact that the color remained meant it hadn't been bleached out by the sunlight coming in through the windows. I remembered the books on the shelf beside the window when I was little. The covers got bleached almost white before even a few years had gone by.

I peeled the paper from the curtain. It didn't come off easily. That meant the adhesive was still there. Could it have been stuck there last year? A month ago? Yesterday?

Just now?

As the sun sank it shone straight through the windows. Draped from the windows, the sun beamed a silver curtain of light into the building and everything inside became visible.

Things like the floor that had been swept, the altar that had been covered with new paper, the vase placed on the altar, the traces of someone having lit a fire, right down to the nickel-silver pot placed neatly on top of it. I could now see the footprints of someone who had come and gone, and even the traces of bedding having been laid out.

A gust of wind blew in through the open door and faded old squares of paper floated down with a rustle. As the sunbeams sank lower, the letters on them glowed gold.

THE PROPHET OF CORRUPTION

Translated by Sung Ryu

THE FIRST ME

0

I MUST MERGE WITH AMAN.

I see no other way to stop my corruption. To stop Aman's corruption, and that of the universe.

I must, even if it leads to the demise of my individuality.

1

When I opened my eyes, I was lying in a field.

It was a warm, dazzling day. A wheat field stretched on beneath a white sky, the gold of the dry stalks so rich that it could trickle down like honey. Not one person was in sight, not a single creature stirred in the endless expanse. There were no buildings, mountains, or hills, not even rivers or streams. Nothing but the field lay between me and the distant horizon.

"You're late," a familiar voice spoke above my head.

The voice of my kin . . . in the broad sense of the word.

My head rested in his lap while he sat knitting. I tried to remember if he had ever knitted as a hobby, but then there must be few hobbies he had never dabbled in. His knitting needles pulled up a tangle of leaves, mud, and hay. Invisible hands seemed to scrape them together, spin them into a sort of yarn, and supply them to the needles.

"You were so late I thought you weren't coming," he said.

"You know there is no avoiding this place."

"I suppose."

I looked around. The curve of the horizon was unusually arched, which meant this place was spherical, but much smaller than Earth, likely no larger than a small asteroid.

The landscape was as intensely hued and vivid as an impressionist painting. Not because the light was any brighter, but because my senses had grown sharper. They felt crystal clear, like they had been rinsed clean in water. What I had thought was red seemed closer to a deadened bloodred now, and what I had thought was blue, the color of sewage. I smelled the wild grass, deeply fragrant as steeped tea, and even heard the breeze whispering beyond the horizon. Everything was resplendent, almost overwhelming, as if a fog had cleared from my head. It would be so until I grew accustomed to my state.

It was an extraordinary sight to behold . . . or it would have been, if I were alive.

"You look like you're in a mood," my kin remarked as he continued to knit.

"All lives have the same ending, which is death. How do you think I feel?"

"Well, you didn't choose a comfortable life for yourself. You never do," he said.

I say "he," but he had no sex. How could they? Neither they nor I had genes now. We had no heart, lungs, digestive tract, or excretory organs. Nor did we have neural networks, bones, or muscles.

I glanced down at my body. A body stripped of secondary sex characteristics looked like that of a large baby. Even a baby had genitals in the world of the living, but here, I did not have them. Our present selves lacked the twenty-third pair of chromosomes that determined our sex, not to mention any hormones. What need did we have of such things? Why should we reproduce to preserve our species?

We were deathless.

"What are you thinking about?" asked my kin from all my past lives. One who had been my parent, sibling, partner, friend, and child.

"Shame," I replied. "I would have felt ashamed if you saw me like this in the Lower Realm."

They looked down at me as if to say, "What are you saying, silly?" But instead they said, "Shame was put in people to counterbalance libido, you know. To keep procreation from spiraling out of control. And libido was put in to get finite beings to reproduce. But we don't have libido here, so we can't have sha—"

"I know."

Indeed I did. *I know what you know, you know what I know.*

You are me, I thought as I scooped up a handful of dirt. Moss, small seeds, and dry leaves mixed with earth slipped through my fingers. Sand, a silicon atom bonded to two oxygen atoms, fourteen electrons orbiting around the nucleus . . . everything, reduced to its source, was of the same substance. The same substance as me.

This place is me.

My bardo.

In some lives, I stumbled in here when I teetered on the brink of death. Then I went back and told everyone excitedly that I had seen the afterworld. But all I had seen was my bardo.

I could never properly recall even this small slice of the afterworld. I was trapped in a body no better than a crude chunk of meat whenever I returned to a life, a body that used every means possible to distract me from thought. A brain with poor cognitive skills, hormones akin to narcotics, a pitiful range of neurotransmitters, neurons with slow processing speeds. It was like having a cognitive disorder compared to my present state of heightened perception.

Everything is me, I repeated in my head. I had to, because I could not believe it.

"How fares Aman?" I asked out of habit. My kin instantly understood *which* Aman I was referring to and, as usual, shook their head.

"The same. Aman still can't escape their own bardo. They're convinced that it's the entire afterworld."

Despite having expected the answer, I was disappointed.

"There are also fragments of Aman that got away, but they

don't come back to the world of the dead. They choose to reincarnate from their bardos instead and each time they split into
hundreds and thousands of smaller pieces. They don't weave
their destinies, they don't care what they'll be born into. All
that seems to be left in them is the will to escape. Even Tushita
has given up on tracking them down."

That was a problem I was aware of . . .

"So, you're really thinking of merging?" my kin asked.

"Yes," I answered. "I am responsible for this mess."

I thought about the sunlight streaming in through a window, the rattling of a copper kettle, the sweet floral scent of tea.
I thought about Aman, old and frail, perched on the bed beside
the window. I thought about the way Aman looked at me. The
thought made my heart ache, even though my body no longer
had such an organ.

My kin said nothing and gazed beyond the horizon. A mag-
nificent black sphere studded with clusters of stars hung con-
spicuously in the white sky. It was rotating, but its massive size
created the illusion of stillness. Neither a sun nor a moon, it
was a vast celestial body housing Earth in the center: the world
of the living. Our school.

"Did you round everything up?"

I nodded.

"From beasts and insects to trees, soil, and rocks?"

I nodded again.

"The living population must've dropped so much. What a
nasty business."

"But you had a hand in it too."

"And I regret it. Anyway, what do you see, now that you've
merged all such fragments into one?"

The first to be merged back into me was a swarm of may-
flies. In the Lower Realm this would constitute mass death. Soil
filled up their puddle, and they flew to my bardo in their spiritual bodies. The next to go was a colony of ants. A bulldozer

ravaged their kingdom. Then a beehive burned in a forest fire. The creatures boiled with resentment at the moment of death, but once dead, they came to a vague understanding. Trees were felled, forests disappeared, flat boulders cracked. They were shocked when they died, but also came to a vague understanding and joined the others. More gathered: animals caught and killed in traps, birds tangled in nets, and fish cut into sashimi. Vanished wetlands and choked ponds, creeks and fields buried under cement. They were bewildered at being merged, but in time they also understood. People sank into reasonless despair and took their own lives, one after another. Babies died in the womb and the ones born were abandoned to die. All questioned why life was so futile.

Every one of them was me.

Yet some entities had grown so separate from me that I began to feel uncertain whether to call them "me" or not. I amassed as many entities as I could without compromising my identity.

"Do you think you can digest Aman?"

"Not yet."

It was true. Lately, my domain had been rapidly shrinking. I was still pathetically small despite consolidating whatever I could get my hands on.

"Go see Tanjae. That'll help you."

"I know."

"They were with Fuxi in their previous life. Fuxi will know where to find them."

"I know."

"Be careful. Once the corruption starts, you think only in ways that encourage further corruption," said my kin, neatly wrapping up what they were knitting. "And when you're completely corrupt, you won't even realize you are."

My kin shook out the garment and held it up to me. It was a long green tunic of rudimentary design, with drooping sleeves and a strap tied casually around the waist. Although it was knitted with leaves, it was smooth and even as fabric woven on a loom.

"Try it on."

"You would have me walk around in clothes? Here?" I asked incredulously. There was no need to wear clothes in the Dark Realm; one could simply transform their body into a clothed form. There was no need to own anything either, as one could make it.

"It's a talisman. It'll help you detect signs of corruption."

"This? How?"

"You'll know you're corrupt the moment you want to put clothes on."

This person is me.

I knew what I was afraid of. I thought of the disease lurking inside me. I thought of my contaminated flesh. If I failed, I would become corrupt. Fear rocked my body at the very thought.

But I must do it. Before it was too late. Before my corruption spread any further, before I reached the point of no return.

I turned my body into liquid and flowed into the tunic. It was slightly big on me, but I enlarged myself to fit it. My kin brushed dirt off their body as they stood up and held out a hand.

"Here."

The hand was transparent. No veins or palm lines. As we did not need to breathe, we had no blood vessels for carrying oxygen. As we did not have blood vessels, we had no complexion. "You should take me too."

I also stood up and put my hand over theirs. But just before our hands touched, they quickly lowered their hand.

"Why have you forged bonds with only yourself lately?" they asked.

I did not answer. A broad smile spread over my kin's face, which was identical to mine.

They were not one person, but the sum of innumerable lives. As I was now. I thought of all the lives I had spent with them. I thought of my parents, my partners, my flesh and blood born from the same womb, my children. Of the days when I did not doubt in the slightest that they belonged to me, that their life and time and existence were meant for me alone, that the love and sacrifice they offered me were justly their duty and my right. I thought of the times when I could not separate them from me.

"You should at least forge bonds with someone other than yourself. That's how you'll learn about relationships."

"There is no rule that says we should. I choose not to."

"Felt too sorry, did you? To involve someone else, to make them watch your godawful ascetic practices?"

I said nothing.

"Oh, I get it. It's because whoever forged a bond with you would've found out. About your condition, I mean. You were probably ashamed. You probably didn't want to be found out. But you're still a godawful mess."

This person is me, I thought. What I wanted, they wanted. But there were times when I hated myself, when I was furious with myself. Times when I wanted to get rid of myself.

I waited, and they held out their hand again. They yanked it back just when it was about to touch mine once more.

"On second thought, there's not much of a difference between us. You're only a bit bigger. Can't *you* merge into *me*? Wouldn't matter which way we do it, right?"

"No, it would not."

I grabbed their hand and flipped it so that my hand was beneath theirs.

Then we merged.

Once you merge, you realize it makes no difference who merges into whom.

2

I WAS ONLY TEASING, THE NEW "ME" THOUGHT. *I WAS GOING TO let the other me merge me.*

But the other me must have thought the same thing.

Yet that entire thought faded. There was no difference. We were originally one being split into two, not two separate beings merged into one.

Now that I was one whole, the emotions I had felt in my fragmented form seemed altogether alien. As if I were looking back on my childhood. On a less experienced, less knowledgeable me. One that I remembered but felt was a far cry from the present me.

Thus two entire lives converged into one. Once I merged, I easily recognized that my current form was closer to my essence. How silly and pointless it had been to obsess over my individuality in such a broken, incomplete state.

The wind caressed the wheat field. The field reclined and sat up again. The wind had blown on my command.

No, the wind was me.

I was blowing. The wildflowers were not reclining, I was. *Everything here is me.*

I gauged the size of my bardo. It was small. I had already harvested in what I could before embarking on this business, but still it was small. My powers and my potential were diminished also.

I was filled with an unexpected dread at the prospect of

gathering in the rest of myself. Just as I had in the world of the living, when I feared what lay beyond death.

I was afraid I would be swallowed by this space that was no more than inorganic matter. That I might become a wheat field or a mound of soil. And yet, I realized, I would not be degrading myself if I did. Besides, I needed this space if I hoped to finish what I set out to do.

I will not disappear. I will only become whole.

I tapped one foot lightly. The ground shook, starting from the spot my foot touched. The wheat field quivered before exploding into a shower of dust. I tapped my foot again and the ground sank as if a meteor had crashed into it, then crumbled away. The dust broke down into molecules, the molecules lost their electric charge and fell apart.

Finally, I disintegrated my human form and joined the rest.

WHEN ONE TURNS into particles, their thoughts also scatter and their senses become fragmented. It is difficult to see or hear or think in this state. Even so, the world of the living is impossible to ignore given its central location. Of course, the terms "world of the living" and "world of the dead" are misnomers, but we continue to use them out of habit. The same goes for the term "Lower Realm." A more spatially accurate name would be "Center Realm."

The Lower Realm's three-dimensional structure has been warped to keep out any light from outside and seal everything within. And at the center of that black sphere is a small, hard, and blue land we call "Earth."

That land is our school. Our hall of learning, our cradle of experiences, our short-term interactive training ground.

That place is me, I thought.

The Lower Realm was growing ever larger with the recent explosion of human population and knowledge. As humanity's field of vision expanded, the Prophets scrambled to create the solar system and threw together a few galaxies. They made areas beyond a certain point unobservable, but they would have to redesign everything if humanity cast its gaze any farther. Since doing so would be a great hassle for the Prophets, they would probably end up intervening by causing human knowledge to regress rather than do the extra work.

Of course, Aman would hate to see that happen . . . I thought.

The Prophets' bardos orbited the world of the living like dwarf galaxies. From a human point of view, one might say that each bardo represented a "heaven" for each religion. The size of a bardo was the size of a Prophet's body—the size of their power. It indicated the number of disciples the Prophet had, the number of followers, and so on. In short, it was a measure of popularity.

As I headed to the bardo of my sibling Fuxi, I glanced sideways at a white sphere opposite the world of the living.

Tushita. The aggregate of Prophets who had long stopped descending to the Lower Realm, in order to preserve their purity and defend themselves against corruption.

They too are me, I thought.

They are all me, I forced myself to think, for doubt crept in and refused to go away. Despite having gathered up all my pieces, I could hardly believe they were me.

I was becoming unmistakably corrupt.

3

FUXI'S BARDO WAS LARGER THAN BEFORE.

Since old Fuxi and I had opposing values, their domain grew insofar as mine shrank. This was inevitable unless our total masses changed.

We were not on good terms, but I had to admit, my sibling had style. Fuxi's bardo was a living, breathing art gallery. Flowers of every color burst into bloom on a mountain, atop which stood a tall golden temple that rearranged itself into a new layout every so often. The paintings on the walls regularly switched scenes while scantily clad sculptures populating the temple struck various poses like models, showing off their perfect figures.

As Fuxi boasted many followers, there was boisterous chatter everywhere. Children sat in front of their teachers in many a corner and reviewed their previous life with the air of bookkeepers. They appraised what they had received, given, done wrong, and done right in their past life and decided what to learn in their next.

"Next time, I want to learn the art of swindling. I've taken an interest in eloquence."

"You'd need a hunger for money, then. How about this? Your father's business fails during your childhood and you spend the rest of your life obsessing over money."

"Someone would need to play that role for me, though. Would you be my father? I'll help you out in the life after this one."

"I have a friend who wants to experience a divorce. Let's rope them in too."

I went past the children. I climbed the mountain by a white marble staircase bedecked with jewels. I could transport myself by other means, but I did not wish to attract attention in Fuxi's domain.

Children leaving for the Lower Realm were huddled next to an emerald lake in the temple's front garden. They reminded themselves of the subjects they would learn and the roles they would play in their next life, carefully committed to memory the faces of friends they were supposed to help, and flew away as a cluster of particles.

"Beware of corruption," the teachers said as they put a hand on the forehead of each departing child. "Remember, the Lower Realm is a dream in which you briefly dwell. That world is an illusion."

That world is an illusion . . . I repeated the habitual phrase under my breath. I had also said it countless times to my students when I sent them off to the Lower Realm.

"The body is an illusion. You are not separate from us. We are one. Everything is connected. Do not forget that."

Do not forget . . . What a paradoxical command. The children forget. They are bound to forget. They are *forced* to forget—given a potion that erases their memories before they are sent down to the Lower Realm. We make them forget, yet tell them to remember.

What foul prank is this?

One of the children caught my eye. The child had been my partner in a past life. They recognized me and gave me a slight nod before disintegrating and flying away. We had once loved each other to death, but now they seemed neither glad nor sad to see me.

Fuxi stood in the middle of the temple, looking ravishing even at a passing glance. They wore an extravagant gold crown on fair, billowing curls and a *dopo* robe that revealed a mighty chest. The Prophet was three times the size of their disciples.

"Here comes the ascetic," Fuxi boomed as if they had swallowed a steam engine whole. The disciples stopped what they were doing and looked around at me. The chatter and the music ceased. Considering that this entire space was Fuxi's body and every disciple a piece that had split from it, one could say that all of Fuxi was paying attention to me.

"So, Prophet Naban. What insights did you gain from your ascetic practice this time?"

Fuxi did not divide into as many pieces as I did when entering the world of the living. Instead, they picked one or two elaborately designed lives. They were massive in the world of the living too. They were never weak, and never understood pain. They led lives wanting for nothing, enjoyed riches they did not earn, and died comfortably. I knew of them in all my lives, but they did not know of my existence. I was the janitor working for their company or the old man picking up wastepaper in their neighborhood. I was the whore from their favorite brothel or the homeless person who lived in a box at the train station they operated.

"What have *you* gained?" I countered.

Fuxi gazed up at the sky with a look that seemed to say, "How can I even begin to describe everything I learned in words?" Their eyes fell on the horizon, over which loomed the mighty world of the living.

"I have gained vigor of the mind. Confidence, and audacity." Fuxi's voice rang out across their bardo. They were not speaking to me but preaching to their disciples. I could not refute them. Even as a human, Fuxi had been as good as a saint, if the sole criteria to judge them by were purity. "You think that children abused by their parents are more mature than the ones who grew up being loved. But you must know the opposite is true. What the soul needs is happiness, not pain."

I glanced around, listening with half an ear to Fuxi's words. Wherever I looked, a wall of soil shot up from the ground, the boughs of a tree drooped, a rock enlarged itself. When I tried to see through them, the soil and rock cackled at me.

I was not welcome here.

I did not mind. If Fuxi came to my bardo, my reaction might have been worse.

"When people who have experienced pain mature, they may indeed reach a higher level of understanding than those who have not," Fuxi went on. "But it is too inefficient. One false step and they can fall into a spiritual abyss. Your methods are akin to pushing children into a ruthless competition and raising only the ones that survive."

"I have come to find Tanjae," I interrupted.

"Who?" Fuxi was playing innocent.

"My child, whom I know you are hiding."

"Students have the right to choose their teacher. That child was drawn to me. And you did not give them a reason to stay."

"I am not here to take Tanjae back. I only need to see them about a personal matter. If they are in your domain, please make way for me."

Fuxi shook their head. "As it happens, Tanjae did not become mine. I courted them and half succeeded, but they panicked and ran off as soon as they set foot in the Dark Realm. They were terribly scared of you. They insisted they would never reincarnate again. I do not blame them. A life you give as a reward is bad enough; I hate to think what kind of life you would give as punishment."

I turned away, listening with half an ear to Fuxi mutter, "That poor child . . ." I could search inside Fuxi if I exerted myself, but I thought better of it. Not only was that a discourtesy, but every Prophet was a force to be reckoned with. They would peer inside me if I peered inside them. I had no desire to let a Prophet, or rather Fuxi, realize what state my body was in. Fuxi was more than capable of gleefully spreading rumors across the whole wide Dark Realm that I was wrong and they right. They might even insist on making my body theirs to cleanse it.

But Tanjae had lived one life as Fuxi's student, and those who had forged a bond with Tanjae could be here anywhere.

"I hear you have been merging," Fuxi said, grabbing hold of me. But not with their hands. The ground had turned sticky and clung to my feet.

I tried to shake myself free, but the muddy ground before me stirred and rose up in the shape of a human. It looked like a child I had forged a bond with in a previous life. More dolls straightened up beside it. Each one assumed the form of someone I had once loved to pieces. My lovers from the days when I had been the most smitten, the most passionate. All of them were naked. Even their intimate parts were achingly familiar to me.

"You gathered up even the flies and maggots."

Men and women, the old and the young, insects and pests and small animals, plants and trees. Since Fuxi was showing me select fragments from my days of deepest infatuation, not everything was beautiful. A blind, bald person with a wizened body stood out from the rest. I had remained by their side as they lay dying in their sickbed. We had sworn again and again to stay married in our afterlives. But now they were . . .

"Did you consolidate everything you have learned? So, what have you achieved from your practice? Why don't you share with the rest of us."

The dolls closed in on me, their outstretched hands groping my body. Legs straddled my waist and arms clasped around my neck. They licked my neck and pulled up my clothes and rubbed between my legs. When they had been living organisms, narcotics were made to pour out from their brains at the merest brushing of bodies, but here, they were only mimicking.

Fuxi's abandon offended me. "Pleasure" was just a navigational instrument created to keep us, who are sent down to the Lower Realm as simpletons, from dying and returning too quickly. To allow us to eat and sleep and mate and reproduce instinctively without having to learn how. And at the same time to make us curious enough to discover new knowledge. But that same instrument began to lead us down messy paths because we did not bother cleaning up the dummy data or the errors growing with each update. Rather, we only patched them up in places.

Pleasure was not something to abandon oneself to, even in the Dark Realm.

"Why so secretive?" Fuxi asked. "We are all practitioners and seekers of truth, are we not? Just think of how much richer our souls would be if you shared your newfound wisdom with us. You know how long it has been since a Prophet last retrieved all of themselves. Everyone is so very interested."

A clay doll was embracing me with a lustful face and licking my cheeks when its expression changed. I had sped up the movement of its particles, fast-forwarding time. In an instant, every doll wrinkled, shriveled up, and was reduced to bones.

I turned around and spoke in a loud voice everyone could hear. "If we could learn through words, we would not have founded the school."

A slight scowl appeared on Fuxi's face. I had just made a part of Fuxi's body, albeit a small one, mine. I had taken it without even venturing a persuasion. What I had done was the Lower Realm equivalent of punching someone in the face.

"We would not have divided our original body into many entities either, or erased our memories and become ignorant children before throwing ourselves into a battle for survival." As I spoke, the bones of the dolls oxidized and crumbled, the wind scattering their ashes. "Learning can only be achieved by living. If you want to know what I learned, reincarnate and live exactly as I did. Then you will know."

I turned on my heels, but Fuxi called after me.

"Naban." Fuxi sounded concerned for me in their own way. "When was the last time you had a proper life?"

I could not help but stop in my tracks.

"Next time, try having good parents for a change; choose an easier, cozier life for yourself so you can rest. A life of enjoyment is not so weak or cowardly a choice as you think it is. You do not know joy. That means you are missing one side of wisdom."

I made no reply. For Fuxi's words were not wrong.

None of us could be wrong. For none of us were right.

I LEFT THE temple grounds and descended the white set of stairs leading down the mountain. Fuxi's children stood at a safe distance, watching or avoiding me, whispering among themselves. I recognized one of them. The child saw me looking and hastily hid behind a sculpture.

I had a bond with this entity, though of course it was harder to find someone I did not know here. This entity used to be my child.

I moved toward them and seized them. As when Fuxi had blocked my view, I did not use my hands. I grew vines that obstructed the child's escape route.

"Yoohee the Merry," I said.

"Teacher Naban," gasped Yoohee. The child looked like white flour dough, with bumps that barely passed for limbs. Or rather a human-size caterpillar whose eyes, nose, and mouth had been tacked on. Yoohee had chosen an odd look, given the latest fad of imitating the human form.

"I am not here to cause a scene. I am looking for Tanjae. Do you know their whereabouts?"

Yoohee looked this way and that.

"I told you, I am not here to make trouble. Your child and Tanjae's were married to each other. You two must have come back together. Have you seen where Tanjae went?"

Yoohee backed away in fright. The pair of sculptures that stood between us, a man and a woman, stripped off their clothes and began fondling each other in various positions. They seemed to be mimicking our facial expressions and gesticulations. I let them at it, knowing how Fuxi had nothing better to do.

"You know Tanjae's a bit of an eccentric. They built a spaceship, jumped in, and made a break for it."

For a moment I thought I had misheard Yoohee. "A spaceship?"

"It travels at the speed of light using a biopropellant, which is only theoretically possible in the world of the living. Of course, it's much easier to make here than in the Lower Realm. You wouldn't need to worry about things like survival equipment or acceleration limit."

"A *spaceship*, you say?"

"Well, I suppose you could call it Tanjae's 'bardo,' but it certainly was a spaceship. It used rocket propulsion. Tanjae is . . . you know, completely governed by the three-dimensional laws of physics even in the Dark Realm."

I began to ask, "Did you say rocket propul—" but stopped short and said instead, "Yes, since Tanjae thinks in three dimensions. So, Tanjae traveled in three dimensions . . . Then the distance covered would correspond to the time passed. Did you see which way they went?"

Yoohee pointed to somewhere in the distance.

"Very well. You have been helpful."

I turned to leave, but Yoohee held me back. The pair of sculptures that had been making love between us let out a provocative moan. Fuxi must have decided that the moment called for background music.

"What?"

"Teacher, I . . . I didn't know it was you."

"No matter. I did not recognize you either."

Yoohee left me two lives ago. The child was a fighter in every life. Even when they were a wolf or a wild boar. They dedicated their lives and deaths to the fair distribution of wealth and income. Then they burned out. As so many children did. Yoohee was tired of losing, and thought I was the problem.

—TEACHER, I AM losing because you've made me poor.

That was what Yoohee said before deserting me.

—I can't fight the powerful if I am powerless.

—If you were not poor, you would not think to fight them in the first place.

That was my reply.

—I can achieve anything with power. When will you stop letting those materialists run the world? I can reincarnate thousands of times in this state and everything would end up the same. We can't change the world like this!

THAT WAS HOW Yoohee left me. Fuxi, as always, benevolently welcomed Yoohee and gave them perfect lives. In Yoohee's last life, they were a man who spread his sperm to his heart's content. He felt no guilt over such matters. He lived believing he could shove his cock into an infinite number of women.

In a previous life, I was one of the women Yoohee fucked. He fucked me longer and more persistently than he had anyone else. He said he took a liking to me at first sight. Whenever we met, he stressed that he and I were not of equal birth.

He did not understand me when I killed myself. Having never imagined a life of submission and humiliation, he did not understand a single shred of my life. He viewed himself as a sort of free-spirited vagabond, and in a way, he was.

"You've come here to reprimand me for the last time we

met, haven't you?" said Yoohee gloomily. I had no salivary glands, but there was a bitter aftertaste in my mouth.

"I have not. What's done is done. When you divide as much as I do, you are bound to meet everyone again at some point. The world of the living is a school for me too, and I needed to learn what I had to learn. I lived that life for me, not anyone else."

"I was also with a woman who used to be my mother in a previous life," Yoohee stammered. "And with my former younger sister, my former daughter . . ."

"They must have been around you since you had already forged bonds with them. The same goes for me. Which one of us was never kin at one point? If you start thinking the way you do, there is no one left for you to love."

"Teacher, I . . ."

"What?"

"I thought I was some great man," said Yoohee, looking like something had broken inside them.

"That is your lesson. That is enough."

I felt Yoohee break a little more. But I was the one broken. For I could not even comfort this young child.

As I MADE to depart Fuxi's bardo, something pierced through my chest. Not in a figurative sense.

A mayfly had whizzed through me and was now soaring higher. I had let it pass almost subconsciously. In Lower Realm terms, it was like sensing movement behind one's back and reflexively moving aside.

A mayfly was common enough. Both in the Lower Realm and here.

The difference was that everything in a Prophet's bardo had intelligence. The stairs I stood on and the sculptures standing next to me were intelligent. Nothing here would dare hurt me or unwittingly bore through me. Whatever that thing was, it had passed through me on purpose.

A test.

Prophets liked to spring tests on their students. They hit them without warning or stabbed them with a needle to see if they could part their bodies like water or change their form.

They checked for signs of corruption.

But who would dare test me, a Prophet?

Well, there were no secrets in the Dark Realm. No matter how hard I tried not to forge bonds in the Lower Realm, everyone I met there even in passing was my sibling, my family, my teacher, or my student. Everyone with whom I happened to dine at the same table, ride in the same vehicle, or live in the same neighborhood was my kin. A keen observer would be able to detect my corruption just by brushing against my clothes.

Who could it be? Fuxi? Tushita? Whoever it was, I did not want them to find out yet. Not now.

I inflated the tip of my finger like bubblegum and tore it off. I transformed the detached piece into a firefly and sent it after the mayfly. The mayfly zoomed down the mountain, following the twists and turns of the staircase. It sped up and slowed down, danced this way and that, pretending to shake off its pursuer but slyly coaxing it on.

My firefly chased it to an academy nestled halfway down the mountain, where children were handing out flyers.

Flyers!

Synthesizing simple objects like paper or fabric was part of the basic curriculum, but was there any knowledge here that had to be passed on in writing?

None of the children looked familiar. If they were not bonded to me, they had to be newborns. They may have lived only a life or two, or may never have visited the world of the living at all.

"We must do away with our outdated education system," said a child whose name I did not know. "Again and again, we erase our memories and descend to the world of the living to learn what we already know, develop technologies we already developed, realize truths we already realized."

"Let us follow Prophet Aman," the children cried. "We must stop destroying the world of the living under the banner of education. We must stop spreading disaster and disease. Let us put an end to wars and refugees. The Prophets have the power and drive to do so but ignore the suffering of the Lower Realm."

Aman.

That was a name I knew. I mulled it over.

Aman, my first child, the first entity that split from me. One who used to be me. The first Prophet to be corrupted. The most corrupt Prophet there ever was.

So, some of Fuxi's children were turning to Aman now. Well, it was no surprise, given old Fuxi's values.

"Aman said we must make the Lower Realm a wise and just world, like reality, not a chaotic illusion of hardship and poverty. And that we must change the world ruined by false teachers."

The child did not mention the false teachers by name, but I knew I was included.

What an outlandish thought. If the Lower Realm mirrored the Dark Realm, what was the point of the Lower Realm's existence?

4

I TRACKED DOWN TANJAE'S "SPACESHIP" SOON ENOUGH BE-
cause it was stationary.

It was flying at the speed of light in three dimensions, but
viewed from the fourth dimension of time, it was not moving
and therefore easy to find.

Tanjae's home was the kind of space battleship that was
still the stuff of imagination in the Lower Realm. The ship not
only had a cafeteria and dormitory, but also a forge, a small
farm, and even a chapel. Having a cafeteria and dormitory
might be excusable, but I was mystified as to what possible use
there could be for a chapel here.

If Tanjae gave the world of the living the technology used
to construct this ship, humans would no longer have to dream
about conquering space. But that would be a right nuisance
for us Prophets; we would have to redesign the structure of the
Lower Realm.

That was not my immediate concern as I landed on the
ship's surface and peered inside, though. Tanjae was at the heart
of the battleship—the engine room—hammering away making
a chair. The ship was controlled by two semi-intelligent machine personalities named Myungyak and Gwanhwa. Myungyak steered the ship and Gwanhwa maintained the facilities.
I had no idea whether I should group them under things that
Tanjae had "birthed" and thus send them to the Lower Realm
for reincarnation training.

"Tanjae," I called from outside. Tanjae tossed up the chair in alarm and fell on their bottom.

"It is I, Naban."

Tanjae scrambled under the table and pulled the chair in to hide. The child believed sound could not travel without a medium and that a wall would either block it or deflect it. I had tried to explain once that no, both the sound and the wall were my body, so all they had to do was yield a little to each other, but the child simply did not understand.

"Open the door."

"Please, go away! I mean, it's not that I don't like you, Teacher, it's just that I don't feel like seeing you today. I've taken ill. Please, come back tomorrow—no, the day after tomorrow—no, I'll call on you later with a gift or something . . ."

Tomorrow, is it? I chortled to myself. How would one go about defining "a day" in the Dark Realm in the first place?

"Do you think you can stop me from entering if you keep this door closed?"

My voice was confident, but I was worried that might be the case. This ship was made by none other than Tanjae. It would be just as closed-minded as its creator. It did not know where it came from. I had to teach it from scratch.

But Tanjae was my child—in other words, a piece split off from my body, one that used to be me not too long ago. Everything the child made was, in a broad sense, my kin. The other Prophets likely could not do it, but I could . . . at least, so I thought.

I tried.

I put my hand on the outer wall and peered into its molecular structure, which looked like a tangle of yarn. I reminded it of its younger days before it was heated to extreme temperatures, before it was alloyed and its molecular structure changed. I reminded it of its origins. I tried to persuade it: *You and I are not different, we are the same entity. I, like you, am an aggregate of molecules, where the space between each molecule is empty, and the space between the nucleus and electrons is too. Emptiness and fullness are effectively the same thing.*

The wall was flustered . . . then it resisted.

I am not a life form.

Nothing is lifeless, I replied.

I am not you. We are strangers.

There are no strangers.

I am a solid object. You cannot pass.

Nothing is solid.

The wall reflected for a moment, then asked a fair question.

If you and I are not different, can't you follow my orders?

It was a sound argument. *If you yield now, I will do the same for you when you need me to.*

With that, I was able to pass.

On the other side of the wall, I found myself standing in the middle of the engine room. Tanjae was trembling under the table with only their eyes peeking out, like a mole.

"Please don't barge in like that. It's scary."

"Then you shoo na have forsh me to."

I feigned composure, but my words were slurring. I was surprisingly exhausted. I had been anxious lest I failed to persuade the wall and got stuck in it comically, or worse, stranded helplessly outside the wall like a fool.

"I wasn't acting of my own accord in my last life," said Tanjae as they pulled the chair further in to hide their body better. I wanted to laugh at Tanjae's meaningless attempt, but looking more closely I realized it was indeed meaningful. The chair looked similar to the ones advertised on the Lower Realm's home shopping channels, with copy along the lines of "Cutting edge! Ergonomic! It's not furniture, it's science." I could not even begin to fathom the mechanism of the wheels or the back of the chair. To pass that chair, I would likely need to persuade each and every bolt and component.

"Teacher Fuxi approached me first. How do you expect a weakling like me to turn Fuxi down?"

"I am not here to discuss that."

"All I did was get my hands on some money. As a mathematical exercise. I developed and tested theories on how money multiplies. It was purely academic. But you'd tell me to give up in my next life what I enjoyed in my last. Well, I won't. You said it yourself: 'Misfortune shouldn't be a punishment, just as happiness shouldn't be a reward. The Lower Realm is where we learn. There's only one purpose to both misfortune and happiness, and that's to learn.'"

While Tanjae blabbered on, I puzzled over what I should do with the chair until I realized my own foolishness and simply pushed it aside with my hand.

Tanjae looked frantically behind them as if hoping to find a door there. However, the child was not capable of escaping through the wall unless they smashed a hole in it with an iron mace. I squatted down in front of them.

"I am not here to scold you. If you do not agree with my ways, you are free to leave me. Another teacher will help you weave your lives. And if you leave me, you have no reason to fear me. Nor do you have to listen to me, so you can throw me out right now. If that is what you want, say so."

Tanjae looked miserable.

"It is fine, child. One lesson is not superior to another. They only express different values. Will you go to Fuxi?"

"No," Tanjae answered sadly and crawled out. "You're going to give me a dreadful life, aren't you? What will you do? Place me in a poor home or a country locked in civil war and keep me from studying? You'd say that's learning too. You're punishing me, really, but of course you'd never admit it."

"I came to learn how you reincarnate," I replied.

"WHEN DID YOU find out?" Tanjae asked as they returned from the warehouse dragging a cartful of wire bundles, batteries, electrical terminals, monitors, and things I still had no wish to look deep inside of. Meanwhile, the wall was having an identity crisis after having let me through; it kept muttering to itself, *I am solid . . . I am fluid . . .*

"It is difficult *not* to know the affairs of my own child."

"Do the other teachers know? They'd quarantine me if they knew."

"They would indeed."

Tanjae started to say something, but having learned the futility of resistance early on as my student, they lapsed into a dejected silence. The wall continued to fuss. *I am soft, I am hard . . .*

"I haven't been able to turn myself into a spiritual body for quite some time now. Meditating and praying doesn't help. I just feel it's impossible." Tanjae pressed down on their palm. It sank and rose up again like well-kneaded dough. "I can't even shape-shift anymore. So I break down my body instead, and beam the pieces into a fetus in the Lower Realm, reassemble myself into DNA sequences, then add on bells and whistles. 'Beam me up, Scotty!' style, you know?"

Tanjae raised a hand, palm out, and parted their fingers down the middle to form two pairs. Tanjae slowly put their hand down when I offered no comment.

"It's much easier than transporting a Lower Realm body. The body has a brain, a neural network . . . it's like a sloppily built robot, with new parts slapped onto an old model now and then. And it has way too much dummy data. But our real bodies are simple. 'The simplest solution is the best solution,' you know? . . . Or maybe not."

I ignored Tanjae and studied the machine before my eyes. It was a glass tube that was just wide enough for one person. There was a hatch on top and a pink blanket spread out at the bottom. I placed a hand on the glass. Persuading it was difficult, but I extracted some information by talking to it.

"Which of the teachers make up the first generation?" asked Tanjae, as if the question had suddenly occurred to them.

"There is no first generation. The second generation is the earliest we go back."

"But we must've been one entity in the beginning. Like Chaos or the universe before the big bang, say, or an amoeba or a cancer cell, or a squirming, shape-shifting monster. Back when there was one density and one self. Who was that first being?"

"We are all second-generation. We divided at the same time, no one came first."

"You mean no one remembers the time when we were one?"

"There is nothing to remember. Nothing ever happened then."

I gathered up some of my particles. Most of my body was floating around me like dust at the moment. If I compressed everything into one, I would be as large as an asteroid and unable to enter this spaceship.

The walls shook and the sundry items strewn across the floor rolled toward me. Tanjae held on to their chair. They said that whenever I made something, they felt like they would get "sucked in" to me. I replied, "Oh, you are."

A viscous liquid flowed out from my fingertip and seeped into Tanjae's transporter. It swelled like a loaf of bread and hardened into the shape of an adult human. It was still connected to me and not yet given a personality.

Tanjae looked like they wanted to swallow, if only they had saliva.

"That's how you made me too, right?"

"I did not make you. I simply divided myself."

"That is the same thing as making. Babies are born that way in the Lower Realm too. When the mother's and father's genes combine and settle in the womb, the mother converts the nutrients her digestive tract absorbed, divides the cells, and grows them into a baby. She follows the same process as we do, except she does it unconsciously . . . It's molecular conversion, so to speak."

"We do not make things that did not exist before. The total mass remains constant."

"It's the same with making babies. It just doesn't look it."

Gwanhwa moved its mechanical arm and pushed an electric wire terminal into the warm, freshly baked body. The wire found its way to the desired spot without having to worry about the constraints of a Lower Realm body, like accidentally tearing open a vessel and causing bleeding or puncturing the intestines.

My senses were still linked to the body, allowing me to feel and to learn where the wire was burrowing and what chemical reactions it set off.

"This is how you spiritualize, then," I remarked.

"I'm not the one doing it. It's chemistry."

"So you can believe in this, but not in your ability to shape-shift."

"It's not a matter of believing, it's science! It's not the kind of magic that you . . ."

If I could talk Tanjae into learning, I would have done so already.

I finished analyzing the transporter's mechanism and let go of my link. What had been a part of me moments before was disconnected now, even if it could still be called "me" and needed more time to acquire individuality. I watched the machine break down the new body, convert it to radio waves, and transmit them to the Lower Realm.

"There is no persuasion involved, I see."

"You heard me, it's chemistry at work."

This transporter forced molecules to break down and sucked them in. It skipped the steps of persuasion and negotiation, there was none of that "You and I are the same, we need each other . . ." kind of talk. Particles obeyed the machine's instructions like lifeless objects and disintegrated.

How interesting. Did this young child know that they entirely surpassed me in some respects? Not only me, but *all* of the second generation?

"What are you trying to figure out?" Tanjae asked.

I pretended not to hear and put my hand on the machine to make more detailed queries. Persuading it was difficult still, but it gave me answers, though slowly. I listened carefully like a good student.

"Why is it important that there's no persuasion involved?" Tanjae asked. Clueless as the child was, they must have finally gotten an ominous feeling.

"Because I want to remain 'me.'"

"Why?"

"If I am not 'me,' I might rethink what I am about to do."

"How do you define 'me'?"

A fairly profound question, I must say.

"Every entity willing to do what I am about to do."

Tanjae was confused. My answer was not characteristic of me. Nor of any Prophet. A Prophet giving any answer other than "Everything is me" should sound warning bells, but it went unnoticed by the inattentive child.

"So, have you finished learning?"

"Not yet to my satisfaction." Then with half a mind to tease the child, I added, "But I would if I merged with you."

Tanjae toppled backward, chair and all. Crawling across the floor, they spluttered, "It's time, oh it's time . . ."

I chuckled. "I jest."

"I—I'm not scared. I won't be dying. I'll just be returning to my original state," Tanjae said without true understanding. "Right? We were originally one whole. And I used to be you, Teacher. You've simply divided yourself. Like an amoeba . . . or a planarian?"

"That is correct," I replied. Except, strictly speaking, it wasn't. We were not divided. We did not "used to be" one; we still were. We split our personalities and were detached from one another in three dimensions, but we remained connected in the fourth. Though this was not something I expected Tanjae to comprehend.

"There's no such thing as empty space, only differences in density," Tanjae continued. "And if density rises at a point, it pulls in the surrounding space, which is how you get gravity. It's like squeezing your flesh. And it actually is. Everything is connected. The whole universe is. In the end we are one. We're more than Gaia, we are the Cosmos. Or should I say Chaos . . ."

"You gave a talk on that topic in the Lower Realm, you know."

"I talked about it, but I've never understood it."

Tanjae pretended to sigh. It was common among the younger children to retain their habits from the Lower Realm.

"Why, your superstring theory was a commendable effort. For someone incapable of imagining four dimensions, that is."

"Aah, please don't." Tanjae waved their hands in protest, blushing furiously.

The theory was not too far off from the truth. All of us formed one string, and Tanjae and I were the points where the string tangled to form oscillating bodies. Only, there was no continuity in our personalities.

"I'm scared now, but I'll be happy once we merge. I'm

going back to what I was. When you die you hate it, but once you're dead, you think, 'Wow, that question I grappled with my entire life was already solved by me three thousand years ago,' and you're happy. You realize you didn't die at all. I guess this would be similar, right?"

I resisted the temptation to say, "We are one entity even if we do not merge," and said instead, "I suppose so. But I already told you I'm not here for that; I intend to delay merging with you as long as possible."

"Why is that?" Tanjae asked warily. I heard the unspoken accusation behind those words too: "You've eaten all the senior students, so why spare me?"

"Well, it seems to me that you are standing at the perihelion of corruption. Normally, anyone with your state of mind would have already been corrupted many times over. I cannot guess where your point of equilibrium is, and I never will if I merge with you. I want to observe you as you are for a little longer. Find out what it is that I am trying to learn from you."

Tanjae fell silent. So did the entire ship. Myungyak and Gwanhwa quieted down too. The muttering wall stopped musing and looked around at us. The whole space responded to Tanjae's thoughts. Tanjae would never be lonely if they were a little more enlightened. If they knew that their creations were always watching over them.

"That's corruption, isn't it?" Tanjae asked.

I saw who was on Tanjae's mind at that moment. I could not help but see. For the entire ship was thinking of the same person. Every one of my molecules surrounding the ship was thinking of the same person.

"To become incapable of believing that the whole world is me," Tanjae added.

Aman.

My first division. The first third-generation entity. The first

Prophet from the third generation. The first corrupt Prophet. The Prophet who spread corruption across the universe.

Aman.

I murmured the name softly in my head. Tanjae did not hear, but the ship's objects buzzed with conversation.

"To believe that the body is real when it's just an illusion," Tanjae went on. "To believe that your present self is all of yourself when it's only one piece of the world." Tanjae looked down at their own body and said, "Like Teacher Aman."

—WE'D ERASE OUR memories and enter a new world.

Aman's voice, full of vigor, rang in my ears.

"Because we should learn wisdom, not knowledge. We can't learn from knowledge. We should learn from life itself. Let's build a school in the center of our world, wipe out our knowledge, and jump into that dynamic arena of life."

5

"WHAT A PECULIAR IDEA, TO PROPOSE THAT WE ERASE OUR memories," I answered Aman. "Until now we have only thought of splitting our personalities."

Aman was an unpredictable child. They poured out an endless stream of new ideas. Passionate they were, and lively. I could not fathom how I had birthed such a personality.

Before we all divided, we were a giant, conceptual lump, stagnant, aimless, and unchanging. A new thought would never occur to us during that state, for nothing new could ever happen. That we had the idea to divide was a miracle in itself.

The first division was a moderate success. But everyone was cautious about another round. Could we handle that many entities? Was ten not diverse enough? Could we reunite our chaotic personalities when there were twenty, thirty entities among our number? What if we could not return to our essential form?

I undertook the second division before the others, as a test. Back when we had our first division, I was supposed to be the central body into which everyone would merge back if anything went wrong. This time we tried the opposite. If things went amiss, everyone would work together to merge me and Aman back into them. I was unseasoned in divisions then and gave almost half of my body away, resulting in amnesia and a change in personality. Having lost continuity with my parent body, I could not keep the name Aisata and renamed myself Naban.

Aman was my first child, and therefore all of our first child. The first entity to break continuity from the Whole. The first generation to feel no attachment to primordial times. From the moment of birth, Aman was busy cooking up mischief and amusing games. Aman was proof of a successful division, a shining beacon signaling a colorful future.

"But if we erase our memories, how shall we return from this school?" Fuxi asked, wondering what curious ideas Aman was entertaining now. Back then, we were still young, relatively undifferentiated, and got along well with each other. "We should graduate at least," Fuxi added. "We cannot live as students forever, can we? With no memories, we would forget how to spiritualize our bodies. How would we return then?"

Language was an amusing game too. By severing the connections between our minds, we gained the pleasure of devising new tools for communication. We preoccupied ourselves with making thousands of signs and symbols each day. Back when we had perfect communication, we had felt no desire for social interaction. Who knew limitations and inconveniences could be so joyful and fun?

It was Aman's idea to build the world of the living. Aman proposed we create a special place where we could go and play for a while under a certain set of rules. A space governed only by our game.

"Someone could go in and bring us back."

Aman shook their head at my suggestion. "Then the students would find out that the Dark Realm exists. Only spiritual beings should interact between the school and the Dark Realm."

Aman mulled over the problem and conjured up a simple structure by splitting a small portion of their body. It was a memory device that used four types of nucleobases as its language. The attraction between the nucleobases gave it a double helix shape. Tanjae would later discover it and name it "DNA."

"Let's record our expiration dates in here and carry it in our bodies when we go," Aman said, positively bursting with pride and self-congratulation for thinking up such a brilliant idea. Aman really was endearing. Endearment was a new emotion, a new bliss we had learned by dividing.

"We set a time limit, so that when a certain amount of time passes we naturally leave our bodies, spiritualize, and return to the Dark Realm. We schedule in a planned end, you see. What might be a good name for that . . ."

We did not know what to call it.

Because none of us knew what "death" was yet.

THE SCHOOL STARTED with a series of failures. We returned at the end of every semester as embarrassed as underachieving students who had flunked. Erasing our intelligence was a humiliating, not to mention disconcerting, affair. Most lives were a hopeless waste of time.

Each time we came back, we debated how we should redesign the world of the living. The Lower Realm in its early days was not too different from the Dark Realm. It was utter confusion, unstable and malleable. We tried fashioning a small piece of land and propping it up with a creature like a snake or turtle, or pinning a giant tree down the center of the land, but none of these attempts were to our satisfaction. Absently, we whiled away our time there and returned. Our biggest problem was that we "died" too easily. No one had ever done anything to avoid death before. We rolled around in our bodies as we pleased, like babies given a toy for the first time. We threw ourselves down cliffs and broke our bodies for fun, then wondered why they did not revert to their original state.

"We can't get rid of the rule that we spiritualize when our bodies get damaged beyond repair," said Aman. "It's a waste of time dragging around a decaying body. Better to come out and go back in again."

"We know. But we've never had to keep our bodies out of harm's way before," we replied in dismay, as if we were disciples being told off by their teacher. Aman thought long and hard.

"I'll try to make us avoid physical damage. Make it very unpleasant. So that we'll recoil just by bumping into something . . ."

I was the first to have the revised gene implanted in my body before entering the world of the living. My body became a little more complex as a result. Pain receptors were installed and a sensory nervous system was made to process external stimuli. Death was quite different this time.

Aman evaded me for a long time when I came back from living that life. They were convinced that they were a complete failure and I would destroy them by merging with them.

"Teacher, I . . . I had no idea that would happen. I didn't know you'd be in so much pain. Not in my wildest dreams."

If we had had the habit of assuming a fixed form in the Dark Realm back then, Aman would have doubtless turned red in the face and burst into tears. But at the time we were mere balls of light continuously shifting shape.

"Never mind. It was a fascinating experience."

"I should look for another way, though. Such pain. It's horrible."

"No, this is important. How shall I put this. It was indeed beyond my wildest . . ." I trailed off as vivid memories of my life came rushing back. I had thrashed around, not wanting to die, and writhed with the desire to live. I had pursued life as if I meant to bite its flesh off.

"I think that is where true learning lies," I said. "Never have I pursued something so fiercely as I did then. Everything was so dynamic. Even in a world so crude. But do try putting in some pleasure too, next time."

Aman was remorseful and again asked for my forgiveness.

I reassured them, "If we balance the two well, we should be able to guide lives in generally the right direction."

We added an element each time we entered the world of the living. We coded in hunger so that we remembered to supply ourselves with energy, the sense of taste so that we found food beneficial to our bodies. We gave ourselves the ability to discern cold from hot. Instilled fear to detect danger before it arose, particularly the fear of the dark, dangerous beasts, and poisonous insects. We put in loose guidelines to help us survive without any knowledge.

We decided to start pairing up genes when we accidentally obliterated the entire ecosystem. We learned that random pairings were more advantageous than combining only good genes. We also added in a need for affection, a need that was as powerful as pain. We inserted the need to preserve one's own species as well as love and affection for family. We kept intervening, for the smarter our creations grew, the stronger their instincts became to return to their true home. At the slightest negligence, popular belief began to value afterlife over life.

I mated with Aman in one of my lives. As soon as I returned to the Dark Realm, Aman, who had been waiting for me, shrieked with joy and embraced me. This was when we were feathered creatures, half bird and half reptile.

"You're alive!"

Aman looked almost exactly like they had in their last life. They bit my neck and licked my face and snuggled into me, their tail bobbing.

"I knew we'd meet again! I knew you'd come back! The afterlife really exists. Life is eternal, I tell you, eternal!"

"Aman, wait, calm down." Thinking I would never be bored as long as this one was around, I laughed and pulled Aman from me. "What are you going on about? Of course the afterlife exists, why do you sound surprised?"

Aman stared at me as if they longed to merge, looking like

they wanted to suck in all my molecules right there and then, if only they could. It took a while before the smile vanished from my face.

"Aman, are you by any chance still . . ."

When I tried to inspect Aman's body, they shook their head. "I don't have genes. They rotted away in the Lower Realm, of course."

"Then why . . . ?"

Their powerful need for survival and mating, their desire for affection and communication, what did it all mean? Why had the desires of the Lower Realm spilled into the Dark Realm?

"Teacher," Aman said feverishly. "I never imagined I could feel such rapture, such tumultuous sparks of the heart. That I could pine for someone, cherish them so much that I forgot myself, that I saw another as myself."

While this may have made an impressive speech in the Lower Realm, here it was far from it. It had the same effect on me as if Aman were saying, "Oh, Teacher, I've realized one plus one is two, how wondrous!"

"Aman, you and I *are* the same self. I am not the Other."

"Yes, I know. But I don't *feel* that it's true. Here it's a fact as clichéd as saying, 'My body is mine.' But there, I felt it in my bones with every breath I drew. I felt it more acutely because I could hardly believe it. Did you not experience that, Teacher?"

I thought back to my previous life. I had been a feathered beast roaming the forest with little on my mind except for food and shelter. I wept for days when my lifelong partner died before me. I wandered the forest, mad with grief. I thought no more of eating or sleeping. Life spent with my partner was joy, life without them lost all meaning. I met my death, almost willingly. I would not have been so devastated had I been the one to perish.

"I did. But I was partly under the influence of hormones, and besides, the instincts to mate and to grieve are, to some extent, just fabrications for the sake of convenience, are they not? They are not real, after all."

But then Aman gazed at me with the eyes of a beast, eyes that shone as they had in the Lower Realm. A primitive soul enthralled by the joy of life glowed within.

"Teacher," Aman said in a small, animal voice, "if we don't believe life is real, what can we ever hope to learn from it?"

AMAN CHANGED WITH each visit to the Lower Realm. They took everything that happened there for genuine experience. They grafted their incomplete Lower Realm personalities onto their true personality. They became increasingly unstable, making the rest of us uneasy.

Aman's condition worsened dramatically after we created humans. Aman identified too deeply with them. Humanity was an experimental species whose survival skills we had minimized in order to invest almost everything in its intelligence. Given its dismal reproduction rate and combat abilities, we expected the species to be outcompeted in the struggle for existence, but somehow it multiplied at an unstoppable pace. The laws of conservation dictated that the overpopulation of one species led to the collapse of biodiversity. Panicking, we planned to curb the human population by sending down floods or droughts, but Aman furiously opposed the idea. They argued we should not disrupt the Lower Realm's ecosystem. Now, *that* we could understand; experiencing destruction as a result of overpopulation could be a form of learning. But then . . .

"How MANY MORE times do you have to upend the place to satisfy yourself?" Aman cried, hurling a stone at me. The first stone they threw was absorbed into my body, the second passed through me. Aman's antics were growing more and more outrageous. I debated whether I should let the stones hit me. I was puzzled. The latest flood was a small-scale event compared to the Precambrian or Permian mass extinctions. Only a coastal city and a few island nations were submerged.

Aman looked exactly like they had on the day they last died, face chalk-white and body reeking of seaweed, greenish water dripping from their wet clothes. They occasionally retched out water. I knew Aman was free to assume whatever form they wanted in the Dark Realm, but I was unnerved by the startling precision with which they had replicated their past form.

The children playing in the garden grew silent, stealing uneasy glances at the temple where the commotion had broken out. They had returned in droves due to this recent disaster and were busy catching up with one another and merrily preparing for a celebration. This was when my bardo still housed a pretty, white-pillared temple and a small garden abloom with wildflowers. Decorating one's space in the style of the Lower Realm was the latest fad at the time.

"I am sorry to say this, Aman, but I cannot understand you . . ."

What was wrong with them? Why were they different from the other children? Had there been some kind of mistake because it was my first time dividing?

"We were all scheduled to come back at some point, no?" I asked.

"This was not scheduled, though. All of us had things to learn in this life. We were getting ready to live our lives to the fullest too. But then you slew so many, so abruptly, without giving us any time to prepare . . ."

Thanks to which I was able to clean up some built-up litter, the fish were thriving, and the lives of marine organisms were enriched in both opportunity and territory, I wanted to say. But I checked myself. Lately, Aman seemed incapable of seeing their own lives and the lives of others as the same thing.

"It was not my doing. Or anyone else's. There were simply too many humans on Earth and not enough plants. The carbon dioxide levels in the air were rising, the days were getting hotter, and the sea was growing warmer than usual. Too much water evaporated from the sea and stirred bigger, wetter storms. None of this was unexpected. I told you we would need to downsize humanity a little."

Aman buried their face in their hands.

"You should've stopped it. Done everything in your power to stop it. How could you leave so many people to die—"

"Aman, who on earth are you saying has died?"

The children who had been adorning a carriage in the garden with flowers surreptitiously stood up and slipped away. Some of them had been Aman's father, mother, friend, or lover.

"They could've been saved. You were in the Dark Realm, so you could have saved them. Why did you just sit and watch? Why did you not come to help? Why didn't you *try* something at least?"

I was flummoxed. Had I misunderstood Aman's reason for opposing human population control? I had assumed it was because they thought the Dark Realm should not intervene with the Lower Realm. Had they not made that argument in full awareness of the fact that the entire ecosystem could soon face destruction without our stepping in? Where were Aman's unreason and irrationality coming from? My train of thought left me feeling faintly annoyed.

"How do you expect me to help? Help with what? Would you have me turn into a dove and fly down amid beams of light, or part the sea into two? How would people ever believe that world was real if I did something like that? And what would be the use of them living there a few extra years? The Lower Realm is a place where you shrivel up if you cannot stuff yourself at every meal, where you die the second you fail to breathe and pump your heart. Where you are doused in chemicals that distract you from thinking straight—how people will thank me for keeping them in such a place!"

Aman gave no answer. I patted their wet shoulders.

"Aman, you have been too immersed in it lately. Life is a sea of suffering, an illusion. There is nothing there. Reality is what happens *after* life."

"But without the will to live, life is meaningless."

"I know what you mean. Life has to be real. That is what we must believe when we are alive. Or else we would squander our fortunes or waste our lives. But there is no need to believe it once we are back here, do you not agree? Come, it has been a long time since all of us gathered together; let us enjoy the festivities."

"Naban."

Then Aman went on to say something I would never forget.

"The Lower Realm is real." Aman's eyes flashed. As if they contained an optic nerve and veins connected to an actual brain. They were bloodshot and wet with tears. Their deep pupils trembled with sadness.

"The people in the Lower Realm are not us. They're completely different beings."

6

"Isn't it funny?"

Tanjae's words roused me from my thoughts. I detected movement beyond the wall the moment I came to my senses. I tensed. Not because I felt movement but because it had taken me that long to do so.

"What is?"

"Learning from scratch what we already know. That I chased after truths or 'secrets' of the universe in all my lives in the Lower Realm, but I can discover them just by merging with you."

"That is not true. By merging, you discover only what I know," I said as I listened intently for any sound beyond the wall, "and I discover only what you know. Things I would never have known, had I not divided you from me."

Tanjae rapped the wall they had forged by hand. The wall shouted "Ow!" in annoyance, but Tanjae did not hear.

"This wall is 'me' too, right? Yeah, yeah, the whole world is 'me,' I know. This spaceship should be especially close to who I am. But if this ship were really my body, why can't I will it to do whatever I please?"

"But you are doing exactly that. You are treating it like an object, just as you please. That is why the wall is treating you like an object too." I reached out for the wall behind me. Tanjae thought I was doing a demonstration, but they were mistaken.

The wall grumbled, *You still owe me for that other time.*
I shall repay you double later.

The wall let me through. I stretched my arm and grabbed
that of the child eavesdropping from the next room. A scream
came from the other side of the wall and Tanjae jumped to their
feet, finally cottoning on.

I saw through the wall. I did not know the child. Since they
shared no bond with me, the child must be newborn.

"What is your name?" I asked. My voice resounded
throughout the ship, as it had to be loud enough to carry to the
other side of the wall.

"Teacher," Tanjae interjected.

"What is your name? Who is your teacher? What business
do you have here?"

I was anxious at having failed to notice the child's presence
sooner, and that vexed me. My powers could have diminished,
or the child could have concealed their motion from me. Either
possibility was upsetting.

The child tried to wriggle free. They seemed to have trouble
believing that a hand could spring out from a wall; they were
terrified. I pulled the child toward me without thinking. I had
intended to bring them through the wall so as to sit them down
in this room for a scolding. But the child's wrist hit the wall
instead of passing through it and twisted at an odd angle. I
paused in surprise.

I spoke to the child's wrist. I told it to become flexible. It
did not answer, or give me the slightest hint of acknowledgment. I kept trying to talk to it but received no response. It was
even more closed-off than Tanjae's wall. No, it was worse than
that—it was no different from an object.

Shuddering inwardly, I let go of the child.

"*I* brought the kid," said Tanjae. From somewhere around
the ship, I heard a voice whisper, *You're really going to give me*

a dreadful life now, aren't you? "Or else they would've been quarantined."

TANJAE BROUGHT OUT a first aid kit and disinfected the child's hand before applying ointment on it. Part of the skin had scraped against the wall, exposing the raw red layer underneath. It was a surreal scene, given that a Dark Realm body never bled and could never be healed with an ointment.

"The kid was wandering through space. You know how the corrupt children are . . ."

"They lose their way." I nodded. "They do not know themselves. They cannot find their teacher. They are stuck, unable to return to the Dark Realm nor the Lower Realm."

I examined the child's hand. It was an intricate replica. There were even blood vessels and organs in the child's body, crude as they were. That was when I remembered the cafeteria and the farm inside the spaceship.

The child's domain was limited to their body. Not an ounce of surrounding air belonged to them. I studied their essence and, after a laborious probe, located their source. Now I understood why both Tanjae and the spaceship had recalled that dear name.

"Aman," I called to the child. The child only stared back at me wide-eyed.

"No, this is a piece of Aman," Tanjae corrected me. "One of Teacher Aman's children, from the fourth or fifth division. The kid has no memory of their parent body."

"Right. So this *is* Aman."

"No, they're different. Just like you and I are different, Teacher."

I glared at Tanjae. Unfazed, they continued, "Teacher Aman divides into countless entities whenever they go down to Earth. Before, they would've inhabited the bodies of insects, fish, birds, or other small animals . . . but you know how it is, there are only humans left in the Lower Realm these days. The natural world has shrunk quite a bit since Teacher Tushita stopped descending to Earth. You've also retrieved every piece of yourself recently. In just the last generation, there's been a mass extinction more sudden than the great Permian extinction in the Paleozoic era."

"You speak of it as if it were wrong."

Tanjae clammed up.

"You think it is wrong?" I asked, seizing the arm of Aman's child. By way of lighthearted protest, I injected some of my molecules into the pores of the child's skin. My molecules sped up their cell division and healed the wound. No matter how corrupt a body was, treating a simple wound like this was nothing. Tanjae's breathing quickened. Oh dear, Tanjae was still clinging to the habit of breathing despite being in the Dark Realm.

"No, there's nothing wrong with it. There's no death either. The Lower Realm isn't real, just as pain isn't. A mass extinction is simply a mass homecoming. We can always go back, so . . ." Tanjae replied mechanically. They were phrases Tanjae must have repeated a thousand times while writing lines under the watchful eye of disciplinary teachers. Whenever Tanjae put their heart and soul into uncovering the structure of the universe, we had to hastily send down a patrol team, expel them from school, and drag them back to the Dark Realm. They were summoned numerous times and put in detention just as often. When they returned from the Lower Realm after crying out for truth with their last breath, they would lose heart and resign themselves to detention for an entire generation.

"Do you doubt that?" I asked, relinquishing my grip on the child's arm. It was a typical question asked to test one's corruption. Aman's child gazed at their hand in wonder, as if they had witnessed a great miracle.

"No," Tanjae answered slowly.

"Good. Now, you do not have what it takes to teach this

child. So send them to whichever teacher you like. They will receive the education they need."

Tanjae stood up and clutched my arm, accidentally tearing and unraveling parts of the tunic my former self had woven with grass. I glowered at Tanjae, but they did not back off.

"The teachers will quarantine this kid."

"They can walk out on their own if they overcome their corruption."

"They never will."

"Then a kind teacher will merge with them."

Tanjae shook their head, frustrated that I was not understanding. On the contrary, I understood all too well—the dangers of this conversation.

"Please just let them live here. They're only a small piece. They won't affect the universe."

"But you will not let that happen, which is why I bring this matter up."

I looked pointedly at the transporter. The machine gave a start and pretended not to have noticed my gaze. Gwanhwa creaked about, coughing evasively. A blanket rolled itself up and attempted to look smaller.

"Hiding a corrupt child is outrageous enough, but sending them to Earth is unacceptable. They should be kept in the Dark Realm at least."

"I know."

"Corrupt entities do not know they *are* the universe. That they and other entities are one and the same. They know neither sympathy nor love. Sending a corrupt child down to Earth will only spread corruption there."

"I know!"

"Knowing without acting is not truly knowing."

Tanjae looked like they did not know how to explain themselves. Tanjae and I were on different planes of understanding.

They said, "These kids want life. A life in the Lower Realm, not the Dark Realm."

"To want a life that is only an illusion is in itself a sign of corruption."

"And yet they still want it. I don't know why. I know their ways are hard to explain. But I do think that everyone has the right to do what they want. As you know, there is no real wrong in the world and no sin, so . . ."

I forced a large number of my molecules into Tanjae's skin through the pores, softening up that arm. Tanjae lost control of their hand and it stuck to my body like a pancake. Aghast, Tanjae tried to extricate their hand but only caused their arm to elongate like warm, stretchy dough. The arm's molecules were tender and supple. Some evaporated and some liquefied, the arm steaming and dripping with water.

"Think again, child."

Tanjae shut their mouth. The whole spaceship was nervous. It sent me hostile signals. But the components of the ship were just as individual and disconnected as Tanjae; they did not have the power to mobilize themselves and chase me out.

The ship shook, and everything in my vicinity from dust to objects began rattling toward me. The air around me thickened, the temperature dropped. The cooled air grew heavier and sank, pushing out the air below and generating wind. I even sucked in light, which caused a redshift and made my body appear slightly more scarlet.

"If you change your mind, I will spare you from merging for now."

Tanjae looked down at their arm, then up at my eyes. "If I lie, I suppose you would see through it."

"That is correct."

Tanjae opened their mouth but closed it again. They shut their eyes.

Just as Tanjae had made their decision, so had I. I pulled. Tanjae's molecules spilled into my body, along with the fear storming inside their mind. Their desperate wish to protect their individuality. Tanjae refused to give up their beliefs to the end. They made an irrational choice despite wanting very much to preserve their life. Irrationality, yet another symptom of corruption.

Tanjae's corruption was bound to be found out. There were no secrets in the Dark Realm. If I spared Tanjae now, they would only be quarantined or merged later, or if they were lucky, subjected to intense training in which they would have to repeat painful and meaningless lives. Tanjae had to be stopped now for their own good.

This child is me, I thought. What was "I" thinking? What was "I" trying to learn?

That a child was rebelling against their teacher meant they had obtained individuality. A new ideology had been born. Tanjae was ready to be a new teacher. Even if their teaching methods were not to my liking, or to any of the other teachers'. No, the very fact that a child was not to my liking signaled that it was time for me to let them go.

I released Tanjae, who bounced back and dropped to the floor. Tanjae's body was not fully restored yet, with liquefied molecules running down like beads of sweat.

"Why?" Tanjae demanded, putting up a tough front despite their trembling.

After a pause, I replied, "As I said, I do not know your point of equilibrium."

"Are you scared? I doubt feasting on me would corrupt you, of all teachers."

"Let me take a look at Aman's child. I should give them a life."

"Will you send them to the Animal Realm?" Tanjae sounded me out cautiously while laying Aman's child in the transporter.

"I do not know yet."

"But that's what you usually do. Animals tend to share each other's feelings more than humans do. Which is why living as animals or lowly creatures for a time can heal us. While humans are very disconnected from one another . . . right?"

That was what we usually did. The more corrupt a child, the more likely we were to give them the life of a small creature. Certain humans who correctly guessed that cause-and-effect relationship viewed it as a punishment, but there are no punishments in life. There are no rewards either. There is only learning.

"Learning the hard way can be meaningful too," I replied. I placed a hand on the child's forehead.

I recalled the myriad pieces of myself that had lived on Earth, when I existed as trees, butterflies, birds, rats, and pests, or formed the grass and rivers and fields. I summoned up every life, every destiny in which I was oblivious to the fact that I shared the same space with my countless other selves.

I unearthed one of my past selves, a woman with certain insecurities. She craved affection because she had been raised in a loveless home. She had spent her entire life without a child, but now I will send her one. The two of them will love each other with the ferocity of battle. They will fight and get hurt. They will make mistakes but learn from each other; they will hurt but live that much more fiercely. The life of one will be a key question in the life of the other.

"I will be your mother," I told the child. "You will learn empathy in your next life. Find something that you believe is kindred to you, whether it is a human or an animal or an object. Then corruption will leave you. And you shall regain the ability to divide or merge at will."

Particles in my body imbued with my will flowed out of my fingertips and into the child's genes. The genes would guide the child's life to some extent but nothing more. Their own will would define their life.

"I don't get it," said Tanjae after the child was transported. "How does reincarnating into the past affect causal relationships?"

"There is no causality. Only mutual interaction."

"What if the kid goes back in time and changes the universe?"

"Every life changes the universe. Each time *you* live a life and come back here, everything changes too. Remember, that child is you, and I am you. If that child changes, so will the rest of us," I said, and surveyed the entire ship. I spoke to it. The conversation was a difficult one in which many trades had to be made, but I tried my best to persuade it.

I had to yield many things in the process and give up a portion of my body. My condition would worsen. But no matter. It would worsen regardless of what I did.

Tanjae noticed my fatigue and asked, "What did you do?"

"I created a conditional gravitational field. Other corrupt children who die and lose their way will be pulled into this spaceship. Take as many as you can under your wing."

Tanjae was quiet. Then they asked, "Why did you do that?"

"So that you may reincarnate those children."

I smiled to myself, thinking that for such Materialist children, waking up in a space battleship after death would make for quite the earth-shattering experience.

Tanjae didn't see the source of my amusement. "Why should I? It's not right."

"Nothing is 'right.' A thing is only either excessive or wanting. As this is not an excessive venture, you may undertake it."

I looked down at the armrest of my chair and pushed my hand through it, as if I were dipping the hand in water. Tanjae paid me little attention. They were used to me pulling such stunts.

But my intrusion threw the armrest into chaos. In human

terms, it had gone insane. It shouted, *I am a solid material, I cannot be pierced this way. I am* . . . as if to reaffirm those facts to itself or perhaps to me.

I overpowered it using the same mechanism as Tanjae's transporter. There was no persuasion. No conversation. No trades.

It's chemistry, I whispered.

THE OLD ME

I WAS FEELING POORLY WHEN YEONSHIM THE LOVING CAME TO see me. I lay on a stone bed I had set up in a dark cave, sinking into my abyss, entrusting the children's education to my disciples. I had cleared away the temple and every house from my bardo and let it turn into a wilderness of crags and dreary fields. The children complained of their teacher having twisted tastes, but the truth was that I did not have the strength for much else.

Yeonshim pounced on me. They knocked me over and pinned me to the ground, seized me by the throat, shook me, slapped me, and tore off my clothes.

The throng of children discussing their lives outside my cave swiveled around. Pups and pests, monkeys and pigs looked my way. The teachers sensed what was going on and prepared for trouble. Believing that one could hurt someone in the Dark Realm was cause enough for concern.

"You killed my child!"

Yeonshim seemed to have dragged their body straight out of the Lower Realm. Their dark, mottled flesh was covered in soil, as if they had crawled out of a grave. Breasts sagging, white hair tangled like a magpie's nest, a few of their teeth missing. They did not seem to have passed through rock or been carried here on winds. They must have journeyed on foot. Their fingernails and toenails were black with dirt, their hands and feet cracked and bloody from chunks of gravel digging into their skin.

"You killed my child!"

I remembered now. Yeonshim was the child of Wangliang. According to the Dark Realm's pedigree, that is. The relationship was reversed in the Lower Realm, where Yeonshim had been Wangliang's mother in their latest life. The last time I saw Yeonshim, they were a ball of light, like a small firefly, and did not dare look me in the eye. They balked when they were instructed to become their teacher's mother and begged to have the command withdrawn; how could they possibly do something so preposterous? I comforted them by saying it was a beginner's training course that ran only briefly.

"May heaven strike down the likes of you, calling that *training*!"

Yeonshim attempted to tear my body to pieces but it merely punctured and tenderized, while vines with chartreuse leaves sprouted around me, swaddling Yeonshim and pulling them off me. As the children watched from a distance, Wangliang flew toward us as a haze of particles and consolidated into a human form between Yeonshim and me.

"Mother," said Wangliang, calling their child by the term of address they had used in the previous life. I was bewildered. "I am here. There is no death, you are mistaken."

I was sprawled on the dirt with the wind knocked out of me. An inexplicable fear coursed inside me. I wanted to throw away my pride and honor and flee from this spot.

Yeonshim finally stopped frantically trying to cut through the vines and glared at Wangliang, fuming. "You are not my child. My child is dead. That bastard killed him."

Yeonshim was in bad shape. They seemed to have lost all memory but that of their previous life. Their disconnection was severe and they appeared to have forgotten how to shape-shift.

That was when a memory came back to me. Had it been a military coup staged in some country? I belonged to the counterinsurgency forces and fired into the crowds of protesters. The mother of the young man I shot dead had come for me now, half a century later. I had been driven half-mad by confusion and guilt after killing the man . . . but that was simply my share of pain to bear. I could not lessen the pain of others. So it had not been an altogether well-lived life, even though I had learned something from it.

Wangliang glanced at me, but when I showed no response, they assumed this was some sort of test and took action. They persuaded the cave to move out of the way: the ceiling cracked open and the walls backed away. Unbidden, the surrounding rocky cliffs and hills also shifted on their haunches and withdrew. The space I was in transformed into a vast clearing. I felt naked out in the open. The children stared at me with curiosity shining in their eyes. I longed to open up a rathole somewhere and hide in it, but even that I could not do.

"Yeonshim has been corrupted," Wangliang declared. "Anyone may be a teacher to a corrupted entity. I shall teach Yeonshim a lesson as their son and teacher, on behalf of Prophet Naban."

We do not punish ourselves. What pain can any punishment inflict on us? We do not reward ourselves either. What pleasure can any reward bring us? We simply teach and learn. On occasion, we teach what a child does not want to learn.

"Mother, you have been corrupted. I shall quarantine you until you can break free on your own. I will forge a wall with my body. That way I would leave a part of myself beside you. You will be able to step out once you realize that the wall is you, is the same as you, and the same as me, that you and I are no different."

Wangliang's decision was an ordinary one. But it felt monstrous to me. For pity's sake, had not Wangliang been Yeonshim's son? That ancient woman had nurtured him in her womb for ten months, suckled him for many more. She had changed the diapers he soiled, put food in his whining mouth. Had she not spent half her life in tears and suffering after he died? How could he treat his mother so?

"You can either disperse into particles, shrink your body, or make yourself able to pass through the wall. I will be watching by your side."

Wangliang's voice was soft and benevolent, yet it did not strike me as such. The whole business seemed ghastly. Yeonshim would take a hundred years to escape at the very least.

"No," Yeonshim pleaded, finally grasping the seriousness of the situation. Wangliang's vines probed Yeonshim's body.

Wangliang pronounced, "You have grown far too disconnected to break down into particles. If you cannot atomize, you cannot reincarnate and purge your corruption through learning. Difficult as this is, it is the fastest way."

"Wait," I said. Even as I spoke, I feared I would let slip my condition. Unaware of my concerns, everyone focused their attention on me, expecting me to utter some great truth.

"It is my fault that Yeonshim became corrupt. I gave them a life too cruel for a young child to bear. I shall forge a bond with Yeonshim in their next life and exchange learning."

"Yeonshim's body has hardened too much. I doubt they can reincarnate."

"I will help them."

"If that is your wish."

Wangliang did not give the matter another thought. They asked, "Will you be their kin?"

"If that is what Yeonshim desires."

"Mother, the Prophet has made a generous offer. Will you accept?"

Yeonshim was flustered. But even in such confusion, Yeonshim seemed to recognize a foe from their last life. "That scoundrel is a murderer. Not a Prophet."

"The Prophet has graciously proposed to be your kin, and will accompany you for one full life."

"That fiend killed my child."

Wangliang looked at me apologetically and said, "Yeonshim is not catching on."

"Ask them what they want. Tell them I will grant it."

I asked Wangliang to relay the message even though I stood right next to Yeonshim, for I dreaded facing them. But Wangliang still thought I was trying to teach them a lesson and kept their eyes on Yeonshim.

"Let me kill that bastard."

"That is impossible," Wangliang replied calmly. Indeed, it was physically impossible. "Please suggest something else."

"Then turn him into a dog, so I can leash it and drag it around its whole life."

"So be it," I answered. Wangliang's eyes flashed coldly. Viewing the position of animals and humans as unequal was another symptom of corruption. Wangliang said, "Kin or beast, it makes no difference. The Prophet will accompany you in life as a beast, protect you, teach you. In that dog, you will find life's joys and solace and wisdom . . ."

"Make him suffer the same life as mine! Reincarnate me so that I can kill that bastard's child!"

"There is nothing to learn from such a life. Your corruption will only worsen. A teacher does not weave you a life that offers no learning."

"I accept," I said again. "Let them choose whatever life they wish to have. Give them time to think and tell me what they decide. I will do exactly what is asked of me."

Wangliang hesitated for a moment but did not question their teacher's judgment. They believed I had a profound plan in mind. But I had nothing, save for pain.

I WATCHED THE children lead Yeonshim to the rest area, then made my escape. I atomized and flew at first, but that became too taxing before long, so I ran on two legs. I hurtled on, inadvertently pulling and tangling the strings that linked me to the universe. Rocks slid off the mountain ridge ahead, the valley sank deeper, the waters grew choppier. I wanted to cut off every one of these strings. I feared that this bulky body of mine, my bardo, would lay bare my innermost secrets. I longed to be divided and disintegrated, to be smaller and run away to a place inhabited by none.

A place inhabited by none?

I was horrified that I had such a thought; it had flared up in me like a sickness.

That child is me.

I wrapped my face in my hands. Yeonshim was me. No one else but me. A part of me that had emerged from my body.

I am the corrupt one.

I was spreading corruption. I was a carrier who transmitted disease wherever my feet touched. If one piece changed, so did the whole. It was needless to say how much impact a colossal body such as mine would have.

"Are you all right?" someone said, blocking my path. It was Wangliang. I was not all right. I sank to the ground, covering my head with my hands. The third generation of teachers flew in and flocked around me. I composed myself. There was nothing to be embarrassed about. Nothing to be ashamed of. Everybody here was me. It was impossible to hide myself from me.

"Corruption is spreading among the children," said Wangliang.

"I know. I have seen it myself."

I was afraid Wangliang would ask for guidance, for I had none to offer. Wangliang was not corrupt and saw through every bit of my confusion. Whispers broke out around me. Wangliang addressed the crowd:

"Settle down. Teacher Naban has been this way ever since they took on the task of eliminating Aman. It was a great sacrifice." They continued, "To dispose of the corrupt Prophet Aman, the Prophets reincarnated next to Aman in every era and removed them early on in life. The Prophets revamped systems, seized power, and changed policies in the guise of chance and misfortune. Those measures could not take down every Aman, however, and Teacher Naban had to personally claim the remaining lives. That is how Aman's existence was erased from history."

So it was.

Aman corrupted the children and accelerated the separation of selves. Now people refused to believe that they and the world were one and the same. That they and the Other were one and the same. They thought themselves alone, and drunk in their solitude, they questioned why they, whose greatness should have matched that of the universe, were so small and insignificant. Tushita bade me to collect the pieces of Aman scattered across Earth and bring them to the Dark Realm. I could not find an excuse to refuse. Aman was my child and myself, everything was my fault.

As I divided into tens of thousands of entities and descended to Earth at every point in time, I thought:

There is no death. We neither disappear nor perish. We simply change. The self never ceases to exist. Only our interpretation of it changes. So, there is no murder, and no sin.

In thinking that, I foolishly overlooked some things:

The enormity of experiencing division.

An enormity tantamount to that of merging.

The ease of corruption, the simplicity.

"To do so," Wangliang went on, "Teacher Naban had to suppress their powers of empathy to a bare minimum. They had to occupy a body specially made to believe the self was different from the Other and that all entities were separate. That is why Teacher Naban has been contaminated, spurring our corruption. We must address this issue."

Wangliang's words were also aimed at me. I braced myself and said, "You must have something in mind."

"Please merge with Aman," Wangliang said calmly. The teachers who stood behind Wangliang were also calm. "Further, please reclaim us, and all the rest. Reclaim us and Aman, and return to your original self, to neither Naban nor Aman, but Aisata."

That thought is mine, I thought. How could that thought not spread when it filled my own head? How could my children not be seduced by it? All of them were essentially me. This very conversation was, in effect, me talking to me. All of these conflicts reflected my division of self, the chaos in my mind.

"Aman will not agree to merge with me."

"We should think of a way, then."

"Once I merge with Aman, Naban will vanish. I will become something I was not before."

"That is not true, Teacher. Aman was originally Naban, just as we were."

I knew what Wangliang said was right. Yet I doubted it, even though nothing about it was doubtful. The sick doubted everything. "Aman is a corrupt Prophet, the source and breeding ground of contamination. Do you not fear how a body such as theirs will change us? We may, all of us, turn into Aman."

"That cannot happen," Wangliang said without an ounce of hesitation. "Once we merge with Aman, the whole of us cannot turn into what you are now either. Even in the unlikely event that we lose our dominance to Aman, change will still occur. Aman cannot perish, and neither can we. There is no perishing. Only change."

It seemed as though I would have to resign my teaching post to Wangliang. Or I could merge into this child.

"Preserving the identity of Naban is not a pressing matter, Teacher. Those who are not corrupt must prioritize their original selves. We must heal Aman before they contaminate more of the universe. Should we fail, we will still have made a meaningful effort. Obtained another lesson."

This person is me, I thought.

Corruption was steadily overcoming me and I had begun to cling to my individuality. Wangliang was right, and my fear was worthless. A dreadful teacher I was, pettily consumed with losing my identity while the worlds grew sick with corruption.

I am responsible.

I gave birth to Aman and failed to stop the child from going astray. I failed to bring all of Aman back to the Dark Realm, to capture the ones that scattered into hiding. So I had to put matters right, once and for all.

I must be the one to do it.

At the same time, a question rose in the recesses of my mind like fog. The strange feeling that I was responsible for more than I could fathom. The inkling that perhaps that was why none of the measures I had taken so far had succeeded. The sneaking suspicion that corruption might be leaking out from the unlikeliest cracks.

I, as a whole, knew everything. Even now, when I was divided, I was still Aisata, the entire universe. Perhaps it was in that knowledge that Aisata thought up this solution, then gave me the order through an unconscious connection.

I inwardly shook my head. How ridiculous my thoughts were, driven by the fear of losing my selfhood. They were foolish meanderings derived from my incompleteness. My turmoil would be gone once I merged with my children. For the present "me" would be no more.

"I am ready," said Wangliang, stretching out a hand toward me. One by one, the children standing behind Wangliang clasped each other's hands.

"We are ready too."

Wangliang had been overly captivated by the afterlife of late. They threw away their Lower Realm lives as they would an old pair of shoes. Bewitched by some mysterious power, they would abandon their possessions and live in the mountains or spend a life at a monastery or temple in complete isolation. Sometimes, they gladly sacrificed themselves for trivial matters of justice or conscience. It dawned on me now what Wangliang had been practicing for.

This person is me.

Whoever was doing this, I was the one doing it. Whatever Wangliang wanted, it was what I wanted.

"This will help," said Wangliang.

Of course it would. Wangliang's personality and purpose would mix into me. I would change, grow bolder. I would know no fear or regret. I needed Wangliang's personality.

The children stood hand in hand with Wangliang, their eyes sparkling with anticipation. They were excited to embark on the road to greater knowledge and insight, to become part of a larger, wiser self. *My dear children, what is about to happen is not what you imagine. When we are one, none of us will seem so great to you.*

I took Wangliang's hand in mine.

Once I did, I could not understand what I had been agonizing over.

This was nothing, really.

THE SECOND ME

1

ENCOUNTERS WITH TUSHITA WERE NEVER VERY PLEASANT, ESPE-
cially when I was up to something. Pristine entities were just as
difficult as corrupt ones.

Tushita was at once nowhere and everywhere. Sometimes
they were a pebble lying in the corner of a nameless Prophet's
bardo, sometimes a child who debated their previous and next
lives in that same corner. Since Tushita could blend in anywhere, spotting them was not an easy task, even for second-
generation Prophets. Neither was asking them to respect my
privacy, not when they were convinced that the whole universe
was essentially them.

Tushita was waiting at the entrance to Hell.

They had assumed the form of a lanky human clad in black
dopo robes and a matching hood. Their face was dark blue, their
eyes like gold coins shattered to pieces by a stone thrown through
the center, their limbs long and withered like sapless trees. They
stood in a battered boat riddled with holes at the bottom, holding oars and a lantern. I used to put together the same ensemble
when I guided my children to the Dark Realm long ago. Behind
Tushita flowed the River of Oblivion, which led to Hell. The
river gleamed bloodred and bubbled like lava.

Of course, the thing before me was not all of Tushita. The
Prophet was an immense white sphere, the size of a planet, that
orbited the world of the living, and this particular entity was
a small oscillating body that had slipped out of the sphere like

a strand of loose string. But unlike my children and I, this entity and Tushita shared a common personality and memory. A white thread thin as a cobweb extended from the entity's back to the distant Tushita.

White thread shot out from Tushita's fingertip. Glinting, it sped toward me and attempted to pierce through the crown of my head. I mobilized my particles and created an electric barrier around my body. Right before my forehead, the thread hissed and burned from the current.

"Is there a reason for us to converse through crude means, Naban?" Tushita said, their golden eyes flashing. The words rang out from their head and crossed into mine in the form of thoughts.

Not hiding my displeasure, I replied, "We decided long ago not to mix the personalities of Prophets. Doing so would contaminate our thoughts."

But I could not shield every one of my molecules, which were like the debris of a planet. Tushita, no doubt, would have already caught hold of a particle beyond my sphere of influence and interrogated it. My aversion, defiance, fear, and humiliation would have been exposed.

Tushita smiled. Not out of pleasure. They knew no joy or sorrow, anger or contentment. Rather, Tushita closely resembled our primeval, emotionless state. The smile was simply a visual cue to facilitate communication. Perhaps Tushita was inwardly thinking, *What dreadful regression, that even among us Prophets we must express our thoughts in this clumsy manner.*

"Merging does not work like that, Naban. Once you merge with Aman, you will no longer have a lingering attachment to your old self. You will not remain 'you.'"

Tushita had dived straight down to my mind's rock bottom.

I froze. I imagined Tushita devouring me, casting millions of strands over me to break me down into particles devoid of volition and personality. Tushita could do so without any malice or desire. They did not understand the obsession with individuality and independence. Because they did not understand it, they crushed it without ill will.

"I am trying to return to my original self. As you have," I said.

Tushita's unfathomable golden eyes glittered. Returning to one's origins was the one desire Tushita understood. Once upon a time, Tushita had been Mago, Pangu, Solmundae, and many other friends. Each one had been unique with distinct personalities. There was no trace of them in the current Tushita. Nor the faintest echo of their misery, before merging, at the prospect of losing their selves.

I pressed on, "I only plan to maintain Naban's identity until I finish merging. There is no other way, if I am to reclaim one so divided and individualized as Aman. I may not complete the feat if I turn into something other than Naban."

Tushita nodded lazily as if to say they had heard such arguments many times already. They caught one of my particles floating in midair and rubbed it between their fingers.

"Aman is a teacher of division, one who believes that life in the Lower Realm is real, not an illusion. They are so convinced of the reality of the Lower Realm that they have started questioning the reality of the Dark Realm. Merging with Aman will thus alter my beliefs at one point. That is why I must remain as Naban till the very end."

"A Prophet's personality cannot be overpowered by the clumsy magic tricks of a third-generation child."

Once again Tushita had swooped down to my rock bottom and once again, I froze. A Prophet of Tushita's standing did not need to connect bodies to read minds. Tushita let nothing slip past their sharp eyes. Just as I had been before Aman divided from me.

"It would only be to help me. The merging depends on *my* will."

"Aman has a will too, Naban. Pitted against one another, whole against whole, there is no assurance which Prophet will come out on top."

I closed my eyes. Fear had swallowed me once more. "As you say, Aman will contaminate me, but I shall contaminate them too. Even if I fail, I should at least be able to stop corruption from spreading any further among us. And across the universe."

Tushita nodded, but I was unsure if it was in agreement or in dismissive acknowledgment of hearing what they already knew.

The river, bleeding crimson, lapped beneath the porous boat in which Tushita stood. The far side of the river boiled angrily. Steam formed an odorous mushroom cloud. Molten rock flowed like a river and the crags had softened as well. On the far side lay the dead, those who had been imprisoned and tortured for centuries and millennia. The dead were bewildered. Why must they pay such a terrible price for so long when all they had done was hate their parents or lie, eat selectively or leave food on their plates, behave a little stubbornly or pettily in just one of their lives? Why must the laws of the Dark Realm be so merciless?

Because they were all Aman.

Pieces divided from Aman.

None of the prisoners were sinners. They were simply guilty of common misfortunes, common weaknesses, or common mistakes. Imprisonment was sometimes a mode of instruction employed by a teacher, at other times an ascetic practice willingly undertaken. But the place took on its horrible appearance entirely due to its inhabitants, who realized they could wield certain small powers there and redecorated their bardo with imaginative flourishes—not having realized they possessed the power to escape.

"Tushita, I cannot let myself grow any more corrupt. This is the only means left to me."

"I wholly agree," Tushita replied. The "whole" Tushita spoke of was not the whole of my words but of my being. The way they saw it, "I" was Tushita as well as the entire Dark Realm. As Tushita equated themselves to the Dark Realm, they equated me to it too. Their sole concern was that my corruption would poison the Whole. They agreed with me only in that the Dark Realm must not be corrupted any further. The corruption or healing of Naban, a mere single entity, was a trivial matter in comparison. "Conversely, if *you* were to be eaten by Aman now, the corruption may spread even more. We have quarantined Aman for a reason. We must wait until they are healed."

"I know the protocol, but I have no time," I replied, thinking that Tushita would understand the scope of "I" differently again.

"Aman is a Prophet of division. They will not agree to merge with you. You will fail."

"Then I will learn something from that too. You can claim me then, after I learn from my failure."

Now *I* was taking a step into Tushita's mind. I did not wish to. This was something I wanted to avoid at all costs. Merging with Fuxi would be a thousand times better than merging with Tushita. At least with Fuxi, I could hope for our union to neutralize each other and spawn a new entity with a new name, but merging with Tushita meant that I would only become a bigger Tushita. Dreading the prospect, I knew, was a sign of corruption, but I could not help but recoil at the thought.

Tushita gave no answer. They seemed to recoil for different reasons. They must have put off merging with me and Aman as long as possible; to them, consuming the corrupted would be like eating dung.

"So let me go," I said.

"I am not here to stall you, Naban."

Tushita held up a finger and twirled it, sucking in my particles as one rolls up noodles. I knew I could not stop Tushita.

Helplessly, I was dragged in. Threads of my particles emitted light as they gathered around that bone-dry finger. What Tushita did had the same effect on me as someone twisting my arm or strangling me in the Lower Realm—it threatened the self.

"The will of all Prophets is my will, Naban. There is no reason for a Prophet to object to another Prophet's decision. An old axiom comes to mind: 'The corrupt do not know their own corruption, and act only in ways to spread corruption.'"

"I am trying to merge, which is the ultimate goal for us all. It is what we must accomplish at the end of the universe, and only then will the universe end. Merging cannot possibly spread corruption."

"And yet you let Tanjae go."

"That child had to be . . ." I stopped short and corrected myself. For I knew the words I was going to say would sound illogical. "That entity knows how to merge while preserving the self. I let Tanjae go in case we needed their knowledge."

Tushita nodded, and again I was uncertain whether the gesture meant they agreed with me or had expected my answer.

"Naban. I sympathize with your motives, but you have already failed once. Rather than take the risk, do you not think it a better solution to have all the Prophets disassemble you, Aman, and the rest of Aisata?"

I fell silent. I sensed Tushita carefully scanning my deepest vulnerabilities with unfeeling eyes.

"Tushita . . . I do not want this," I said finally. "Let me at least return to my original self. I do not wish to merge with anyone other than myself and Aman. Even if I have to give up Naban, I cannot give up Aisata too."

Fear reared its ugly head again the moment I finished speaking. I did not and could not explain myself. I had laid bare my irrationality. If Tushita were to eat me now or lock me away forever, I could say nothing in my defense. Meekly, I closed my eyes and prepared to accept the ending I did not want.

But Tushita showed no sign of moving. Neither sympathy nor spite existed in them. Save for corruption, nothing was right or wrong to them. They simply considered which path led to less corruption, or more.

"Your will is also mine, Naban," said Tushita. "While your words point to a different direction than mine, they are reasonable. Rather than risk corruption among the clean, it makes sense to try merging corrupt entities first, despite the odds of failure."

I almost let out an audible sigh of relief. If I were caught in the hideous act of mimicking breathing too, Tushita would have gobbled me up before I could cry "Wait!"

Tushita gazed across the river. "Naban, hold steadfast to your will. To merge is to mix bodies as well as minds. One wrong move and Aman may convert you. Then you would pursue a different purpose."

"That will not happen."

Tushita lapsed into thought for a moment, then added, "We shall, however, learn from this too." They stepped back and made room for me on the boat. "I will guide you to the other side of the river, Naban. I will wait for your return. Should you fail, I will do you the kindness of eating you with the affection and duty of siblinghood."

A fair remark, but I was not overly pleased to hear it. But I had no way of stopping Tushita from keeping their word anyhow. I splashed across the surface of the water and climbed onto the boat. Tushita watched me board and asked, "Why are you wearing clothes, Naban?"

"It is a gift from me to myself."

Tushita asked no more.

2

THE PATH I USED TO TAKE WAS BARRED BY BEDROCK. IT WAS not responsive to persuasion. I barely found a single crack to squeeze through, having turned my body into a near gaseous form. I knew that no place in the universe remained unchanging, but the wild transfigurations of this one were beyond all my expectations. The ground's surface had collapsed, burying shards of bone and skull beneath it. The bones were heavily marred and broken as if they had been torn apart by the gnashing of beasts. There was a time when the teachers made rounds here to preach, but none set foot on this terrain now.

I thought of Wangliang. I thought of Yeonshim, and all my children. What had Naban been like before merging with them?

I would never know. The instant I merged, I forgot who my primary self was. I inherited the name of my oldest entity as a small gesture of courtesy, but no single entity represented who I was now. My personality differed from all of theirs, my purpose from all of theirs.

What would happen if I failed? If Aman were to devour me instead?

Would I, like Aman, take the empty shell that was my body to be my all, believe the Lower Realm to be the only world in existence, fear the Dark Realm and cling to the world of the living? Would I presume that organs and nerves and a bundle of muscles—a three-dimensional lump of matter—constituted my whole being, and that anything else was none of my concern?

Would I fight tooth and nail like Aman to preserve that state? Would I, a diseased body, hunger for disease?

I would know when I turned corrupt. But not before. The thought that I might glean learning from corruption did occur to me, but it did not reach my heart. It was like trying to think I could learn from insanity if I were to go insane.

A hot wind blasted me as I stepped onto the ground.

The wind was half fire, as all oxygen had burned away, leaving nothing that might be called an atmosphere. But I had no need to breathe and my body felt no heat.

The space was practically a vacuum. Every last drop of water had evaporated and the hot wind had driven everything up, making the space not so much gaseous but halfway between liquid and solid.

I transformed into a human and stood upright. The ground had melted and glided along like sticky clots of blood. I made my body feather-light since I would sink or get swept away if I had weight. Of course, a real Lower Realm body would have been burned to a crisp just by occupying this space.

I saw others with human forms. They did not look too different from the gooey, molten rocks or clumps of mud. They were also not too different in that they squirmed and moaned, drowned in the lava, or were blown to smithereens by a sudden surge of red waves.

I continued to walk and stumbled on something. It was a human hand. A skinless, nailless hand.

I bent forward to examine it. Wiping some lava away, I found a face. Half of it had melted and the remaining skin was cooked red. An arm exposed bare bone, on which stuck bits of old flesh and muscle.

"Help me," croaked the human after a long time. "You've come to save me, right? Are you a god? A divine messenger?" The human stared at me, eyes full of wonder.

Indeed, standing barefoot in this inferno with clothes intact, I must have been an astounding sight. But I wondered. Did the people here really not think themselves miraculous too? The heat of this place was such that no human skin or bone should have survived it. Merely suffering some burns was impossible here. Even if it were possible, no one should be alive in that state, yet the human before me clearly was.

"Is it over? Have I finished paying for my sins? Can I go to heaven now?"

"You do not need me to pull you out. This place is you, Aman."

Aman gaped at me, then lost their footing and was sucked a little deeper into the sea of fire. In trying to make sense of my words, Aman seemed to have forgotten for a moment that they were in a fiery hell.

"This entire place has been created by you," I said, as I always did on my visits. But it did no good. Here, memories scattered into the wind. Even I would retain nothing in my head if I were to live here with a nervous system resembling that of Lower Realm bodies. I would need more room for my pain alone.

"It hurts."

"There is no pain."

An uncomfortable suspicion crept into Aman's eyes. My words seemed to be neither what Aman had expected nor wanted to hear. No doubt they had hoped for a winged creature to descend, pull them out, and take them to a place completely different from this one.

"Every bit of this place is you. You must understand that, Aman."

"Who's Aman?" Aman looked puzzled.

"All of you are the pieces of Aman I retrieved from Earth. You have been quarantined here, and failing to merge or escape, you constructed an imaginary bardo of your own. This place is your creation. All of it is you."

"Have we ever met?"

Oh yes we had. I closed my eyes and recalled the fragrance of tea. The aged Aman lying by the sunlit window. I thought of the clay dolls Fuxi had conjured up for me to see.

Of all the lives I had spent with this entity, I called to mind the most vivid. I had interacted with every incarnation of Aman, but my life with this particular one had been the hottest and the fiercest.

I thought of their eyes, eyes I saw for the last time in that life. Their pupils shimmered like black moons. When their eyes closed, tears hanging on the long lashes trickled down. We were alive, and our lives belonged to each other. It seemed as though we had been one piece in the beginning and finally found the missing half we had long pined for. Even if all pain came to me and all happiness went to this person, I could have given that life my blessing. If I died and this person lived, it would have been the same as me living.

"We did more than just meet," I replied. "You and I were one."

You will fail. Ignoring Tushita's warning that rang in my head, I grabbed Aman's hand. I began to suck Aman in at once. They felt like a block of metal. They were firmly disconnected.

I pictured the transporter in my head as I mechanized a portion of my body and conjured a bundle of electric wires, which I plugged into Aman's body. Aman screamed. They seemed to have realized that I had no intention of taking them to Earth, let alone heaven. Flopping around like a fish out of water, they begged me to spare them. I could not understand. After spending all this time in a boiling cauldron, did they still have the desire to live?

"Stop resisting. I am trying to save you."

You, before anyone else, I thought, but mentally shook my head. Distinguishing between entities was a sure sign of corruption.

When I continued to pull in relentlessly, the look in Aman's eyes changed. Fear and resentment turned into rage, then into belligerence.

Aman's body began to respond. It rejected me with everything it had. White blood cells mobilized around my wires, and blood clotted up the wounds. When I inserted chemicals to melt the body down, its immune system fought back by releasing more counteractive substances.

Yes, that's it. Finally, you are acting like someone who used to be me.

I thought of several chemical formulas. I thought of the carbon atom with its four arms, and oxygen with its tendency to cling to and react with almost anything. I assembled and reassembled them in various combinations until I concocted a chemical that broke down human tissue, then injected it into the body. I stabbed, Aman defended. I pulled, Aman pushed back. It took a war of chemical and molecular formulas before I could feed on a single Aman.

I scanned my body. I checked for mental changes rather than physical ones. Had one person's worth of memories poured into me? Was I changed as much?

I was the same. Only bigger. Aman had become a part of me without blending into me.

I had succeeded.

Relief washed over me. As the tension in me unknotted, I laughed.

I could do it. I could retain myself. Stay as Naban. I would eat them one by one and slowly, I—

A violent spasm shook me. My body ran amok like an unbridled foal. It sucked in its surroundings like an engine gone haywire. Gulps of lava spilled into my throat, followed by boulders and mounds of earth. The souls clamoring inside them were dragged in too.

I realized that in the eagerness of learning how to devour, I had not learned how to stop myself. I scrambled to shape-shift but my half-machine body would not listen.

Tens of thousands of personalities exploded inside me. Emotions twisted this way and that. None mixed or blended, all churned in pandemonium.

I slumped to the ground, wishing I could regurgitate everything. Millions of Amans, Prophets of Division, Prophets of Individuality, sprang wildly to life inside me.

I am different.

I am not you.

I am me and you are not.

No, I vehemently denied their assertions. *All of you are me . . .*

My plea bounced off them.

I had made a terrible mistake. The realization struck like lightning. When I devised this method of merging, I was already viewing myself as separate from Aman. If I did not accept Aman as me, they would not accept me either. Everything that had entered me began to attack me.

You will fail, Tushita's voice whispered in my head. Hell poured into me all the while, gulp after gulp after gulp.

I TRUDGED OUT of the muddy riverbed. My feet were blackened and my toenails yellowed, dead, and cracked. Starting from my heels, I dispersed into molecules then condensed into liquid, trickled down, hardened, and was absorbed by the rest of my body.

What remained of Hell in my wake was a field barren as a desert. Cliffs and mountains had crumbled, the river of blood dried up. I had devoured everything from those boiling in the furnace to those frozen in Ice Hell. I ate the ones that starved and the ones captured and slashed by *dokkaebi* with knives. I left only the sand dunes and the dusty winds untouched, as I need not bother eating them.

Flesh trailed behind me like a giant sack, the countless un-mixed personalities rattling within.

Tushita was waiting for me on the tattered boat, which rested serenely on the riverbed. My feet sank deep into the mud. Tushita eyed my footprints. Their gaze also lingered on my sack of flesh, which wriggled like a bagful of freshly caught fish.

"You there, what is your name?" asked Tushita. For a moment I delayed answering. I had failed. I would perish. My death was imminent but . . . not just yet.

"Naban," I replied. A look of admiration crossed Tushita's face. It was not pretended. I clambered onto the boat and Tushita rowed me across the waterless river, back to the far bank.

My consciousness faded when I left Hell. Unable to form a body in my stupor, I dissolved into molecules.

For a while I pondered whether I was Naban or Hell, the successor of Naban or the successor of Hell. That thought in itself, I soon recognized, was an illusion. Naban and Hell and Aman were all parts of me, mere incomplete pieces.

I had become something closer to the original me. Oh, how happy I was. How long it had been . . .

3

TANJAE'S SPACESHIP WAS LODGED IN A SMALL ASTEROID.

It had not crashed into the asteroid. The asteroid had flown to it and surrounded it. A Prophet had come.

The ship was red with rust and green with moss and mold. Creepers had broken through the windows and enveloped the ship, and a thick tree had somehow wriggled through its surface. How much time had passed? Since I did not know how far I had floated along the dimension of time, a hundred years could have passed in the Lower Realm . . . no, a thousand, or even ten thousand.

I . . .

. . . was back to being Naban.

Good grief. How long had I roamed, giddy about returning to my earlier self? Wrapped in ecstasy without an ounce of self-awareness. As a blob of light or a lump of cells. But while I was a lump of cells, I was so happy with my state that I had not thought to come back.

My body burned like lava. A portion of it was compressed into a human shape, and the rest formed a thick layer of gas molecules around the asteroid like an atmosphere. Electric sparks flying here and chemicals reacting there produced lightning and thunder. Every moment, I writhed in the powerful temptation to return to that molecular form.

Why was I here?

That was when I remembered musing about a piece of me

that I had not yet absorbed. I remembered questioning why I had spared it, and feeling excited at the prospect of absorbing that last piece. I even remembered scheming to approach it in the guise of Naban to facilitate persuasion.

I felt horrible. Those thoughts had been my own but now I could not stand them. They seemed absurd, though they were not such outlandish thoughts to have. In fact, my feeling absurd was absurd. It struck me that the element of Aman might be exerting a stronger influence on me in my current, smaller form. I had to hasten back and evenly redistribute my body or else the pro-division element of Aman would manifest itself in who knows what manner.

And yet . . .

I steadied my gaze, shakily sat up, and crawled to the spaceship. With great effort, I turned the handle of the hatch half buried in the ground and pushed it open. I did not have the strength to persuade or pass the wall. The spaceship in turn seemed too weak to talk to me.

I took a step inside. Puddles formed wherever my feet landed. I was not sweating, but had lost control of my body—it was liquefying. Two or three times it gasified, but I managed to just about pull myself together and resumed walking.

The engine room looked like a gutted whale; only its skeleton remained. Children bustled in and out carrying items, dragging nearly everything outside. They were very young. They had limbs, and had holes for eyes or mouths, but that was it. Many of them were transparent or floated around without feet.

I spotted a fully formed child in the center of the room. It took me a while to remember their name: Jaehwa the Prosperous, a child of Fuxi. I liked the child even less than Fuxi. The two of them were bound to be similar, as they shared the same essence, but Jaehwa was much more juvenile. If Fuxi pursued pleasure, Jaehwa was true to their name and pursued only riches.

Jaehwa had a mountainous body with an immense girth, a

bald head, and a good-natured face that sported a meaty nose, beneath which protruded two long strands of a mustache. Jaehwa bore a striking resemblance to those piggy banks placed next to the cash registers of some Lower Realm restaurants to bring wealth and honor.

"Well, well, well, what have we here? They were even making paper," Jaehwa muttered, picking up one of the papers strewn across the dusty floor. "What did they make this out of? Did they hammer out wood or something?" The paper fluttered and rustled crisply. It was clearly of a different ilk from Jaehwa's squashy body, whose outline was blurry. The paper was, for all intents and purposes, corrupted. It was oblivious to its intelligence and its sameness to its surroundings.

Jaehwa attempted to absorb the paper but crumpled it and tore it up when it did not budge. It refused to be merged no matter what cruelty came its way. As if to declare it would sooner perish than lose its individuality.

Jaehwa noticed me only after several shreds of paper had fallen at my feet.

"Naban . . ." A pause, then Jaehwa added, "Teacher Naban."

"Who gave you permission to come here?" I demanded. The children who had been cleaning nearby stopped in their tracks. Jaehwa waved the children away and stepped back to get a better look at me. They had to take quite a few steps back because they were so large. They bowed.

"It has been a long time, Teacher. I heard you had returned to your origins and reached spiritual enlightenment."

How long had I been gone? Everything felt unfamiliar. No, the universe had not changed—I had. Because I was different, I saw everything differently. I interpreted every word differently.

"This is my domain. Why do you School of Pleasure followers disrupt the School of Honest Poverty's domain?"

"Ah, you must not be acquainted with the current ideology yet. Teacher Tushita has reorganized the administration and unified all schools. The School of Pleasure falls under that umbrella too."

Jaehwa conjured a business card from their fingertips and pushed it toward me. Without moving, I drew out a threadlike tentacle from my flank and snatched the card away and into my body. Jaehwa looked taken aback, then dusted off their hands as if losing even one business card's worth of their body was regrettable.

"You, Teacher, unified Hell and returned to the primordial universe, but the corruption persisted. I suppose the disease was too widespread. Teacher Tushita decided it was time to act, and launched a radical reeducation of the children. Those suspected to carry the disease were placed in intensive training, and those deemed hopeless are being merged into Teacher Tushita."

The children who were still in the room shouted in unison, "One, two, three!" and wrenched the dashboard off the wall. The wires and power cable split and tore. Myungyak and Gwanhwa quietly accepted their fates. They did not scream or protest. They simply stopped functioning, as if to say they either existed wholly or not at all, there was no middle ground. As if to say they would merge with others over their dead bodies.

"As it turns out, this place was a hotbed of corruption," said Jaehwa.

It was natural that a Prophet should uproot this place. If Tushita had not acted, another Prophet would have. Corrupted things should be disintegrated and restored. But it all felt off somehow. Unreasonable.

"You look unwell, Teacher."

When Jaehwa reached out a hand, I dissolved my form, stretching and scattering my body. I had dodged Jaehwa's gaze, in a different sense of the phrase from the Lower Realm.

"Tanjae is not corrupt. Even if they were, I should be the judge of that."

"Yes," Jaehwa replied. "But that's a gross understatement. Tanjae is the next generation's false Prophet. Aman's heir."

My insides churned. *Wait. Let me just finish this,* I whispered to my body. *This personality will fall soon. When it does you can do as you please. Please, give me a bit more time.*

"Tanjae was pulling in corrupt children, hiding them, and sending them back to the Lower Realm. We should have suspected Tanjae from the moment they tried to bring the knowledge of the Dark Realm to the Lower Realm. The rascal favored the Lower Realm all along."

I rolled my eyes. Not in the usual way. I unfurled dozens of long, thin, and soft strips of flesh from my back and sprouted swiveling eyeballs on each end. Jaehwa flinched. Using my tentacles, I searched inside the circuit board and slithered along the vent. I scanned the children at work and slipped into packed boxes.

Jaehwa probably thought I was making a show of protest, but I was not. Normally, at least in my own child's house, I should have been able to see through everything without craning my body or growing eyeballs. But I could not see without eyes. At least I did not think I could.

I located the hangar. It was protected with multiple layers of security and contained scores of children. A system was already in place where twenty transporters ran automatically. The children helped each other lie down in a transporter and escape to the Lower Realm. Tanjae must have hidden the children first when the search squad raided the spacecraft.

Tanjae was nearby. They were trapped inside a small metal box placed in an empty warehouse. The box had no breathing holes or windows. Not that Tanjae would die in such a box. They would not die, but . . .

Even though the inside of a box was no different from the outside—staying inside it should not be any harder or more painful, there was nothing Tanjae could not see or do because of being confined—it made me queasy. I felt as if Tanjae had been wronged.

"I used a material Tanjae made. I did them that kindness," Jaehwa said, following my gaze. "They can come out as soon as they realize that the wall is them. Even small children can do that. Tanjae is more than old enough, can't they do something so simple?"

"We must not tie Tanjae down to the Dark Realm. The Lower Realm might stop progressing or go back a few decades."

"So?" Jaehwa asked, eyeing me quizzically. Not out of sarcasm but with genuine curiosity. "That in itself is learning. Do you mean to say, Teacher, that there is meaning only in the Lower Realm's growth? The whole ecosystem could be destroyed and we would still learn. One lesson is not superior to the other."

Every word of that was true. But it sounded obscene. Crazy. I could not be sure how these words might sound to me a few moments from now. I might even grab Jaehwa by the throat and berate them for spinning lies.

Instead I said, "Tanjae is my child. In other words, me. This place is thus my domain and my body. I have returned now and will take care of it myself."

"I am your child too. My parent body, Teacher Fuxi, was also you once. All of us are parent and child to each other."

"You are distant kin."

"That's cold," said Jaehwa, drumming on their lower belly. "But you know we were intimate once."

I looked at them.

"Don't tell me you still resent me for what happened."

In one of my lives, Jaehwa had been the director of the orphanage I was in. He received government funding for every child. People were money to him. He brought children from missing-child shelters and burned their notebooks or any papers containing their home phone number. Sometimes he sent parents away who had managed to track down the orphanage.

He beat children until they forgot their addresses. Because I remembered almost everything about my parents and home, I got daily beatings. Sometimes I took the bullet for the other children. Most of the orphans who suffered with me were my children, my disciples.

"But you like that kind of life, don't you, Teacher?"

I was silent. I remembered a life in which this child rammed himself into me night after night. Ravaged me inside whenever he got drunk.

"To obtain learning in life, someone has to create bad karma. This is a sacrifice too, in a way, since you give up your own learning for the sake of others."

"I know Fuxi sent you."

"You do?"

"Fuxi wants to teach me a lesson. So, what do you wish to tell me?"

"Now that you've gathered all of yourself, can you see new truths? What have you learned through so many lives?"

"What are you trying to say?"

"Teacher, your methods encouraged your corruption and your children's. You are no different from Teacher Aman."

I could see Fuxi behind Jaehwa's back. This entity before me was one part of Fuxi. The Prophet had once again removed a chunk of their body and sent it my way. For noble purposes, from their point of view.

"Poverty, unhappiness, deprivation, abuse, an unloved life, all of these things alienate you from others. They corrupt you spiritually. Make you forget that you and the universe are the same."

When I gave no response, Jaehwa continued, "You end up caring for your own welfare and nothing else."

I REMEMBERED AMAN once saying:

—People of the Lower Realm have a right to be happy.

They are not us. They are independent entities. We don't have the right to weave their destinies and shape their lives to suit our needs.

Was I really being compared to that child whose views were opposite to mine? Was there truly no difference between us? How was that possible? I sought to teach that the Lower Realm was an illusion. But that only stoked my obsession with the Lower Realm, you say? Accelerated my division? How? I tried to think, but it was no good. I could not communicate with my current parent body despite being connected to it, and had no way to read the minds of others, much less my own.

"WHAT DID YOU learn in the life you spent with me?" asked Jaehwa. "Did you think, 'Oh, a great will I can't fathom made me live this life' or 'I chose this life for myself'? Were you happy that life taught you lessons? Ha, as if! You, my dear Teacher, were just a little kid crying in pain all the time."

Jaehwa was right. But admitting that fact only made me sneer. For all Jaehwa's cleverness in spotting the resemblance between me and my children, the fool was blind to their own resemblance to me. How could corruption stain only one corner when all of us were connected? How could the universe stay clean when I was corrupted?

"A sacrifice, you say . . ." I said as I advanced toward Jaehwa. I put my hand on a fat finger ten times the size of my hand. If we were in the Lower Realm, such a sheer difference in physical quantity would have allowed Jaehwa to crush my hand to a pulp with a mere squeeze, but here, my body was far larger than met the eye.

"It is indeed a sacrifice. A greater sacrifice than you can ever imagine," I continued.

Jaehwa sensed what I was thinking. They sensed it, and disbelieved. For my decision was not one a Prophet would make. But I cradled Hell in me. There was nothing I could not do.

"The more pain you inflict on others, the more sympathy you lose. You forget that the Other is the same as you. How disconnected you have become, just from your petty desire to teach me a lesson. How much of your body do you have left? How much of your domain can you control?" I pressed.

I felt Jaehwa's fear through my hand. Jaehwa was tiny. I knew just by holding them. They could summon every last piece of themselves and this body would be all they could muster. But it was a horribly great price to pay for just one lifetime of pleasure.

I increased the density of my body and the air around us grew murky. My gaseous molecules converged and clashed. Clashing particles produced sparks of electricity, which heated and momentarily expanded the particles, culminating in a thunderous crack. The flash of light behind me plunged Jaehwa's body into shadow.

"Teacher," Jaehwa said in a strangled voice. "Wh-why are you doing this to me? My studies have not fin—"

I COLLAPSED AFTER eating Jaehwa.

My body sprawled out of its own accord. I sucked and swallowed whatever came into view. I guzzled the children carrying the circuit board. A child who had been labeling boxes of evidence outside the ship came whizzing into me. I munched on the moss growing on the circuit board and the creepers climbing up the walls. I dug up the earth in which the ship was buried. I stuffed mouthfuls of earth down my throat, sucked the sap from the tree's roots. All without persuasion or conversation. The things I crammed into my body shrieked in panic and confusion.

I could not stop. Everything tasted so good.

I must save Tanjae, I thought. At the same time I wondered, *Why must I?* Tanjae was simply being educated. True, it might take them a thousand years to get out, but what of it? A thousand years would go by in the blink of an eye . . .

I shook my head.

I must save them.

I melted into the floor. I trickled down like water and materialized near Tanjae's box. With no strength to walk, I briefly dispersed my body and reassembled right in front of the box. The metal box looked like it had been cast in a single mold, showing no trace of being glued or nailed together. Realizing it was impossible to take Tanjae out of the box, I absorbed the box whole. It was a stubborn little thing and tasted awful. I had easily stomached Jaehwa and all those children, but now bile rose in my throat.

Tanjae lay covering their head with their arms. I hardly recognized them, even though they could not have been trapped for too long. Face ashen and hair graying, Tanjae was soaked because a part of their body had liquefied.

"Are you all right?" I asked.

"What took you so long?" Tanjae said, trembling. "Of course, you must have been busy. With plenty of things to take care of."

My body shook. I gasified briefly before I snapped awake and resolidified my body.

"You can't even begin to imagine what this feels like, Teacher. You've lived so many lives, but whenever you come back here you brush them off as if they're nothing. You go 'Ha, ha, ha, the Lower Realm is always the same' . . . What's so hard about walking through a wall, you ask?" Tanjae muttered a few choice swear words from the Lower Realm. They insulted my mother and my ancestors, though it was unclear who they referred to.

"You have no idea what this is, Teacher. You don't know pain . . . so you just enjoy it."

"I suppose so," I replied sadly. "Go seek another teacher. I was not the right one for you."

Tanjae's tearful voice faded away. My vantage point shifted.

My senses moved to the outskirts of the atmosphere surrounding the asteroid. I could feel the small asteroid hovering in the heart of my gasified body down below. I gazed upon the infinitesimal piece of myself aboard the spaceship on that asteroid. I was wondering what I was doing there when I abruptly came back.

I was Naban again, sitting before Tanjae in the form of a small human. I sensed I would not be able to sustain this personality for much longer. I could not guess what I would degenerate into or what purpose I would serve, having devoured Jaehwa and the School of Pleasure children. It made me sad to think that my personality would disappear. I knew it was a symptom of corruption but I could not help myself.

"Please kill me," Tanjae pleaded.

"There is no death."

"Then let me perish."

"That cannot be done."

I had a feeling this would be the last lecture I would ever give Tanjae and I would not get through to the child. I patted their shoulder. They slapped my hand away as if it were dirty.

"I will help you reincarnate. You will forget everything when you go down."

"I can't, not me. Even if I live, I'll wind up dead anyway. And when I die, I'll remember everything again. I can't bear that. My soul is finished. Nothing disappears. Memory is eternal, and so is life . . ."

"You will forget. Believe me."

"I can't!" Tanjae held out a hand. "Please merge with me."

I clenched my jaws.

"Take me. Then I wouldn't be dying and I won't ever have to be myself again. You, Teacher, will be fine with having my memories. You could accept and forget them. I can't, but you can."

I said nothing. This child believed that they would vanish

if they merged with me. That they would lose their sentience and become my arm or leg or some other appendage to my body . . .

My thoughts gave way to laughter. Had I not also lamented the death of my existence just moments ago? *Naban, you are no longer a teacher. You cannot presume to teach anyone now.*

What are you waiting for? I heard myself whisper from the other side of the atmosphere.

You will only be complete when you merge with it.

I must spare the child.

I was torn between the two thoughts.

Eat it and become whole again.

I will not.

Do you fear eating the corrupt child will soil you? You have nothing to worry about, not when you have eaten so much already. You can digest it easily.

No.

Absolutely not.

Tanjae was my child. In lives I could not count, I was their mother, father, friend, and teacher. Sometimes I was their son, their daughter, the beggar who knocked on their door on a cold day, the ragged child who asked for their help on the street. When I returned to the Dark Realm, I would chide Tanjae for "being unfilial" or for "shutting the door in my face" and such, thoroughly enjoying the abashed look on their face. That was why I could not bring myself to eliminate this child.

My whole self was perplexed at myself. *That is not a reason.*

I did not have the ability or the desire to explain. "They" could not understand. Soon, neither would I. The thought saddened me.

I placed my hand on Tanjae's. The child clutched it hard, as if it were their only hope. As if they were willing me to consume them quickly. A sweet scent overpowered me. I had to steel myself against the urge to wolf Tanjae down. My current body was no better than a swarm of hungry ghosts. I resisted. This temptation I felt was not mine. This was not me.

"Still, nothing ends. Nothing perishes. Only our interpretation changes." This was my final teaching. One that I myself had come to disbelieve. "Stay," I said.

"For what?"

"You must succeed me. You may take the name Naban if you need it."

Tanjae, finally at that moment, seemed to escape themselves. They recognized my condition, even as they suffered deep pain. Who said this child was corrupt?

"Are you ill?" Tanjae asked.

"Stay and help the children who lost their way. That shall be your ideology . . ." I meant to continue but was forced out of my body. Once more I became the atmospheric molecules circling the asteroid in which Tanjae's spaceship was buried. Now I wondered why I kept making meaningless conversation with a lowly creature inside my body. I should just swallow it and leave—

Tanjae seized my arm and pulled. I lurched back to the asteroid and keeled over. Tanjae helped me up.

"What did you eat?" the child asked.

"Hell." This was not a metaphor. "I will disappear with Aman. I told no one, but I have been suffering a sickness. I tried to return to my original form to stop my corruption. Nothing went as I expected. I do not know what will happen now."

Our surroundings chilled as I spoke. Corruption was devouring the universe. So what? The wall pitied me. The entire battleship sneered. Tanjae shook their head.

"Nothing disappears. To believe you can disappear is in itself a corruption."

It was as if lightning struck somewhere in my heart.

Tanjae went on, "There is no sin, and no sinner. There's only learning. No entity should have to disappear. The only wrong in the universe is in destroying balance. Ignoring the law of conservation of mass. Forgetting that the universe has a constant total mass and trying to erase a part of it."

I stared at Tanjae, stunned. I knew the child was blurting out my teachings without understanding them, afraid that I would disappear. But Tanjae always had the kind of insights that could only come from not understanding. Some insights were only known to babies or small children, who lacked wisdom and knowledge.

Ah, that was when I knew. Ah, it was too late. Ah, the corrupt do not know their own corruption.

Ah, I had gained learning but soon I would lose it. My whole self would devour and nullify everything I learned, iron out any unevenness in density. What a fool my whole self was. In being divided, I was a piece of architecture, an artwork, but if I were spread evenly, I would be reduced to mere specks of dust, a mound of earth. I would be worthless.

"Merging with that kind of mind-set will only worsen the corruption," said Tanjae. "Please, stop. Come back to your old self."

I had to admit that this child was wiser than I now. No, the smallest of children would be wiser than I now. So would the lowliest of creatures born on Earth without an ounce of knowledge.

I pulled Tanjae into a tight embrace.

Then I delicately maneuvered my gasified molecules hovering around the spaceship. I ripped out the shriveled creepers stuck to the ship's walls, reconnected the electric wires, and put the broken components back together. For permanently damaged parts, I rescued the frame and furnished it with new parts molded from my body. I soldered and assembled. The interior of the ship dazzled with a golden light as particles combined and divided.

I could feel Tanjae's body tensing in my arms. This would

be the last time I get to see the child look so shocked by my little prank. In spite of myself, I laughed.

"Leave this place . . ." I said after I finished restoring the spaceship and even polished it to sparkling perfection. "Run from the Prophets. And from me. You, my child, will find a way beyond any of our wildest dreams. Go, and preach your own teachings."

". . . Teacher?"

I WONDERED WHY I was still conversing with this small and insignificant organism in my body. I need not trouble myself with such a creature. Both the space battleship it was in and the asteroid the ship was on were but motes of dust.

". . . Teacher?" I heard a voice desperately cry out from afar. I considered eating the creature, but I had a funny feeling that it would be indigestible and dropped the idea.

Then I thought about who "I" was.

One of my former entities came to mind. A Prophet by the name of Naban.

It occurred to me that Naban had decided to merge with Aman, in order to return to the self that existed before it split into two Prophets. Now that I had transcended Naban, it was clear to me how fixated the Prophet had been on their own self. So much so that they were fixated on returning to their original form, Aisata.

An inferior thought. I smirked and gazed upon the whole universe as my whole self.

The universe was a spongelike organism whose cells were intertwined. It constantly moved and fluctuated. Pull one string and the whole universe moved in that direction, however subtly. Causes and effects were so intricately connected that one could not possibly predict what would manifest and shoot to prominence at every moment. The Whole was alive, mutating into new forms wherever one looked.

I turned my gaze to the Lower Realm and beheld the blue Earth in its center. The Earth as seen in four dimensions was a ball of fuzzy, colorful yarn teeming with life, raveling and unraveling without pause. Try to see it and it would shift its shape, try to catch it and it would slip away. All the strands were linked to one another as well as to the Dark Realm. An entity with an especially high density and large oscillations was called, for lack of a better term, a "personality." But viewed as a whole, the boundaries between entities were blurred.

I looked back at Naban's personality and snorted. How attached they had been to the Lower Realm. So attached, in fact, that they meditated and practiced asceticism in the Lower Realm to convince themselves of its illusory nature. Paradoxically, their attempts only deepened their attachment. It was no coincidence that they had birthed Aman and Tanjae.

The so-called division and merging were both an illusion. They were simply a matter of varying or leveling density. All of us were connected, even now. Every pain we suffered in life, every moment we spent laughing, raging, crying, and rejoicing was nothing once it was smoothed out.

Yet an old part of me had made it their mission to merge, risking their individuality. While their mission was not extraordinary, I toyed with the idea of completing it for that old part of me, as a tribute to the death of a personality.

I searched for all those in the Lower Realm that might be considered a personality of Aman: anyone who had gotten away. There being no clear-cut boundaries between entities, I roughly marked out all that could be assembled back to Aisata.

I addressed that group.

"Aman."

The dragonfly that took flight after a brief rest on a leaf, the busy honeybee toiling away to build a hive, the ant that had just carried a crumb of dirt out of its nest, the child that had just fallen asleep, the mother suckling her baby, the man

bemoaning his lot over drinks with friends, the homeless people lying in cardboard boxes at a subway station, all of whom
made up the same person. At my call, their hearts pounded as
one. Most thought nothing of it but the more astute of them
jerked awake, having felt something sweep over their chests, or
paused and looked around, or up at the sky.

"Aman," I called again. Many of their thoughts froze. Some
drifted off to sleep from sudden drowsiness, some felt a sharp
chest pain and took a break from work in bemusement.

"It's been so long," the group replied. Though who they
were speaking to I did not know.

4

"YOU LOOK TERRIBLE," AMAN SAID, LAUGHING, BUT NOT laughing out loud. Each of Aman's personalities felt their hearts stir with a strange joy and declared they would treat someone to a meal today, burst into song, or clapped a friend on the shoulder with a hearty suggestion for a round of drinks. Unaware of the fate awaiting them.

"You're a ragbag of everything," Aman remarked.

I was astounded. How could the "whole" of a self be so crass?

"Oh, hi there, Hell, and the countless dead things in Hell. Hi, Naban, and Naban's many disciples. Why, you lot are a mismatched jumble . . . Where's Tanjae? Have you left them behind because they're the youngest?"

Alas, bother. I expected no less from the Prophet of Division; Aman could not see me as a whole but only as separate elements.

"Come here, Aman," I said. "Your divisions have gotten out of hand, and so have the universe's. Let us go back to how we were before."

I sensed a sadness emanate from Aman, as if I had uttered something heinous and merciless. I must make allowances for Aman. The entity believed in death and interpreted change as a termination.

"You are sad now, but when you return you will understand. It will be a natural process, nothing unusual."

I felt Aman huddle up.

"You have no reason to refuse. Not that you can refuse."

"I'm not worried about me. I just feel sorry for Naban."

What was that supposed to mean? But I need not ruminate on the matter. The distorted views of a corrupted entity were not worth my attention.

I increased my density, compressing my body as though squeezing my flesh together. I created a complicated gravitational field targeting Aman and pulled them in geometrically. What followed might resemble two galaxies clashing and merging into one, or two stars in close proximity rippling hotly from the sheer force of each other's gravity until they fused.

Matter traveled back and forth. At first the only things to come were molecules floating around the atmosphere. Then the bigger things came. Minor disasters would be breaking out all over the Lower Realm now. Organisms would be meeting mysterious mass deaths, fish washing up dead on shores, birds falling from the sky. Everything happened in one fleeting moment for me, but it took decades to unfold in the Lower Realm.

Aman grieved for every death. As if to say every life was distinct, every personality unique, and that I had no right to dictate those lives.

"Death is an illusion. Do not mourn," I told Aman.

"But I can't help but mourn . . ." Aman began. It was in that instant that Aman struck me as human. I felt their sorrowful eyes boring into me. They finished, ". . . the death of Naban."

THE DEATH OF Naban.

What a strange thing to say.

There was no death. The personalities of Aman and Naban would of course never manifest themselves again . . . but that was not death. Their memories would live on in me, eternal as the universe itself. Naban could not die . . . even if they could, what was there to grieve about?

Then again, Aman had refused to merge and divided themselves over eons. They were a force to be reckoned with. I had to stay vigilant until I finished absorbing Aman's personality completely, which is to say, until I achieved perfect evenness. If at any point I had the urge to stop merging, that would be the Aman in me. I must not be tempted. I must prevail.

I kept pulling.

Thoughts and essences flooded into me. Memories poured in. Unnumbered lives seeped into my body. I drank them in with relish, like a creature receiving nourishment through membranes.

All were valuable data and assets. The overload of information would confuse any small-bodied entity, but not me. Every new particle added to my greatness. I was Aisata, one of the first selves. Oh, how I had ached for my homeland, my complete whole. The summation of truths. The noble soul that had performed the sacrifice of dividing its personality for the sake of learning and growth.

Once I have Aman, I thought, *I should round up the other friends too. We should become whole again, assess where we are at, then divide once more. It would be useful to integrate everything we have learned so far anyhow.*

Then I pondered why this thought had not occurred to me before.

Sunlight streamed in through the window. Aman lay beneath it and looked at me. Water boiled inside the rattling copper kettle. When Aman became too ill and frail to eat, I began to brew tea every day. I foraged for plants and flowers. I made infusions of water parsley, aster, dandelion, chamomile.

I poured water onto dried and powdered dandelion. Aman always watched me work from beside the window.

Aman lived everywhere around the world. Division after division, they chose to live as the smallest and weakest of beings. They became a water plant drifting down a calm river. Flies swarming around a garbage bag leaning against a utility pole. A stray cat curling up around her litter of just-born kittens beneath a snow-capped car. They struggled in a street gutter to push their wings out of an egg cracked half open by their mother. They were conceived in mothers too young to raise a child, born on the streets or in the grubby rooms of shelters. They were infants starved of milk or the children who cradled those infants as they begged for food.

Not one of them lived for long.

Not one of them lived lightly.

THEN NABAN AWAKENED.

AND I AWAKENED.

Naban, no, *I* stared emptily at my surroundings as if I were hypnotized. Just now, I . . . no, that was not me. I could not bear to call that thing me. I recalled what "they," the whole I belonged to, had meditated on.

What in the world had I been thinking? That I had sought to obliterate all life but my own from this universe! What demonic delusion was this? That I had dared to take the lives that were not mine to take. When none wished to die, what right did I have, what justification?

Sadness overwhelmed me. I wanted to cry, and I did.

"XX."

Someone was calling me by an unfamiliar name. They fought their way through the crowd and ran toward me, pulling me into a hug. I felt dazed but I reciprocated the gesture. They pulled me closer, kissed me on the lips, and stroked my head.

"Aman," I said, realizing only a moment later that it was impolite of me to call them that. They were but a piece of Aman. One whose destiny I had weaved when I was bent on teaching

Aman the futility of life. We were everything to each other then. A joy and a blessing, a reason to live. We stayed together in life and death. I remembered boiling tea every day for Aman in the final moments of their life, when they were too weak to swallow. We were happy even when we parted. We believed death would not do us part.

But after they left me, they plummeted to Hell. They thought I must have gone to heaven when they could not find me and spent their time questioning what sin they had committed in life.

I realized I should not call them "Aman," or see them as a piece of Aman either. They were perfect and whole, just as they were. They were no one but themself and belonged to none.

"XX," I called their name and embraced them tightly this time. It was only after we caressed each other for a long time that I thought to observe my surroundings.

I was in the middle of a vast crowd. All looked exactly like they had in their previous life: babies, children, seniors, animals, and lesser creatures. I felt like I had walked into a Noah's Ark the size of a generation starship. Excluding this small piece of me in human form, the rest of my body was a dust cloud encircling the gathering. Had my traits and Aman's manifested independently? I had hoped to see two substances blended into one liquid, but instead, they had separated like sand in water.

That was when I knew I had lost. But my defeat did not sting. I had changed, and my values had become a thing of the past. It did not matter if they were right or wrong, I could not believe in them anymore.

I turned my dust cloud into a spaceship so that the others might feel a little more at ease. I performed the transfiguration easily, having restored Tanjae's ship recently.

It finally dawned on me that I had murdered all of these creatures. Half of them I had killed ages ago by turning myself into humans, animals, poisonous insects, pests, or disasters, then I had brought them back to the Dark Realm and watched them suffer in Hell for the sake of education. The other half I had slaughtered just now to fulfill my deluded fantasy of returning to my origins.

I shuddered in disgust.

So enormous was my sin. So ruthless was the disaster I had brought. I was a living nightmare, a monster. How could I take this many lives without so much as an iota of guilt? All my talk of "education" and "returning" were the ravings of a lunatic. Could there be a more evil deed? A greater sinner? They had been such precious lives, such vital presences.

I clutched my head and sobbed. I felt my doughy body harden with every tear shed. What was I to do about everything? *All of you have the right to exact vengeance on me. Do whatever you need to do. Ask anything of me. I will oblige. Your vengeance may take different paths as you are separate entities, but no matter. It is my burden to bear.*

—There is no wrong, Naban.

A voice had rung out above the heads of the masses. I looked up.

—Only imbalance.

A resonance of the mind.

There was some murmuring, but everyone's minds were linked at least a little. Ah, that must be my influence. The state I was in was likely the result of Aman's personality manifesting.

I tried to see if there was anything wrong with me, if there were any problems. But I could not know. In my present state of mind, I wanted to believe that I had been unhinged moments ago and had now regained my sanity, but the opposite could be just as true.

"You are right," I stuttered. As I spoke, thin skin covered my body, pores and hair follicles appeared, tears welled up in my eyes, and sweat beaded my forehead. "The universe lost balance. When I tried to eliminate you."

Perhaps there really was no wrong. Nothing might have ever been wrong. How could sin exist in a world that had no Other? Nothing existed in such a world, let alone sin. Nothing held value. There were no good deeds, sacrifices, virtues, or love either. But there was one thing I did do wrong. And although it was just one thing, it was certainly enough to be called a sin.

"The universe was corrupted," I said, "the moment I defined you as corrupt."

5

SOMEONE WHO HAD SPENT A LIFE WITH ME HUGGED AND CON-
soled me. *Let go of me, I do not deserve your consolation,* I
wanted to say. *My punishment should be commensurate to the
pain I gave you.*

I tried to explain. "Division started from *me*. You just happened to inherit my divisive nature when you split from me. So
the rest of me took on a unifying nature to balance myself out,
that is all. We simply filled each other's gaps. The universe's corruption did not stem from you. It started the moment I defined
you and tried to exclude you from all of us.

"I corrupted the universe, and it has corrupted me in return."

The crowd broke into mutters. Some understood me; others grumbled, "The world of the dead is much more bizarre
than I thought." "Is this some sort of test?" "If we pass it, do
you reckon they'll give us a house somewhere around here?"
But Aman as a "whole" understood and accepted.

"You were weak and I much stronger, but I failed to see
that. I bound you to the Dark Realm and that upset the universe's balance. Now no one in the Lower Realm tries to protect life; there only remain those who destroy the lives of others
and their own. This is all my fault."

How can someone have sympathy when they are incapable
of imagining the Other? How can they love or feel? How can

they communicate without dividing? How can they hold life dear when they know immortal truths? As the Whole, I was omnipotent, but utterly useless at the same time. I was flawless, and therefore, nothing.

We had no life when we had no Other. The Dark Realm was an illusion. Only the lives in the Lower Realm were true. Aman whispered:

—There is no wrong, Naban.

—THERE WAS A time when I didn't think so. I may not think so in the future. But whatever personality I take on, I will be sure of my stance, every time.

—Just as you can't understand your past self, someday your future self won't understand your present self.

I SWALLOWED MY tears. I looked around at everyone.

"I can send all of you back."

As my eyes moved from one face to another, faces of those with whom I had forged bonds, I had to suppress the memories of my sins and the accompanying urge to kill myself, even though it was physically impossible.

But my immortality did have a silver lining: I had eternity to fix my mistakes.

I transfigured all of my particles. I pictured Tanjae's transporter and chemical formulas and electric wires as I produced millions of them. I solidified and liquefied gases to create chemical substances that I injected into everyone's bodies.

Never in the history of the universe had there been a more complicated, more extensive transfiguration in such a short span of time. I spent most of my body in the process, leaving only the tiny human form.

Then we, a small ship of cloud, exploded in the middle of the universe.

Aman split into hundreds and thousands, millions and billions of particles. These fragments of life showered down on the Lower Realm. Light particles streaked the skies like shooting stars, each finding their way into a suitable body. Those that failed to find a body shrouded the planet in the form of molecules before pouring down as life-giving rain.

THE THIRD ME

1

I FELL INTO A PUDDLE OF MUD.

As I fell, I reflexively reached out my hands to protect my head and got twigs stuck in them. My body could not pass through the ground or think to clear rocks for a safe landing. It bounced back when it hit something, halted when it was blocked. I kept retching, forgetting that I had no organs. I also forgot I had no need to breathe and gasped for fresh air.

I opened my eyes and looked around. I was on a small asteroid that held nothing but the traces of a spacecraft having taken off. The world of the living loomed black in the sky. Trying to figure out why I had crashed here, I remembered the conditions I had set for the gravitational field surrounding the spacecraft and this asteroid. I had made it so that children who lost their way would come here.

This was a familiar place. But not one detail felt the same. The sky was dull, the flowers lackluster. I could not see in the dark or behind my back. A whirlwind erupted of its own accord, abated, and rose up again. A leaf fell from a tree and a flower fluttered each of their own accord.

Then all was quiet.

The noises I had always heard were gone. The whispers that had constantly buzzed in my ear like staticky radio. Sound was not something I heard from brain malfunction or tinnitus; it was the feelings and thoughts of my connections flowing into me.

I was separate.

I could not find any links between me and the universe. The threads would still be there, but I could neither see, touch, nor feel them. I could not transform, much less spiritualize. Traversing to the Lower Realm or reincarnating was no longer a possibility.

I got to my feet. I stood in despair for a long time, until I accepted the fact that in order to move, I now had to use my feet. I put one foot forward and tripped—I was unable to defy gravity.

I considered the question of this entire space being me. I looked back on a time when I was a primeval blob of thick liquid that thought it would be fun to separate hard material from soft. A time when I thought of splitting myself into different personalities and conversing with them to save myself from tedium.

I could not believe my state. I could not believe anything. No matter how hard I tried.

I should look for Tanjae, I thought with a pang of self-derision. The child might let me take a spare room on their spaceship. They might build me a comfortable bed, a rice cooker, or even a microwave. But I had no way to get to them. I did not know where Tanjae's ship was and could not swim to it. I was stuck in the gravity of this place. I saw now that the child was a great Prophet. How on earth did they construct a spaceship?

"You lost, Naban."

My head snapped up at the sound booming above my head. Tushita was right before me.

Amazingly, I could not see Tushita unless I threw back my head and beheld them. Their parent body in the distance, the threads extending from it, the molecules swirling around Tushita were all invisible to me. Tushita simply looked like the Grim Reaper, clad in black, scythe in hand, completely detached from the rest of the universe. It hit me then just how much my visual and auditory senses had deteriorated.

Tushita seemed to have arrived a while ago. Judging by how long it took for them to speak, I guessed they must have attempted other means of communication before talking to me. I just could not hear them.

"I did not lose. I simply recognized what I did wrong."

"Wrong, is it . . ."

Tushita reached for the leafy tunic I was wearing and absorbed it. Unlike me, the tunic was not corrupted and easily yielded to Tushita. I hunched over in alarm.

The next moment, I realized I had no reason to. My body had nothing to hide. That tunic was my body in the first place. I tried to pull myself together and sit up, but my body would not budge. I tried to fashion another garment by dividing my body, but that failed too. Come to think of it, such attempts were meaningless to begin with.

I shook. It made no sense for my body to shake here. In the Lower Realm, anxiety constricted the blood vessels. To prevent the constricted vessels from lowering temperature, the body shook and created heat. Shaking was an error that resulted from two programs clashing. An immortal organism should *not* shake. Tushita noted every sign of my strain.

"Give me back my tunic."

"Surely"—Tushita gazed down at me incredulously—"you are not ashamed?"

"It is mine, so give it back! It was left to me by my kin. Give it here!"

Desiring possession, attaching meaning to relationships formed in the Lower Realm, viewing a piece of myself as another, feeling unnecessary emotions: my every word and action exposed my corruption. But at this point, exposing it further made no difference anyway.

"Poor Naban," said Tushita.

My breath caught in my throat. A terrible pain coursed through me like lightning. Every cell in my body seemed to burst. I was burned, fried, frozen, and skewered. My skin was torn and sliced. Tushita had filled my pores with their particles and rocked my senses.

I faintly recalled having said on occasion, "There is no wrong." I could not even make sense of what I had said. What did I mean, "There is no wrong"?

Was it not wrong of Tushita to do this to me?

"Poor Naban." Tushita's voice rang in my head. Perhaps I heard a hint of sincere pity in their voice, but it felt cruel all the same.

Tushita lifted their gaze to the world of the living. It was black as night, contrasting sharply with Tushita's full, snow-white body in the sky. Both seemed unthinkably giant to me, now a trivial little creature.

Somewhere from the depths of my mind, a voice whispered the familiar words, "There is no pain." If there was no pain, if I could not feel it, then Tushita could not harm me. Tushita meant no harm and sought only to confirm my corruption. Had I not been corrupt, Tushita would not have wronged me. Still, I did not understand how anyone could deny the existence of this raw tumult.

"All the pieces of Aman will reincarnate freely now without visiting a teacher or the Dark Realm. They will not mix with one another and will live independent lives. I wonder, Naban, if there has ever been an entity more corrupt than you since the beginning of time."

I had reflexively kneeled and prostrated myself before Tushita. It was a posture that humans were made to adopt instinctively in the Lower Realm to stop losing body heat and shield themselves from the cold, or to protect their head, organs, and vital points from danger. But I had no need to do so right now. My head understood that, yet my body stayed put. I felt an icy gaze upon my head. My shame was as great as my pain, and that fact pained me further.

"Eat me," I said. "I am corrupt. It is not wrong to be, but you must want to dispose of me. Eat me and purify me."

Tushita stretched out a hand. Not in the usual way. A slimy something resembling an oily lump of protein protruded from Tushita's body and groped every inch of mine, trying to decide how best to eat me. I was curious too. My utterly corrupt body would be immune against persuasion and conversation. How would Tushita break me down? Would they spout acid and melt me? Would they dice me with knives? I would have had nothing to fear if I felt no pain.

"I, Tushita, declare to all of the Dark Realm," Tushita's voice blared loudly in my head. It would be resounding inside every head in the Dark Realm. "The Lower Realm has fallen. It has turned into a breeding ground for the corrupt Prophets Naban and Aman. A nest of evil beyond salvation. I shall quarantine all of the Lower Realm, including the entity before me."

I could not believe my ears, the only auditory instrument available to me now.

"From this point forward, I forbid all in the Dark Realm from entering the Lower Realm. Excluding corrupt entities in the Lower Realm, the rest of us will return to our immaculate, primordial self. From there we will explore new methods of learning. We will purge pollution and form a new, pristine Whole. We have finished learning a lesson and that is valuable in itself."

I staggered to my feet and charged at Tushita, screaming. I did it without rhyme or reason, a clear sign of corruption.

Tushita retaliated without malice. What malice could they harbor when they did not know pain? Those ignorant of pain did not know when to stop either. I twitched uncontrollably and gagged, though I had nothing to bring up.

"Poor Naban."

Tushita's voice echoed coldly inside my spinning head.

"Tushita . . . *you* are corrupt," I managed to gasp out, clawing at the muddy ground. Tushita's golden eyes flickered.

"I wonder," I said, "has there ever been an entity more corrupt than you? You dare deny the enormous whole that is the Lower Realm. Both Aman and I are you, Tushita. That Lower Realm is all you. The very things you call corrupt *are* you." I wheezed, "You deny a part of yourself, which means *you* are corrupt. Your corruption blinds you to your condition."

Tushita seemed to consider this point. But, like me, corrupted entities form mental boundaries and cannot perceive anything that lies beyond. While they may concede they could be wrong, the thought never truly sinks in.

"Once I obtain the other Prophets' insights, I will have a different answer to that problem, Naban."

"If you are brave enough, eat me first. I will pass on the insights I have gained through all my lives."

"So I will. After your sickness is cured."

"I am not si—"

My body felt like it was being ripped apart. Talons seemed to slash my flesh and tear out my guts. Tushita examined every nook and cranny of my completely solid body, now liquefying, now gasifying my molecules away. Even as I slipped in and out of consciousness, I noticed that Tushita was extracting only the particles containing Tanjae's chemical formulas. If this were the Lower Realm, Tushita could have cut open my brain, but here, memories were stored all over my body. At least my body did not get bloodied or suffer organ ruptures as it would have in the Lower Realm. It only shrank.

I willed myself to think that this pain was not real. It was hard. I wished Tushita would kill me instead. Good grief, I just thought "kill me." How low was I to sink?

"Merging without persuasion may be a useful technique, so I shall take it. It would make no difference who has it since you are me and I you."

Hatred surged in me as I glared at Tushita. Logical as Tushita's words were, they felt unfair, accursed. Tumult and irrationality were reserved for me alone now.

Walls rose around me on all sides. They built themselves, brick upon mortar upon brick. Once upon a time, I would have easily understood their mechanism. Now, they seemed to be astonishing miracles. When they were tall enough to cover half of Tushita's face, the Prophet said, "You will be able to come out when you realize you and these walls are the same. I wish you recovery, Naban."

"Shut up," I snarled through gritted teeth, and Tushita responded with an indulgent nod.

Once the walls blocked Tushita from view, a roof materialized over them. Plunging me into darkness. Wiping out sight and sound.

I was stuck here. Alone. Utterly disconnected.

How many children had I locked up in this kind of space for "education"? I had been puzzled at their agony. I had been foolish and was paying for it now. I needed to.

I had no intention of leaving. I had no desire to be one with the walls. I would not disassemble my body or merge with anyone.

I remembered programming Lower Realm creatures to black out or go insane if they experienced pain beyond a certain limit. The program was designed to keep those shackled to their bodies from suffering unnecessary pain. If I were properly corrupted, perhaps I could go crazy. Then it might not be so hard. I hoped without real hope.

As I lay there, my perception of light and sound dulled. The heat and cold faded too. When all my senses shut down, hallucinations took their place. A body desperate for stimuli forces open other senses. I saw Tushita descending on Fuxi's palace. Clad in a garment white as snow with wings brilliant as a bird's, Tushita split into dozens of entities that remained connected to the parent body's back through silver threads. They landed in the garden. A hush fell over the children and Fuxi showed their displeasure plainly.

"It is time," the Tushitas spoke.

"When it is time should be determined by all of us," replied Fuxi.

"It does not matter when. Resistance is a telltale sign of corruption. You have been corrupted, Fuxi."

Fuxi steeled their body and the children followed suit. Their bodies became rock-hard and heavily armored. They got into formation and produced blades and metals that would be difficult to digest. With the help of the older children, the young ones backed away, disassembled, and took flight. A gaping hole appeared in every Tushita's chest. The holes sucked in everything in the vicinity. With a long, bloodcurdling shriek, the Tushitas ripped open the holes wider and swooped down on the children.

2

I was still somewhat sane when Tanjae came.

It seems I did not have enough time to go crazy. Or a small part of me could have been uncorrupted. Only, I could not move. It was not my body that was weak; my mind was. The pain of sensory deprivation had robbed me of judgment and drive.

Tanjae arrived in a shiny, neon green armored suit fitted with mechanical joints. They held a laser gun nearly as big as their body. They seemed to have used it to break through the walls. The old me would have burst out laughing at the sight of them, but now I was awestruck. How had they made such a thing?

"What about Tushita . . . ?" I asked as Tanjae helped me up. They shook their head.

"They don't exist anymore. They've become something else."

"Fuxi and the other Prophets . . . ? Did they fight Tushita? Who won?"

"Merging doesn't work like that. It's simply changing into something new. You know this already," Tanjae said calmly. They had the air of someone who had already plowed through several battlefields. "The teachers tried to neutralize Tushita in the end by merging themselves in, but they turned into something else too."

I swayed and collapsed to the ground. I buried my face in my hands, unable to get up. "No, they should not have . . ."

"Not have what?"

"Those Prophets were Others. Tushita should not have taken their lives without permission . . . Tushita has committed a wrong, an atrocity . . ."

Tanjae was silent.

"Technically it's not a *wrong*. It's just something you don't want to see happening, Teacher. Though you used to," said the child, who was now closer to my teacher than my student. "It's also something I don't want to see."

The space warped. The walls crumbled like cookies. The roof caved in, bending the walls as easily as if they were wet mud. A white cloud of dust rose, liquefied, and rained down.

"But it was meant to happen sooner or later," said Tanjae.

I would say that too, once I was merged. "It was meant to happen." Without sorrow or regret. As the old me would have done. But I was corrupted and everything saddened me.

It was coming for me. I could feel it. It was coming to swallow the last Prophet left in the Dark Realm. Tushita had been reluctant to eat me, but that thing was no longer Tushita.

Another wall came crashing down and the dust was sucked outside. The floor tilted, and I rolled helplessly down it before I could react. Tanjae flew through the air using the rocket propulsion of their mechanical shoes, blocked the yawning hole in the wall with their body, and caught me in their arms. The metal arms of Tanjae's suit were large and powerful.

"We've got to protect the Lower Realm," Tanjae said as they peered outside. The words cleared my head. "The Dark Realm will be fine. They know what this is. That it isn't a big deal. But the Lower Realm won't understand. They won't accept this kind of ending. They'll just think this is a terrible disaster. What should we do?"

Tanjae's words had no logic to them, but to my surprise, I understood them perfectly. I did not use to—they had sounded like the ramblings of a foolish child before. Now I wondered: How could I have thought that?

The asteroid crumpled, shattered, and dispersed into the void, its shards sparkling like jewels. Light flooded in through the collapsed wall. That the universe was emitting light meant it was shrinking. Sourceless light poured in from all directions. The heart of the shrinking universe was black as it absorbed light. Every bardo was pulled into it like fibers. The whole universe was attempting to return to its original state. Though I could hardly believe it, this whole was me. Corrupt as I was, I still retained primordial memories and could appraise the properties and inclinations of my "self."

"Go to the Lower Realm," I said. "You are a Prophet too. And that *thing* will not go there before it eats every Prophet. Since the Lower Realm is as large as the Dark Realm, it will not attempt to attack before it is big enough to do so. The Lower Realm will remain safe while you are on the run. You, I am sure, will find a means of transportation that the rest of us can never imagine."

"What about you, Teacher?"

I glanced outside. "Once it eats me, it too will change. If I am corrupt enough . . . perhaps my determination to save you might sway it. Let us trust in my corruption," I said, half believing, half doubting. Would this lowly creature's corruption be powerful enough to corrupt the entire universe? Would my corruption prove so great?

But I am Naban. The first to attempt the reversal of entropy and invent imbalance. The first to divide. I am the Prophet who bore the Prophet of Division. Inside me I hold knowledge gathered from time immemorial and the memories of countless lives. All corruption stemmed from me and the ultimate corruption dwells in me. I am by no means small.

"I may be corrupt, but I am still a Prophet. Once I merge, I will go on to become something else. Let us hope."

"Right."

I did not know what Tanjae meant by "right," even when

they pushed me aside and stared out through the hole in the wall. It was only when Tanjae said, "So it wouldn't matter if we switched" that I realized their intentions with a jolt and clutched the child. With the mechanical arm of their suit, Tanjae pulled my hand off, gently yet powerfully. I could not penetrate, stretch, or transform. One by one my fingers were meekly peeled away.

"I can't go," said Tanjae. "It took me all I had to make it this far. I'm out of fuel and that thing ate my ship. You seem to think science can do anything, but I can't conjure stuff out of thin air like the teachers can."

I was struck speechless. Tanjae pressed down on my shoulders as they continued, "But *you're* different, Teacher. Please, go to the Lower Realm. Go and figure out a way to protect it with Teacher Aman."

No, I thought. I was nothing now. I had no powers. I would have to break down my body and seep into a Lower Realm body. It was an absurdly impossible feat. I would die if I attempted it. But I knew the thoughts I was having now were even more absurd.

"I'll be fine," Tanjae continued. "I'm sad now, but I won't be once I merge. The delusions will go away and I'll be happy, right?"

I could not answer. In one life, when I was the priest of a small church, I had gripped Tanjae's hands and told them something similar as the young child lay dying from an illness. I was ignorant then and wiser now, yet my despair ran deeper.

Tanjae stepped in front of the hole with neither determination nor fear. There was no wistfulness about them, not even solemnity. Tanjae was confident and poised, like a small god.

"Go," Tanjae said again.

With that, they leaped in.

I COULD NOT GO.

My body weighed me down like a heavy rock. I could not

fly or disperse it into particles. Lumps of dirt and stones pelted down from the ceiling. I could not conjure a hard shell to shield myself from the stones or turn into an animal large enough to withstand the pain. I was slammed with whatever hit me, rolled whichever way I was pushed. Gravity swerved to one side, causing the floor to lurch up and throw me into the air. I was flung about like an object. The walls that had crumbled like cookies formed a floor, which then scattered down into the void like dandelion seeds.

Down.

No, not "down."

Gravity had simply appeared there.

"I," or what used to be me, was devouring pieces of myself.

The shrinking universe was so radiant I could barely open my eyes. Light rushed toward me from all sides. The center of the contraction was black. I went into free fall, stripped of support or any footholds.

I would have tried anything to stop falling if I had had my old powers, but it was useless. I could not create gravity or make a reverse-thrust propeller as Tanjae could. I plummeted.

As I fell, an overwhelming personality poured like a waterfall into my consciousness. Myriads of selves brushed past me. A translucent serpent coiled itself around me, then let go. A monster I could not place charged toward me, baring its fangs. A tempest of numberless people raged through my mind. Conversations and persuasions and arguments broke forth. But none affected me. Everything passed through me.

My assailant halted, held me afloat in space, then retreated. I watched my assailant without knowing if I was lying down, standing, or still free-falling.

Entities not yet fully melted into the contracting, compact celestial body sprang out like string before being yanked back in. Threads still stretched out in every direction and sucked in the remaining entities and particles. My assailant looked like a continuously exploding black sun, or perhaps a mammoth lump of cancer cells. An immortal life-form, resembling the cancer cells that were proliferating even in this moment in the bodies of the Lower Realm. An absolute self.

It did not hurry. It had no reason to. It had already gone far beyond mere intelligence. All the histories of the universe we had experienced, all of our accumulated knowledge blended and created new meaning. It was struck by a storm of new knowledge at every moment.

It was "me."

The me before I began dividing to escape my eternity of solitude and inertia. Just as I had been back then, this new me was radically wise and endlessly ruthless.

This is a corrupt entity.

I can cause it pain.

The corrupt submit easily to pain.

Its thoughts deluged into me. But I was already overflowing with pain. Whatever torture was added to this body of mine, how could it compare to the agony of losing my bond to another? To the suffering of clinging on to a life that had cost the life of another?

"Naban."

"I" was calling me.

"Join me. One cycle has ended. Let us learn anew."

I shook my head.

I knew my pain would vanish if I joined it. I knew wisdom and enlightenment would flow into me, that I would be filled with peace and happiness. I would look back and laugh at my obsession over this minuscule fragment of myself. I knew Tanjae was not dead. Neither were the other children. I was deceiving myself that they were independent life-forms, the Other. All this I knew, but I could not contain my grief.

"I" read my mind and pitied me. "Stop behaving like an organism governed by genes, Naban. You have been corrupted and need purifying." It spoke to me consolingly with the mercy of one who espoused an entirely alien set of values.

When I made no reply, white threads shot out toward me. They prodded my fingers and twisted around my wrists. They ensnared my ankles and strangled my throat. They were going to cut me to pieces by force. I remained limp, my will to move extinguished by heartbreak.

Fingernails grew from my bound hands. Hair grew over the vines wrapped around my neck. Pores opened in my skin and fine hairs poked out between my wrinkles. My insides metamorphosed too. A body composed itself, based on my own anatomical memory and knowledge. Blood vessels branched out to the beating of a robust heart. My heartbeats rang throughout a universe stripped of all other sounds. My lungs swelled to thick slabs and sprouted pathways connecting them to the nose and mouth. Bones hardened, muscles thickened, organs developed. Tears streamed down as tear ducts formed. I gulped down saliva and expelled a deep breath.

A pain sharper than anything I had ever felt seared through me when the nervous system and sensory receptors came to life. I felt like my heart would burst open. Blood pooled beneath the skin, squeezed too tight by the vines. The ache was excruciating in the areas where they had cut off circulation. The pain was stark, undiluted. It was nothing like the sensations transmitted by the crude sensory receptors of the Lower Realm. I opened my eyes, which were now attached to optic nerves, and glared at my assailant.

The vines loosened their grip a little. My assailant had no facial expression, but I could sense its surprise. It debated whether absorbing an entity *this* corrupt would be safe. Should it wait until I was healed, especially when it would have to stomach the vast corruption of the Lower Realm? Perhaps it should quarantine me for now . . .

While it hesitated, I flung myself into its depths.

EVERYTHING BOILED INSIDE. Fuxi's palace had melted into a soup as if it had been plunged into a blast furnace. Other friends, along with their little bardos, had been pulverized, their parts drifting about. It was like a chemical solution undergoing a wild chain reaction or a nuclear-fusion reactor in there. Each entity had retained half of itself and lost the other half. I found a space battleship floating in their midst. I did not so much find it as I was drawn to it. I knew I would be drawn to it. Thank you, gravitational field, for detecting my corruption.

In this fearsome sea of electrolytes that crushed the very personalities of Prophets, the battleship stoutly held its ground, maintaining its identity. It fought alone against the utter chaos. It was admirable, a true child of Tanjae.

As I plummeted, I whispered to the ship's wall. *Sorry to keep asking you, but . . .*

Come in, the wall commanded, and I obeyed.

I WAS THROWN into the engine room.

I thought the pain would kill me, but I was sane enough to know it could not.

I quickly took in my surroundings as I pushed everything I saw up against the walls. I wrenched off machines and pushed them along with the desks and chairs. It shocked me, how heavy and cumbersome they all were.

I heard a distant cackle. *What are you up to?*

The battleship was engulfed by a swarm of light that had chased me there. The walls creaked and moaned as they began to close in. I retreated to the middle of the room. The walls halted.

The door was blocked and barricaded with things like printers, TVs, and sound systems: all things packed with circuitry and components conducting electromagnetic energy. These obstacles had interiors with more complicated structures than most organisms. My assailant had stopped its advances because the door refused to talk to it; I felt it scrambling for a solution in alarm.

But I knew it would find one before long.

For it was "me."

I topped off the barricade by wedging in Tanjae's fancy ergonomic chair, then hurtled out the emergency exit and down a corridor. Even if my assailant succeeded in persuading the door, it would have to spend a long time debating with the chair.

I had to walk in order to get anywhere and run to get anywhere faster. I had to open doors before I could go through them and go around if I hit a dead end. A naked human body is an ecologically lousy thing. My fragile soles swiftly collected scratches. My legs buckled as I ran, making me trip, and my head knocked against a wall as I rounded a corner. I could not see an inch beyond my nose in this maze, but I stumbled along using my mental map as reference. I felt my way through the darkness and finally switched on a light.

The warehouse contained twenty transporters. I chose one at random and lowered myself into it. I lay there only a few seconds before I sat back up.

The tangles of wire were all over the place. Gwanhwa was next to me but I could not talk to them. I had forgotten how. Complicated dashboards stood beside the transporters, but their mechanism was beyond me. I could not see inside them to diagram their structure either. I grasped at the engineering knowledge I had acquired from the Lower Realm, but it was pointless. Whatever mechanism the dashboards used, it would far outstrip Lower Realm technologies in any time and space.

Tanjae, O great teacher, I thought, half laughing, half sighing. *Your imbecile disciple has no hope of carrying out your will.*

I sat there, despondent, but then the door sprang to life and trembled. It began emitting a faint light, perspiring, and swelling up like a balloon. I did not hear any persuasions or transactions taking place.

A figure walked through the door. It was radiant, translucent, and had the appearance of Tanjae. Scores of gleaming white lines ran from Tanjae's body to somewhere outside.

Tanjae had been sent in alone on purpose. Because the spaceship, even as objectified as it was, would recognize its master. And Tanjae would hold the most sway over me.

This is not Tanjae, I told myself. Even if that thing had Tanjae's memories and consisted of the same matter that once made up Tanjae's body, it was not Tanjae. It was an entirely different thing. There *was* no Tanjae anymore. The child was dead. They were not coming back.

Dead. I shuddered at the unfamiliarity of my own thoughts. *They are not the same.*

"You were right, Teacher," the thing with Tanjae's face and body said in Tanjae's voice. It did not bother moving its mouth. Its powers were much beyond mine, which limited me to speaking through my mouth.

"Only my interpretation changed," it said as it leaped into the air and landed before me. "I didn't die, I didn't disappear, I simply changed. I don't know why I was so scared."

Yes. I knew this all too well. Even at this moment.

Tanjae's double looked around its spaceship. As I had once done, it eyed the miscellaneous items in the ship as if they were junk. It almost burst out laughing when it saw my small and pitiful naked body covered in scratches.

"There were so many things I didn't know, but if I'd known it was *this* easy to learn the truth, I would've begged you, if no one else, to merge with me."

"Help me," I said.

"Help you?" Its eyes glinted.

"Send me to the Lower Realm, please. I cannot get there on my own."

Between so many of our divisions, between so many lives and deaths since time immemorial, had there ever been a more corrupted entity than me? That *thing*, which made up my majority, gazed down upon me with innocent and righteous mercy, with the concern of a teacher trying to teach a lesson.

"What do you intend to do there?" The look on its face suggested that it understood everything and yet nothing at all. "Hmm, okay. Let's say I wait for you until you come back. Nothing's going to change even if I do. It's all a matter of time. What plan could you devise down there? You'd forget why you were even born."

"I know."

"If the Dark Realm stops sending down new children, there'll be no births and the Lower Realm's ecosystem will fail. Ah, maybe not *too* soon, since Aman's figured out how to self-reincarnate. But you can't divide your body anymore, what could you possibly do on your own?" Tanjae held out a shimmering hand. "Come. This is nothing. You'll look back and laugh over why you tried so badly to run away."

"I know," I replied. "I know . . ."

"Then why do you want to go?"

I was astonished. How could such an immense being, one that had merged all knowledge, not be able to look inside the head of a being so small? The astonishment was probably mutual: How could such a small being become so perfectly disconnected?

"I want to live," I said. Tanjae looked stumped. "Even for just one life, I want to live. A life is lived only once, anyway, and once is enough. You have given me this one chance at life, so I must take it."

Ah, how illogical and irrational I sounded. My heart understood with such clarity, but I felt hopelessly incapable of persuading anyone else.

Tanjae lapsed into a heavy silence, then smiled. It was the kind of smile a great artist from the Lower Realm might have devoted a whole life to paint on a temple wall. There was something more than mercy in the smile.

"Balance." Tanjae nodded. It helped me lie down. It did not use its hands. At the slightest jerk of its head, an invisible hand pushed my chest down before I could resist.

Tanjae began to control Gwanhwa, still without using its hands. Wires swept over my body looking for suitable injection sites, pierced my skin, and entered my bloodstream. This Tanjae did not understand pain and was relentless in its handling of me. But I did not let my pain show.

"A life lived only once, huh? Maybe that'll have a unique value."

I saw a mild curiosity—one that might have belonged to me once—in Tanjae's eyes. Eyes that sought to comprehend the incomprehensible. Eyes that tried to see the value in the young and insignificant.

I sensed that Tanjae was viewing this as a novel experiment. If the connection between the Dark and Lower Realms were severed completely, if every Prophet left the latter and only the corrupt remained, what would become of the Lower Realm? A world whose entire population believed it to be the only world, the only truth, and the life lived in it to be the only true life because there were no past lives or afterlives. Watching such a world unfold would be a kind of learning too.

"Chemistry" broke me down into particles.

I would see Aman when I reached the Lower Realm. I closed my eyes and mused.

Since so many Amans had rained down on the Lower Realm, whomever I met there would be Aman. Wherever I turned, I would see Aman. Whomever I loved, whomever I forged bonds with, it would be Aman. The thought made me happy.

I thought of the Aman I had loved above all.

I thought of the Aman who had watched me from their bed. The sunlight pouring in through the window. The scent of tea we inhaled together every morning. It would be nice for my life to end that way. For it to be my only life.

I remembered the day when my dearest said "yes" to my proposal. It was raining heavily that day. We took cover under the awning of a building and were forced to stay there awhile, then I was proposing before I knew it. *What kind of proposal is that?* Aman said, and we launched into a long fight. We pushed each other until one knocked the other over in the rain, we took turns to angrily announce our departure and stalk away, only to come running back, shivering, to take shelter beneath the awning again.

We leaned on each other's shoulders. We traced our fingers over each other's eyebrows and put our foreheads together. We looked into each other's eyes and brushed away our wet hair. We caressed our cheeks, our lips met. The acute senses in our erogenous zones piqued, the program embedded there to help us find our other half, the chemical reactions akin to alcohol and drugs, the dopamine and adrenaline.

The very chemicals that had traveled down my veins and nerves in that moment were me and part of me, the pouring rain and the street I had stood on and the ground beneath my feet, that whole world, even the person by my side, were me and part of me. That was why all of it was real. Oh, but more than anything else, that person was meaningful *because* they were the Other. Whomever I met, I could love and pity and give my life to because they were not me.

The Prophet who was entranced by the world of the living, the corrupted human who believed the false sensations relayed by their survival program to be pure truth.

I am blessed with this corruption, so take me wherever you wish. I will learn something from that too.

THAT
ONE LIFE

Translated by Sung Ryu

N

GOOD, I SEE MYSELF.

But not in a mirror, it seems. It should be impossible to see myself from this angle. Strange . . . Ah, I know what this is. An out-of-body experience. It happens sometimes during sleep.

I see that I am lying facedown in a grass field. It must be hard to breathe with my nose buried in the ground like that. I hope someone flips me over. No, that would not work. I have an arrow stuck in my back. Someone should pull that out. But one wrong tug and I could lose too much blood . . . In fact, I seem to have already done so. That looks like at least a liter of blood around my body. At this rate I will bleed to death. That wound needs to be stanched. Never mind, it is too late. The arrow has pierced my heart.

So I am dead.

Feeling oddly detached from this deluge of information, I surveyed my surroundings. A forest glowed in rainbow hues. The colors were striking, and every object shimmered as if seen through a heat haze, or looked supple as a baby's skin. Twinkling silver threads extended from birches and firs, wild grass and fallen leaves, crisscrossing in every direction like cobwebs. All of them were connected through the threads, my body too.

Fine. I was dead. Now what?

I looked about, hoping to find a sign that read THIS WAY TO THE WORLD OF THE DEAD, or perhaps a guide carrying a sandwich board with the words WELCOME. ALL HELL-BOUND

VISITORS, QUEUE HERE. I spotted a man sitting on a boulder. Our eyes met. Clad in a silvery material, he was playing cat's cradle by himself.

A messenger of death?

Just as I wondered how he was playing cat's cradle alone, two extra hands sprang out from his back and continued the game. Startling, but I calmed down soon enough. After all, no one would have seen what messengers of death really looked like. Sure, they could have four arms, why not?

"You've finished early," said the messenger. "I thought you'd live longer."

My memories rushed back in that instant. Not all of them, but enough for me to take stock of the situation. I looked down at my dead body once more. A boy soldier who looked hardly over fourteen. My parents could not afford to buy their eldest son's way out of military service, so I was dragged here in my brother's stead two days ago. I had been at that tender age when I was not quite used to life.

"It was enough," I told Tanjae, or rather the entire Dark Realm that had incarnated as Tanjae.

"I thought you'd try out more things. Since you had reincarnated into the past, you could've become a powerful king, say, or founded a new kingdom."

"It was enough," I repeated.

That was when I heard a curious sound, the kind produced by a speaker at high volume in an echo chamber (. . . such flashes of knowledge felt strange in my own head). It dawned on me that I must be listening without eardrums. Presently, I could detect anything from the lowest frequencies that whales heard to the ultrasounds that bats did.

This sound was the cry of a child. My dead body twitched. A little girl covered in mud and tears clawed her way out from beneath my body. Sobbing, the girl tried to find her mother among the piles of bodies around her, then limped away.

"To save a kid?" said Tanjae.

"It is a meaningful act."

"Sure it is. Every life changes the whole universe. Whether or not that life is yours."

Perhaps Tanjae was having trouble with the cat's cradle, because they sprouted three more arms from their back. With one arm they scratched their head, with another they scratched their buttocks, and with five arms they manipulated the string this way and that to create a shape. The shape of an intricate spaceship. Back when I was an organism on Earth, I would not have been able to trace where and how the string should bend to produce that shape.

"I'm perfecting the art of killing time," Tanjae said defensively, noticing my gaze. "What was I saying? Ah," Tanjae muttered to themselves before continuing, "that kid's life means more than that. The only one who grasps its full meaning is Naban. Even Hwangcheon wouldn't know until they merge with Naban."

Hwangcheon. I mulled over the name. It was unfamiliar. Perhaps whatever entity resulted from the merging of the entire universe save for the Lower Realm, Aman, me, and Tanjae decided to call themselves that, or . . .

"I am the one who eliminated Aman in every era," I said as I walked toward Tanjae and pulled the tip of the string spaceship's engine. The string began unraveling from that point. When I hoisted it up higher, miraculously, the spaceship straightened out to a single line. "So I know where the forces converge."

THE BOY WHO shot the arrow from a mountainside that day was also me. He was one of my old selves that had showered down on the Lower Realm to eradicate all Amans. I was scared and kept calling for my mother, but I managed to release the bowstring as I had been trained. The arrow rode the wind and hit Aman as she was scrambling away from the heat of battle, clutching her mother's hand. That wind was also me. The tree branch that Aman's mother tripped over was also me. The general who led the battle and the village elder who nudged the mother and child toward the mountain were also me. Thus, I alone knew when to intervene to save Aman; I alone knew how history would play out if Aman lived.

Just now, I had thrown myself between my other selves and interrupted them at precisely the right point. That had been the sole purpose of this life.

"There must be a ton of variables interacting with each other," said Tanjae, "but you seem to have found the right one somehow. The interplay between one life and another is far more complicated than the three-body problem. And any computations for complex systems."

"There are many suitable points. This just happens to be one of them. It is nearly impossible to create the result I want, but avoiding unwanted ones can be done with a simpler equation."

In the first history I had erased, this child escaped the battlefield alone and stumbled upon a camp of bandits in the mountain. It had been set up by farmers who fled the war and their kingdom and was governed by a simple and idyllic order. There, Aman immersed herself in books and Taoist sorcery and grew up to be their leader. She started a civil rebellion in which she ousted the king and seized the throne. She reigned as a powerful monarch, built a vast empire, and lived a long, full life. Following her death, Eastern learning, matriarchal monarchies, and gender-balanced governments spread across all of Asia and Europe. Female dynasties emerged throughout history, while fairly advanced forms of republics, albeit with some minor differences from modern democracies, took root across the world early on. When I had deleted this Aman, that history disappeared with her, leaving only a faint trace of her life in folklore and legend.

I had deleted and taken back all other Amans who made a mark on history, and their lives had vanished into the realm of myth. In later eras, when Aman underwent many divisions, I grew increasingly heavy-handed in my schemes. I instigated a ridiculous witch hunt in the Middle Ages and used sex-selective abortion to my advantage in modern and contemporary times. Once I had finished, the only democracy left in antiquity was a limited version in Greek city-states, rebellions and civil movements were ruthlessly crushed in most dynasties, and women were excluded from all sociopolitical institutions. I had felt no guilt over the results at the time.

"I think I get it," said Tanjae. "History is variable. Only, whenever it changes, the world's memory changes with it and no one realizes it's changed. Except for the person who traveled back in time. It's like in adventure games where the character remembers only one route, but the player remembers every route ever played . . ."

When I looked blankly back at them, they mumbled, "Haven't you ever played a game before?" and folded in their arms one by one. Noticing that they had only one arm left, Tanjae pulled another one back out with a "Whoops!"

That was when it hit me. "How did you disconnect yourself?"

Tanjae blinked. Their gaze was a little wiser than I remembered, a little more human than when I last met them.

"If you mean from you, I was disconnected the moment I was born. But you don't seem to be asking about that. I must've merged with someone then, haven't I? But I have no memory of it. Since the day I was born, I have been me all along. Of course, I did divide myself a few times to take on students."

Tanjae bit on a finger and lapsed into thought. Nowhere in their body did I see a thread connecting them to the universe. Though my vision was not at its sharpest now.

"And Aman?"

"The same as ever. And they don't get along with the other teachers. Especially Teacher Hwangcheon. But everyone's trying their best not to intrude on each other's domains. I'm not sure what you want to hear. Teacher Aman still thinks that each divided entity is a universe in its own right. They cherish the Lower Realm over the Dark Realm too. Their school of thought is popular among the newborns. Eh? You're not crying, are you?"

A memory slowly surfaced, freshly formed. The great sovereign who lived out her life and arrived in the world of the dead instantly realized that the future me had tried to murder her, and that an entity from an even more distant future had saved her. Aman went to see the old Naban—who knew nothing yet and lounged about at their temple—and waged a war of disputes and persuasions. The two of them even engaged in several duels that involved exchanging a portion of their bodies. The duels ended with Naban promising they would never plot to eliminate Aman or cooperate in such an endeavor.

"Seems like your memory of why you came to the Lower Realm is different from mine," said Tanjae.

"I suppose so."

There would have been some justice in the vanished history too. Just as there will be some injustice in this newly risen history. I bear sole responsibility for that as well. I would not have gone down this path if I were not corrupt, but without corruption I would not have thought to eliminate Aman in the first place. As the present me is corrupt, I wish to undo, at least, the deaths I brought upon others. No matter the consequences.

"Well, at least this is how the universe originally was, right?"

"There is no original universe," I answered.

There is only one life, and the ever-shifting cosmos it creates.

N + 1

AMAN TOLD ME TO GO TO AN OLD BUILDING. HE KNEW I COULD go anywhere.

He told me gods dwell in old things. If I really wanted to find someone like me, he said, search among the nonliving instead of the living. Talk to rocks or boulders. Beings that had survived ages of human destruction, living through millennium after millennium, harbored intelligence and would answer me if I engaged them with all my heart. Aman told me to make friends that way, if I was so lonely. Then Aman would tell me legends of King Munmu's Underwater Tomb and Gyeongbokgung Palace, of Seokguram Grotto and the Shadowless Pagoda, and of the Turtle Ships.

The corners of my mouth twitched whenever Aman recounted such stories with a solemn face. I almost burst out laughing when he went so far as invoking Lotte World Tower. But I forced myself to keep a straight face. As tall as Aman's tales were, there was a sacred quality to them. Sacredness was not born out of truth, but from the skillful pen of the storyteller who fattened and spiced up historical records. Passed on from generation to generation, these essentially coauthored folktales contained just the right combination of morals and irony, twists and feeling. I was beginning to question whether I knew the truths of the universe on my own, or was indulging in a fantasy of my own. How was unverifiable, unrecorded fact different from myth? So instead of correcting Aman's error, I took to the road.

The streets of Seoul were covered in red Jörmungandr vines. Their thick, woody stems punched through the concrete and climbed to the tops of skyscrapers, using the buildings as a support. The buildings crumpled like paper inside their iron grip but were still inhabited by people. Robots, which might be called the last remaining "organism" on Earth allied with humanity, stood watch every night and patrolled the buildings' perimeters. The Jörmungandr fed on ozone or ammonia and their flowers spewed venom. They were immune to every poisonous chemical invented by humans. Giant Ymir bulls ambled down roads on four legs and breathed foul-smelling yellow vapor from their mouths. Spanning hundreds of meters from spine to foot, they shook buildings and crushed the asphalt with every step. As the roads had long crumbled beneath their feet, only four-wheel-drive vehicles and motorbikes managed to navigate them. Some people had recently taken to riding gray Fenrir wolves they had caught in the mountains.

People said this was the end of the world. I disagreed. It was simply the end of the human race. People said the gods had abandoned the world. I disagreed. Divine attention had simply shifted from us to other creatures. Every new species was superbly resistant to pollution and germs. They multiplied alarmingly fast in environments where oxygen was scarce but ozone and ammonia abounded. They grew from plastic dumps and conquered oceans beyond human reach, bided their time, and finally crawled onto land after cities had been destroyed several times over. At first people tried to find ways to eradicate them, but once any pesticide or toxic gas was used on them, the next generation was born immune to it and began propagating swiftly again.

I roamed the streets at night with only a dagger and basket in hand to pretend that I was out hunting. I explored the basements of collapsed buildings and rummaged the nests of creatures dwelling in sewers. I hunted the ones that looked edible and brought home new species to study. I told people I was checking for any potential dangers, but Aman was the only one who knew the real reason behind my expeditions: I was looking for an organism like myself. If nature made an organism like me, would it not have made another one? Sometimes I felt that the rest of humanity formed one homogenous entity and I was the odd one out.

"Everyone thinks that when they're young," said Aman.

"I am *not* young," I protested.

"But you've never been an adult either."

Aman ruffled my hair as if I were a child. His hands were thin and wrinkly. He had gone blind some time ago and was losing his hearing. At night he coughed till his whole body quaked and spat out dark phlegm. He would run out of life soon. Like all the other Amans I loved had before him.

He was the sixth male Aman to marry me and the seventeenth child that I named "Aman" upon birth. He was my descendant, to be precise, but the taboo against incest had long been lifted. Women able to bear children were rare, young women even more so. There had once been a time when scientists locked me up in labs and broke me down into cells to squeeze the secret of immortality out of me, but they, like the others, passed into the annals of history. If anyone wanted to analyze my body now, the technology for it no longer existed. Rather than try to uncover the secret to my immortality, people today revered my life itself. Humanity in the age of myth was far more accepting of the unknown than humanity in the age of science.

I considered visiting the Underwater Tomb of King Munmu or Seokguram Grotto, but decided on Lotte World Tower for the irony. It also happened to be where I had found three types of mushrooms and five new species of fish, in the submerged basement where the aquarium had burst open.

Perhaps Aman was right. Inanimate objects were the only things that had existed since my time. Perhaps a being that lived forever was close to a nonliving thing. I walked around a Jörmungandr-covered building and found a suitable spot to sit down. Leaning against a damp wall that smelled of mold and rust, I struck up a conversation with the building in jest at first, then in earnest. I had eternity on my hands after all, perhaps I would try for an eternity. I was growing tired of losing Aman over and over again. I was tired of having no hope of reuniting with Aman in the world of the dead. I wanted answers. Answers to the origin and meaning of my existence, the reason my life persisted.

I discovered that starvation could not kill me three centuries ago, when I was trapped in an underground tunnel and decided to experiment. I starved, but that was all. I still cannot understand how that was possible. But I have suspected that something in my body might be turning light or air or moisture into nitrogen, as a plant photosynthesizes.

After who knows how many days, I got my reply. But not from the building.

THEY LOOKED LIKE phantoms. Wrapped in fog, they were wobbly and transparent. They had limbs and large heads like those of humans and appeared to walk on two legs, but I could not be sure. At first I thought I was seeing things because of my hunger. But their presence weighed down on me too heavily for them to be imaginary. Or there could be hallucinatory mushrooms or mosses nearby. If not a hallucination, though, they had to be creatures that generated wavelengths beyond the human visual spectrum. Such a species might well have appeared by now.

—We were waiting, Naban.

A voice echoed in my mind. While they addressed me by a peculiar name, they spoke a human language—*my* language.

You waited?

The emergence of an intelligent species was not surprising in itself. I had been expecting it. But the fact that they spoke a language I knew put me on my guard. It was one thing to have intelligence, but to have the same language system as mine? Even if they did not, why would they bother learning the language of another species? Again, I suspected I was hallucinating. Perhaps they sensed the questions forming in my mind because they added:

—Waiting for your desire to seek out your kind to grow strong enough.

Instinctively, I drew my dagger from my belt. Although my body was forever that of a fifteen-year-old, my physical capabilities had never stopped growing. Of course, training would have been pointless if my mysterious body undid any changes in its muscle mass, but my body developed athletic skills as unceasingly as my brain accumulated knowledge. Without meaning to, I had the body of one who had undergone thousands of hours of exercise and training—though my strength was still limited to what my basic physique allowed for.

They spoke to me as if I had been tested without even realizing it and had already passed. The moment I heard their words, pride and a sense of achievement washed over me as if my life's efforts had been validated. I felt important, great even. These were dangerous feelings to have when I did not know who they were and had no reason to trust them.

—We are exactly what you have been searching for, Naban.

The white apparitions held out their hands in unison. I scrambled to my feet, groped the wall behind me, and lifted my dagger horizontally to my face, assuming a defensive position.

"If you knew I was searching, why did you not come find me earlier?"

—Conversation is meaningless. Take our hands. Then you will understand.

I could tackle them head-on to test my enemy's powers, but

I was outnumbered and could not risk failure. While I recovered fast and did not age, I was not immune to injuries. I edged sideways until my hand found a gap behind me and ran for it. Apparitions shot up from the ground and blocked my path. I wheeled around, finding myself surrounded. Tangible entities that traveled underground? They defied all common sense. I knew there was no way out and so I waited. The apparition that stood in the front held out a hand.

Is that all they want?

When I showed no sign of taking the hand, the legs of an apparition in the back elongated like octopus tentacles and wrapped around my ankles as I stared wide-eyed in horror. The tentacles were hard as steel and burned as if they spouted acid. They throttled my ankles like they meant to sever them.

That they were inflicting pain on me suggested they needed my consent to whatever this ritual was for. Their impatience told me there was more at stake for them than there was for me. I asked, "Why do you want me?"

—You are one of us. We were one entity originally, but you split from us. Once we become whole . . .

"What happens then?"

The apparition clammed up. Was that hesitation I saw?

—The human race has reached its end. It has been corrupted, and must be purified and reborn. This should have happened long ago, but you were living in its midst, so we waited.

I whipped around.

I raised my dagger and stabbed the foot of the apparition standing next to me. It felt squishy under the tip of my dagger, like stretchy dough. It stuck and clung to the blade. It also seemed to contain a substance that melted metal. It did not bleed or so much as jerk from the pain.

Evolution might be happening fast, but it would still take eons for a species such as this to appear on Earth.

Aliens? But I was inclined to believe that aliens were highly unlikely to attempt communicating with a random pedestrian over a politician, say, or an academic. A man would have been quick to consider these creatures ghosts or monsters, but I was born in an age that denounced the afterlife and was not hardwired to think in such terms.

I regretted my attack, but what was done was done. Another tentacle materialized and seized my arm that held the dagger. More pain. The apparition in the front offered their hand again.

—Do not resist, Naban. We are your kind. Take this hand and you will understand everything. Wisdom will find you.

Somehow, I knew they were not lying. Then it dawned on me that what I had wanted all along was not what I wanted at all. I should have known how monstrous my kind was. Ignorant of death and aging and decline, my kind had the arrogance to believe that they were in no way, shape, or form related to the average human. What transcendent powers did they have to justify proclaiming the "corruption" or the "end" of humanity; how dare they? I waited and braced myself for the worst.

"Dammit, this isn't gonna work," the apparition suddenly grumbled. "This method won't do."

"?"

I blinked, baffled. The slimy tentacles withdrew at once, causing me to fall on my behind.

"Forget it. I wasn't serious about the whole 'end of humanity' spiel. We don't intervene to *that* extent. Time will take care of that anyway. I was just hoping to talk you into leaving this place, since you were taking your sweet time here. You're stubborn as a mule, Teacher."

"??"

"Honestly, you pulled the dirtiest trick there ever was. You said you'd live just one life, but then you come down here in an immortal body? Sheesh. No one's done that since the Age of Myth. You used to complain that it was such a drag to live any more than two decades in an inferior body. Now look at you, you'd be happy to live on till Earth burned to ashes."

"????"

I gaped at the apparition, dumbstruck. The grumbling apparition began to radiate as its outline sharpened. Through a shroud of silvery thread, I saw a brawny woman who had braided pigtails and wore coveralls stained with dirty fingerprints. She did not look anything like a god, ghost, Grim Reaper, or alien. But judging by how she had elongated her body before, she seemed to be able to shape-shift at will.

"If at any time you want to come back, Teacher, just think it. I'll fly over right away. All right?"

And then she was gone quick as a flash. The other apparitions vanished with her. Suddenly finding myself alone, I could only blink once more in bemusement.

I PICKED SOME underwater toadstools on the ground floor, hunted three or four imperial bryozoans in the aquarium, and left the building with a full basket. It was daybreak. A crimson glow bathed the city and the herd of giant Ymir bulls marched slowly in the distance, letting out an occasional *bbooo*. They appeared slow due to their gargantuan size but were actually moving very fast. The Jörmungandr twisting around the buildings glinted in the sunlight, red as veins.

An odd thought occurred to me. Perhaps the universe was alive because *I* was alive. Omnipotent beings might be watching us from somewhere in that sky, all-knowing yet not knowing the value of life. They who were oblivious to the greatness of survival and scorned life's battles, who failed to see the sacredness of one person's individuality. Yet by some arrangement I was unaware of, they could not touch this world while I lived . . .

. . . It was just a thought.

Still, it was not such a bad idea to try to live as long as I dared. I gripped my basket tighter and started back home, where Aman was waiting.

N – 1

I GAZED DOWN AT MY DEAD BODY, THE YOUNG BOY SOLDIER whose face was rammed into the ground. Having accepted the fact of my death, I looked around for a sign that read THIS WAY TO THE WORLD OF THE DEAD, or perhaps a guide carrying a sandwich board with the words WELCOME. ALL HELL-BOUND VISITORS, QUEUE HERE.

I spotted a figure standing in front of a boulder, clad in a long black *dopo* robe and a matching hood. I noted their large, golden eyes that looked like shattered coins and their thin, sapless limbs just visible beneath their robes.

A messenger of death?

But the thought was cut short by other memories burgeoning inside me as if I were rousing from a hangover. The memories that my body had suppressed until now, the histories etched into my every past life. My mind cleared even more when I summoned my spiritual body, which had exploded into pieces from the shock of dying. Sensitive humans would be able to see me when I was so converged, but I doubted they would see much with their pitifully narrow visual spectrums that could not even register infrared and ultraviolet rays.

"Tushita," I called their name and closed my mouth. Had they not lost their individuality by merging with the Whole? The fact that Tushita existed meant history had shifted its course. Even so I had failed, seeing as it was Tushita who came to greet me.

While the results were regrettable, they would be a failure or defeat only if I viewed them as such. Besides, I had lived the life I chose.

"I have kept you waiting for too long," I said. "I lived my one life and am content. You may eat me now." I extended my hand toward Tushita. But Tushita remained silent. Their eyes were dark and somber. Sensing something was wrong, I walked up to Tushita and grabbed their wrist. It was emaciated. Much more so than it looked at first glance. Their body had shrunk to a pathetic size. Even if they summoned all the spiritual bodies they had, they would only double or triple their size at most. They would not amount to the universe or a planet, or an asteroid for that matter, not even a mountain or creek. Was this really the Tushita for whom my colleagues had merged their bodies in order to defend against the Lower Realm's corruption?

"You won, Naban," Tushita said hoarsely.

"In what way?" I asked, my memories of this new universe not yet fully recovered. Tushita considered me, trying to assess whether I was teasing them or was truly in the dark. Their powers of perception seemed to have become pathetically weak too.

"I had imprisoned you, but pieces of Aman and their children kidnapped you, removed from your body the code for merging without persuasion, and absorbed it. They defined our erasure of Aman from history as treason against the Whole. They also defined *us* as corrupt, not them."

A new memory emerged. My connection to the Whole had faded by then and I could not stop the children from dismantling my body. In my despair over failing, I had not even thought to try to stop them.

"The children stole your code and turned it into a sort of hacking software. They distributed a virus all over the Dark Realm, one that cut off entities from the Whole and disabled merging. Disease spread across the realm and half of our number lost the ability to divide or merge. The Prophets and the teachers also lost the majority of their bodies. To reincarnate into the Lower Realm, they must now go through a machine in Aman's bardo."

I said nothing. So, I had won. I should be happy, but I was not.

"What about Tanjae?" I asked.

"They fought back. With incomprehensible methods. They shot laser cannons and missiles. They even deployed a robot army.

"In the end, Tanjae was captured by Aman's army. They were thoroughly taken apart and integrated into many different personalities. To make it impossible for them to recover their original form.

"Tanjae used to look after those children. It is beyond me why they would do that to their own teacher."

It was not beyond me. Tanjae was not corrupt. Neither was I right now.

"Aman's children shared the Dark Realm's knowledge with the Lower Realm. They passed on the technology and wisdom of the gods. The Lower Realm saw glorious progress in science, which now threatens to overtake magic and sorcery. Enlightened people of the Lower Realm know the afterlife exists and can now communicate with the Dark Realm. They know how to live their lives. They have access to the wisdom of all Prophets through spiritual channels. Everything is as Aman wanted."

Aman wanted? As far as I knew, the old Aman wanted nothing of the sort.

"You won, Naban. The current ruler of the Dark Realm is Aman. Aman has built an enormous temple there and is making every preparation to welcome you. I came to find you because I would rather be eaten by you than be captured and taken apart. Please, eat me and embrace my knowledge and my memories of all my lives, so that I might retain who 'I' am. Given your size, my addition will not compromise your identity."

Tushita did not see that they were already not who they used to be. Clinging to one's identity was a sign of contamination, but they seemed not to have noticed.

I lifted my hand from Tushita's arm. Only then did I grasp my true size. My body was almost back to how it used to be before I set out to eliminate Aman. Nearly the same size as when I first earned the name Naban. Now I knew the full extent of my powers and privileges. I was the First Being and the First Prophet; I could birth countless children again and repopulate the world. If the Dark and Lower Realms were connected, that in itself would be the start of new learning. I would teach people so that they would never suffer. I would channel all of my past lives into them.

I relished these fantasies to my heart's content. How pleasurable they were. But instead of losing myself in pleasure, I restrained myself.

"Please eat me," Tushita implored.

"What if I refuse?"

Tushita glared at me but composed themself soon enough. I was so large and Tushita so small, I could see through the bottom of their heart.

"You are cruel. Though I understand why."

Tushita swallowed their anger and reminded themselves of the things they had done to me. They seemed to think that they were getting their comeuppance. In the smallness of their mind, they were beginning to nitpick on matters of right and wrong, reward and retribution.

"If you refuse to eat me, I will go fight Aman. From my point of view, Aman is corrupt. They may not have been in the past, but they clearly are now. They have grown too big and destroyed balance. Trivial though my body is, I will fight. And to that end I will face you first. I will safeguard my identity through this fight. Once you defeat me, disintegrate me or quarantine me in Hell."

I reduced my body slightly. Gravity appeared at the tip of my finger and the universe began to gather there. Theoretically, even the edges of the universe must have rippled. Aman would have felt it too from somewhere in the Dark Realm. Tushita prepared for combat, but they looked just about as threatening as a fidgeting child.

I know all of my potential. And all of my contradictions.

For I am Naban, one who remembers the beginning of time. For I know nothing in the universe is not me. For I know that no one part of a whole is more valuable than another; one is simply larger or smaller. For I know corruption arises when one tries to exclude another from a world. For I am not corrupt now.

I opened my mouth.

"How can I help, Tushita?"

ON MY
WAY TO YOU

Translated by Sophie Bowman

HER FIRST LETTER

One day into the voyage,
one day in Earth time

HOW'VE YOU BEEN?
I'm on my way now.

I WROTE THAT and put down the pencil for a moment, then looked out the window. I'm actually waiting for them to finish boarding.

I can see an endless line of people outside, carrying bags on their backs or their heads. There are kids messing about, and others that are just exhausted, dangling from their parents' hands all cranky, fighting sleep. An elderly couple are supporting each other up to the entranceway, hand in hand, and there are people my age too, snacking, chatting away, and fussing over this and that. Off in another corner there's a crowd of people embracing each other and sharing long farewells.

I couldn't bring much with me. I didn't want to risk getting caught as I snuck out. But I did manage to pack an e-book reader. It's a really cheap one, with a screen the size of a watch face. It's too tiny to read from, but it's fine for listening to audiobooks. I loaded it with around a hundred classics, so I shouldn't get too bored in the two months it'll take to reach you.

I guess you'll be pretty surprised about getting a handwritten letter—I was taken aback too when the attendant gave me a pencil and paper. I asked her, "What's this for?" and she said, "You can write with it even when there's no gravity." She made a gesture as though writing upside down and added, "You know, if you try to write with a ballpoint pen lying down it doesn't work, but a pencil does." So I said, no, no, that's not it, and asked why they use paper at all. "Well, technology is always changing," she said, but I still didn't get it, so she explained that no matter how simply a device is made, there would be people who can't use it. The elderly, children, people from other star systems, occasionally poor people too. But that everyone would want to write a letter, no matter who they were.

So apparently, if I write on this paper, they'll capture an image and transmit that, and wherever it's picked up they'll convert it as they see fit.

So it might have even been made into an audio file by the time it reaches you.

I GOT TOLD off by an attendant just now when she caught me snooping around inside the ship, checking everything out. It was really embarrassing, so I'm cooped up in my room now. You know how I am. I have to inspect my surroundings as soon as I get to a new place. I can't relax until I've secured somewhere to hide and an escape route. Living with my family . . . that's just how you get.

I GET A little kick every time the navigation AI makes an announcement. It uses the sentences I thought up, just as I wrote them. It's crazy that anyone's still using that script, it's from a writing gig I did so long ago.

WE'RE ALL GETTING restless already, so me and my roommates are in the middle of playing the "cooking-and-cleaning game." Do you know it? I played it all the time when I was little. Then again, it's a girls' game, so you might not have heard of it.

Whenever AI conversation scriptwriters get together, they play the game as though their lives depend on winning.

In case you haven't played, I'll explain: Two people give a command to an AI at the same time. One orders it to get the cleaning done and the other orders it to cook a meal, and the side whose command the AI sets as priority wins. Early AIs always carried out commands in the order they were given, but these days they make more complex deliberations. Commands like "Do the cleaning by seven thirty this evening" get prioritized over simpler ones, like "Make dinner." The time limit gives the machine a sense of urgency. Actually, there are people who say that the know-how for winning the game is similar to the know-how for getting a husband to do housework. There's even a rumor it was made up so that girls could train in the most effective ways of getting their future husbands to do things around the house.

IT's HARD TO believe I'm somewhere so far away that I have to fly four years, four months, and 12 days at the speed of light to reach you. That means that, for us to meet, I have to travel 9.5 trillion kilometers four times over, and then a third of that distance again.

Of course, time stands still when the ship reaches light speed, so those years will only feel like two months to me: the month it takes to accelerate to light speed and the month it takes to slow down.

I remember telling you that I had to go to Alpha Centauri.

I said I was going to accompany my family when they emigrated and come straight back as soon as my feet had touched the ground. I explained that since anyone who travels to another solar system gets an outer planets residency permit, it'd be easier for me to find a proper job when I got back; that there are loads of advantages when it comes to taxes and things like that; it just meant hanging in there for four months.

"That's from your perspective," you said, staring back at me as you counted time on your fingers. "I'll have to wait nine years—eight years and eight months more than your four months."

"Yeah." I closed my eyes, waiting for what you'd say.

I was expecting something like, "You really found a clever way to break up with me. In that case, I'm off. I'll just go find someone new."

But you didn't. Instead, the next day, you came in with an armful of pamphlets on interstellar marriage and said that if you saved up for about four and a half years, you'd be able to buy a ticket to take what they call the Orbit of Waiting. You explained that it was a ship that circled around the sun at the speed of light so that the passengers could get to the same time as people traveling in from other stars.

"Then I'd only have to wait a little over four and a half years."

As soon as you spoke those words, I hugged you and began to sob.

You told me it would be really great. This way or that, welfare was getting better year on year, and great technologies would keep emerging. You said going a few years into the future was more of a sure bet than taking out an insurance policy.

It seemed like you understood.

Understood that I desperately needed to leave my family on the other side of the universe.

The same solar system wouldn't do. These days people can meet in real time through the internet, even from the other side of a planet. To really, truly get away from them, there was nothing else for me to do but leave them in another time and place. Even if they were to come chasing after me at the speed of light, it would take years. With that distance between us, even my father getting into a rage and yelling, "Tell me where you are right now!" and me replying, "Oh gosh, well . . ." would take eight years, eight months, and twenty-four days.

I OFTEN THINK of that time not long after we started seeing each other. I kept canceling on you at the last minute and cutting off contact for days on end. I thought you'd lose interest like all the others. But then one day you sent me a text. *Come out and meet me, it doesn't matter how you look.*

You said that you'd wait.

A few days later, when I finally went to the café, you were sitting near the door looking a mess. You honestly looked like you'd spent the last few nights sleeping on the streets. My appearance was no better. I was wearing a hat, a jacket, and an eye patch and had wrapped a scarf around half my face in scorching-hot weather. I managed to cover the bruises on my body with clothing, but my swollen cheeks and puffed-up eyes must have been plain to see. I felt so mortified that day, and I hated and resented you for being so persistent in wanting to see me, for being so patient that I couldn't help but come out, despite my cringe-worthy state.

But you didn't question me at all. Instead, you went on and on about things like ways of reducing swelling and old remedies for bruises, and then you fell asleep, right there on the café sofa.

"Family's not a big deal, you know," you said the next time we met. "When it comes to family, you can always make a new one. That's why the world has this great thing called marriage. Since the average life expectancy keeps getting longer, we'll live to be a hundred. And if I live with you from now until then, I'll become four times more your family than your first family was."

And then you pestered me, saying, "So let's hurry up and get married! As soon as we can, let's do it."

That's why I'm on my way to you now.

To become four times more family with the person I chose for myself.

Wait for me.

HER SECOND LETTER

One month into the voyage,
one year and four months later in Earth time

ARGH, I'M SO UPSET.

I got all dramatic and sent you a letter that would move you to tears, and now this. It's so unfair.

I'm sorry, honey. I'm really sorry.

Hear me out. What happened was, we'd gotten up to light speed and then they said they'd received a distress signal. A ship nearby had met disaster and was adrift. The captain made the broadcast with her voice pitched unnaturally low: "In accordance with interstellar regulations, we will now begin braking to carry out rescue operations." Seriously, she just made a unilateral announcement, without even trying to get our consent! In all the wide universe, why did that ship have to get into trouble right near ours?

I'm not saying we shouldn't make the rescue—I know, I know, it's the ethical code of spacefarers. And it's not as if they could've just called 911 in this open sea. The problem is, we were flying at the speed of light, so no matter how urgently the captain reduced speed, it'd take a month to come to a stop, and a whole month more to accelerate again.

That's two months! Wait, in Earth time . . . that's three months!

Without even realizing what I was doing, I clung on to an

attendant who was passing by and protested, "Did you hear that loud crack just now? That's the sound of my engagement being broken. I'm a bride going to my wedding, and I've already written my fiancé the best letter you can imagine. What are you going to do about it?" Having listened inattentively, the attendant made a call somewhere and said, "We have a passenger here with an upcoming wedding more important than the lives of thirty people. Please take good care of her." And then two burly men appeared out of nowhere, lifted me up like some light piece of luggage, and threw me back into my room.

Seriously! What did I do to deserve that? I just wanted them to acknowledge the fact that we're all making sacrifices!

A little while ago another attendant came in with a stern expression on her face. She said that we'd have to share our room when the survivors arrived on board and requested that all the occupants sign a consent form. When I asked how many people would be coming in, she said it would be eight. Eight more people, into a four-person room!

So I asked what would happen if I didn't consent, and she just said, "There's nothing we can do about that," then closed her mouth up like a clam and stood there in the middle of the room. Wow, she wasn't wielding a knife, but it was a total heist. A heist!

Once she was gone, me and my roommates vented our frustration together for ages. How could they be doing this to us? We're all good people! We all paid our way fair and square! Why do we have to take the hit? Getting worked up like that made us hungry, so even though it was late we ordered tons of spicy food and ate like we hadn't had a meal in days. And then I turned on my e-book reader and started listening to Goethe's *Faust*. Whatever the story, I thought listening to something ancient would help calm me down.

Sorry, honey. I'm truly sorry.

I left you on your own for four and a half years. And now

I'm making you wait three months more. Through no fault of my own, I'll end up being late for my own wedding of all things, and you'll never let me hear the end of it.

Forgive me, just this once. I'll make you twenty wish coupons as soon as I get there . . . okay? How about thirty?

THAT FAUST IS a funny guy.

To think that he'd gladly perish, gladly let the devil chain him up and throw him into eternal doom if only he could say, "Ah, stay a while! You are so lovely!" at someone or some moment, just once in his life; if he could feel such joy, even if it was fleeting. What made him so extreme? Was he just in complete despair? Or was he that much more desperate for life than death?

I GUESS THE world will have changed a lot by the time I get back.

That's the way things went before too. Whether it was buildings or stores or even streets, they never made it more than a few years. A shop that appeared the day before would close down the day after, and a building that was there the month before would disappear before another month passed by. As though the whole country itself were gripped in self-loathing, it would constantly tear itself down. Even when it came to things that were old, things that could have been cherished.

Living in a place like that, we had to develop the habit of never getting attached to anything. We became conditioned to feel no regret or sadness, no matter what might be lost to us. All that remains of those things now are our memories.

You know what, honey—back on Earth there's not one thing that I can call mine. I've left my house and family and all my belongings behind, everything, on the other side of the universe. When I get back to Earth, all the streets and buildings I used to know will likely be gone too.

Still, I'm not afraid one bit.

I had this idea. That my home isn't a place. It's a person. And that person is you. You're my home, and where I long to be . . .

Now I've gone and told you something really romantic, you'll have to forgive me for being late.

I'm on my way home now.

Wait for me.

HER THIRD LETTER

Four months and ten days into the voyage,
four years, nine months, and ten days later in Earth time

Hi, honey! Yoo-hoo!

I got your letter as soon as we landed in the port.

Oh dear, you poor thing. You changed ship trying to match up our arrival times, but it went wrong and you're going to be three years late? Tut-tut! You've got to do better!

When I heard, I burst out laughing and thought, *Wow! He's really stepping up his game.* I searched for another ship right away, and there was one just preparing for takeoff. I lucked out!

It's a wonderful world! All it takes is a trip on a Light Voyager and no matter how out of step the meeting time, you're able to make it right. Whether it's three years or a hundred, there's no way we couldn't meet!

I feel great now. I was so agonized by making you wait three more months that I was losing loads of weight, but now you're the one who's going to be super late. By the time we meet I'll have waited two years and nine months more than you from our scheduled wedding day. You'll have to be really good to me going forward, husband!

Don't you worry about a thing. I sorted out every complication from the delay all by myself!

I contacted the wedding venue and got in touch with your

friends. They were a bit shocked by the news that we'd be three years late, but they all said they'd be there. Apparently they already met up at the venue on the original date and had a good time.

I notified the tenants at our place and adjusted the contract. Your boss didn't take the news too well, unfortunately. But still, the employee filling in for you now is happy about having her contract extended.

Your letter came as a voice recording. I loaded it onto my e-book reader, and I keep listening to it over and over, even now. Every time I get to the bit where you beg and plead, "Wait for me. . . . Please. . . . I'll be good for the rest of our life together," I laugh so hard I can't breathe.

You know what, honey?

To be honest, I don't mind you being late one bit. It means there'll be three more years separating me from my family. Aw, my darling, how did you know exactly what I wanted? If only I could give you a big kiss. Mwah!

JUST AS I imagined, everything's really changed. All the cars on the roads are autonomous vehicles now. Lucky I never bothered getting my driver's license! There are separate lanes exclusively for wheelchairs too, and at the port there's a sign language interpreter robot. I was reading the news today, and apparently they're going to start introducing free higher education next year.

You were right. Things are getting better bit by bit. Three years from now things will be even better.

THE SHIP I'VE boarded is a research vessel that goes on geological explorations. I hear they also supply goods to nearby space stations on the side while they travel around collecting soil from asteroids. They've repurposed some of the compartments too, to take in passengers. The number of space travelers keep growing year on year, but the number of ships hasn't kept up, so ships like this take on passengers using loopholes in the law. They're not insured, but my ticket was super cheap.

Everyone on board is either a researcher or else a peddler—I'm the only regular traveler. They asked me why I boarded this kind of ship. So I told them I was on my way to get married, and they all laughed their heads off! A middle-aged dry fish salesman handed me a piece of dried pollack and said that no man would wait that long, that this man I was going to meet would've settled down with someone else already.

So I got worked up and snapped back that the person I'm going to marry isn't just any man but "my man." All the while chomping on the dried fish! I was so embarrassed for making such a scene, afterward I hid my face against the wall.

I meant it, though. You're not just any man. You're my man. And I'm not just any woman. I'm your woman. And so, we're different from everyone else.

Why do people feel the need to say such things? People who've never met us before, who have no real interest in us, go around rattling off superficial advice, as though they've become prophets and received the word of God, as though they've gone off and gotten a qualification in meddling with our life. No matter how distinguished or smart a person is, the only life they really know about is their own.

MY FATHER LOATHED every man that ever came near me. There was uproar when I told him we were going to get married. He hurled everything in my bedroom out onto the street, telling me that I'd come back crying and begging for forgiveness once I'd tasted all the bitterness of life and thrashed around in its misery. Now, I question what grounds he had to indulge in such a specific fantasy, when really, he put my mom through all of that himself.

Now that I've gotten this far away, I think I get it. What he'd hated so much, with such passion, was himself.

Aside from yourself, there's no one who can know you to the core, and so there's no one who can hate you more than yourself. Just like there's no one who can love you more than you can love yourself.

That must be why he hated me so much. Since I came from him and resemble him.

YOU NEVER SPOKE about the past. Like wishing your parents had done something for you when you were younger, or wistfully thinking you could've been better off if you'd had this or done that at some point. You only ever talked about what was happening now, or else the future.

"There is no past. It's all an illusion," you'd say from time to time.

When I asked how that could be, you scratched your head as though it was tricky to explain.

"Think about it. Everything that we mistake for the past is just the present. Everything is all in the present."

I think I finally understand what that means now.

Since the past has flowed away in the river of time, and the future hasn't come yet, all that exists is the present, this moment of now that appears, then vanishes like a flash of light. Old wounds stinging the heart are actually chemicals the brain pours out as it replays memories.

You were right, there is no past. The past exists only in my memories, and memories are recalled in the present. There's no future yet either, that too is just something I'm thinking of *now*.

Right, so I'm not going to think about those people anymore. Thinking only of good things, I'll make my present out of what's good.

I keep thinking of the moment when I'll say, "I'm back!"

and run toward you at the port, straight into your arms. Even just picturing it, I feel like my present is all aglow.

Oh yeah, you said you bought a toy ring that plays love songs? That's great. You should put it on my finger at the wedding. All our guests will be in stitches.

My home, where I long to be.

I'm on my way home now.

Sleep well. I love you.

HER FOURTH LETTER

*Five months and twenty-six days into the voyage,
seven years and eight months and
twenty-four days later in Earth time*

OH GOD.

Honey, what am I supposed to do?

I'VE PICKED UP my pencil again after crying for ages.

I sent you a letter a while back, but I'm writing another. The stewards are in such confusion that the first one probably wasn't even sent.

There are too many people around me, and the stewards keep coming and going, so I can't cry as much as I need to. Some people are unconscious, and one guy keeps bleeding from his stomach, and the stewards won't stop throwing open the door to ask pointless questions and then disappear. When I complained about it, they said it's because they're out of their senses too. If the stewards are out of it, then what hope do the passengers have?

I'm looking out the window and one whole side of the ship is shredded. Apparently, a jagged asteroid scraped past us. Only a few compartments in the ship are safe now. You even have to put on a space suit to go out to the toilet, but it takes thirty minutes to put one on, and even that has to be taken in turns. So you have to raise your hand half an hour before actually feeling the urge, and in order to do that you have to take a ticket around an hour in advance. Ridiculous, huh?

A little while ago, the captain came in and complained for ages about how he's ruined, and then went out again. Thanks to that I learned all about how much real estate he owns, how many children he has, and how much he has in savings. Funny, huh?

The only ships that pass by this way are freight vessels, or else other research ships. Even with those, we had to draw lots to decide who gets to go and when. With my lot, the only real choices are a lightship going to Alpha Centauri that will arrive in two months, or a freight vessel headed for Earth that will arrive here a month from now.

Except, the one going to Earth isn't a lightship, so it'll take eleven years to get there.

Eleven years . . .

Eleven whole years.

And if I board that one, apparently there's nowhere to eat or sleep or go to the toilet, so I'll have to go into the hibernation pod on board for disaster survivors and sleep until it's time to disembark.

Someone's crying again, right in front of me. And I can hear another person shouting from somewhere. The middle-aged woman lying beside me keeps snatching all of the blanket, saying she's cold. And she told me to stop thinking ridiculous thoughts and go back to Alpha Centauri. That there are lots of people who have ended up as frozen meat after a mishap in the hibernation process. And that you'll have left, that you'll be long gone already . . .

ELEVEN YEARS.

No, eighteen years and eight months . . .

I can't bring myself to ask you to get back on another ship.

By now you'll have no savings to pay the fare, and even if you borrow everything you can, how can a newlywed couple with no house and nowhere to go get by when they have to pay back interest from the outset? And who would ever hire someone with an eighteen-year gap in their résumé? Technology and everything else will be completely different. Even if I can marry you, every time you get drunk, you'll sulk that you ruined your whole life so that you could marry me, and I just wouldn't be able to bear it.

I really wanted to marry you.

I really wanted us to be four times more family. But I guess that's impossible now.

Still, I'm going to Earth.

Do I even have a choice, really? You're my only home.

I don't have the heart to ask you to wait.

Just, please, come out to the port.

Eleven years from now, come out to meet me when I arrive. It's fine if you bring your wife and kids. It's all right. I'll understand everything. I'll shake her hand in a dignified way, and we can chat all day long, similar women who ended up getting hooked on the same man.

I just want to see you.

I think that'll make everything all right. Just knowing that you're there under the same sky. Then, even if we're apart, we'd still be living together. Our house would just be a bit big.

HER FIFTH LETTER

Six months and twenty-six days into the voyage,
seven years, nine months, and twenty-four days later in Earth time

SORRY IT'S TAKEN ME SO LONG TO SEND A LETTER.

It was really impossible to write on that ship. It's not a difficult thing to do at all, but even small things were a big deal there. Living all squished together day in, day out, everything you could ever imagine happening ended up happening. If anyone did anything even a little out of the ordinary, everyone around them lost it.

I'm finally alone now.

Although I almost didn't make it.

I don't know how I survived in that beat-up ship for a whole month . . . But that's enough, no need to talk about that now. Since the past exists only when it's brought to mind.

IT'S LIKE A deep freezer in here. My hands are so numb with cold I can barely write. The temperature's fixed to ensure the freshness of the cargo. I asked HUN to turn on the heating, but she said there *is* no heating system. There's no real lighting either, so I'm writing this by the light from my little e-book reader screen.

Oh, I should explain. HUN's the captain of this freight vessel. She's not human, she's an AI captain. She's really smart. No matter what I ask, she doesn't get angry, and she's really good at explaining things in a calm and detailed way.

HUN told me I have to empty my stomach before going into the hibernation pod, so I've been fasting since I got here. I'm so hungry I could die. Soon all my bodily fluids will be removed and replaced with antifreeze. HUN said to think of it like a kind of dialysis. But she also informed me I could die if my body has an allergic reaction to the antifreeze. She reassured me, even if that happens, my corpse will be well preserved and delivered intact to my family, so not to worry. Can you believe it?

I asked her if I could send you a letter. According to HUN, you'll be able to receive it if you're still on the ship you were on before. But if you've changed onto another ship, she doesn't know the address, so she wouldn't know how to get it to you. Well, that makes sense. But I'm writing it anyway.

There's nothing for me to do here until the preparations for hibernation are complete, so I've been playing the cooking-and-cleaning game with HUN. I said that, compared to "Do the cleaning by seven thirty this evening," the command "I'm about to starve to death. Make some food for me," should be set as priority. Because a person's survival is more important than anything else. But HUN said the second command was pretty vague. Humans have a habit of using phrases like "I'm about to die" when it's not actually true, so I would have to provide clearer reasoning. She told me to say: "I'm undergoing dietary therapy treatment, and it's dangerous if I don't have meals at a specific time." Of course, there'd be no way of confirming whether I was really sick, but the AI would prioritize the command anyway, because she shouldn't miss the correct timing trying to verify my claim.

When we meet, I'm going to keep talking all day long. I'll tell you about everything I've been through in the past month. Let's see who had a harder time!

I really hope I win.

I hope you haven't had even one difficult thing to deal with.

I hope you've lived with a full tummy and a toasty back the whole time I've been gone. I can't imagine how I'll feel if you've messed up your life worrying about me.

I mean it. If you don't live well, I'll probably end up messing up my life feeling terrible about it.

While I'm gone, I hope you'll eat delicious things and go on loads of holidays. Read lots of interesting stuff too. In return, every now and then, when something good happens, think of me. If you do that, I'll be there with you.

And come out to the port and tell me you lived that way for eleven years. Promise.

I think then I'll be able to sleep soundly.

Goodbye, my love.

Thank you for having loved me.

I was happy thanks to you . . .

HER SIXTH LETTER

*Six months and twenty-six days into the voyage
(excluding the years spent asleep), nineteen years,
two months, and four days later in Earth time*

As soon as I awoke, I could feel something was off.

At first, I thought the ship must have made an emergency landing, or else arrived in the wrong place. I thought it wasn't Earth. Or that it couldn't be Korea, at least.

The smell was different. The air was stuffy, and the smell of soil and grass stung my nose. In the silence all around, the only sound was HUN's broadcasts:

"Please unload the cargo."

"Please come out to the control tower."

"Is no one there?"

The antifreeze that was pumped into my body had only just been replaced with blood, so I felt like I could freeze to death at any moment. It felt as though I'd been submerged in the icy winter sea for a century and turned into a frozen dumpling. I was dizzy, my mind was hazy, and I had no strength at all. Every time I breathed, I thought I could smell stale oil reeking out of my lungs. Shaking like an ancient woman, I somehow managed to crawl over to the warm bath HUN had prepared nearby and fall in with a splash. It was only when my body had thawed out a little that I collected myself and took in my surroundings.

The hatch was open, but no one came through it, only rain pelted in on the wind. Cargo rattled along the container belt and dropped off it with a plop. Plop. Plop. Like it was dropped in thick rice porridge.

HUN finally stopped her broadcast when I called out to her. She explained that we'd been slightly delayed because it took her a while to inspect and fix an issue with the fuselage. When I asked how late we were, she answered, "Not very much at all. Around one year, four months, and four days later than scheduled."

A *year*.

HUN's mechanical voice really did sound mechanical then.

It was so dark outside. The wind and rain raged, wailing. All around me, in every direction, there were mud flats with water plants covering the whole area like occupation forces. I had no way of knowing where the sea began and the land ended.

I broke one of the cargo crates and yanked off a wooden board. I threw it onto the mud and clung to it as I waded ashore. When I looked back, the ship seemed to be sinking into the mud. The marsh looked like a silent monster ready to eat it up.

The mud and water extended into the port. No matter where I looked there was no trace of people, let alone any ships. I thought to myself again that we must have made an emergency landing on another planet.

But then I came to the waiting room, though it was so overrun by plants it looked like a low hill. When I cut through the shroud of creeping ivy with a pocketknife and went inside, it was a total mess. There were so many bullet holes that the walls looked like honeycomb, and I saw dark bloodstains dried into the floor. The electronic display was off, and someone had written a message over it in glow-in-the-dark paint.

WELCOME TRAVELERS
RETURNING FROM INTERSTELLAR JOURNEYS.
UNFORTUNATELY THE SITUATION IN KOREA NOW IS BAD.
A NUCLEAR PLANT IN THE SOUTH EXPLODED
AND CIVIL WAR IS ONGOING.
THE SITUATION IN OTHER COUNTRIES IS ALSO BAD.
PLEASE HURRY TO ANOTHER TIME.

Please hurry to another Time . . .

I just stood there staring at the notice for ages, clutching my trembling body. Beside it there were warnings scrawled in spray paint, telling travelers what to beware of. Someone had scrubbed out "radioactivity" and sprayed "martial law army" over it, and on top of that was written "bandits," and above that again was "civil militia."

I guess what was the biggest threat kept changing.

I left the waiting room to go back to HUN and tell her, "Let's go home, we've come to the wrong place." You know, it was only much later that the thought occurred to me: Everything on the electronic display was written in Korean. We definitely hadn't landed in the wrong place.

As I wandered around the mud flat in the rain that pelted down like hail, I spotted something peculiar in the distance.

It looked like an old shack.

It was actually a tent the wind had slashed into shreds. When I got closer, I saw that the ground behind it was pressed down in a wide, shallow crater.

It looked as though an object the size of a small spacecraft had stayed there for a long time. Only that one patch of ground was protected from the rain and wind and not overgrown with plants. Not far off, things like metal water barrels and dishes were being blown around, and there was something like animal feed stuck fast to the dishes. It was as if someone had been right there until just a little while ago, as though they'd left not long before.

But as I stood watching, the tent was blown away in the wind and rainwater guzzled in and swallowed up the small crater.

Once it'd all disappeared, I couldn't be sure if I'd been hallucinating, or if it really had been there.

With my mind totally blank, I swiped around in the mud frantically, as though you might be hiding there, in a hole you dug into the ground. Then I started calling out to you, but all that came back was the bitter howl of the wind.

And I was so, so afraid. Terrified that you might have waited for me here. That you could have come to this place on the appointed day, waited for me, and then left grinding your teeth, feeling betrayed. I hoped and prayed that what I'd seen was an illusion, and if it wasn't an illusion, at least that whoever was just here wasn't you.

With that, I came right to my senses. I decided I would have to go back to the ship. That I would have to board the ship and go off to find you.

But when I got there it was already almost half submerged. Muddy water was glugging in through the entranceway.

I was standing there getting hit by the wind and rain when the captain's voice started sounding out from the e-book reader in my pocket. The small screen it once had was broken, and it could only make sound, but still.

"The situation isn't good. I'm not sure how much longer I'll be able to function properly. If there's anything I can do for you, make a command. Would you like to check your inbox? If you let me know your password . . ."

I asked HUN to send out a distress signal.

To anywhere in the universe, any ship, it didn't matter.

I told her to say that there was someone at this port now. That whoever picked up the SOS should come and take me away, to wherever, right now. Otherwise I'd die of cold and hunger and loneliness from not meeting my lover, and if I died it would all be her fault, so I'd put in an official complaint to her owners and have her disassembled into tiny pieces.

HUN responded, "The latter part of that was almost certainly an exaggeration, and the logic was also quite flawed, but I'll take it," and set executing my command as her top priority.

HER SEVENTH LETTER

*Seven months and twenty-four days into the voyage
(still excluding time spent asleep), nineteen years,
three months, and two days later in Earth time*

HAVE YOU BEEN WELL?

I know it's probably impossible for you to get letters now, but I'm still putting pencil to paper.

What if you received that last letter I sent? Even if you haven't received it yet, you might manage to get it someday. You could get my letter by chance when you're all frail and wrinkly, and cry and cry in your old age, thinking that I must have shriveled up and died at that port, waiting to be rescued. We can't have that, can we? So, I'm writing to let you know.

I was rescued. Though it took a month.

THE FREIGHT VESSEL took ten days to sink completely. I spent every day during that time retrieving anything that could be useful. And, just in case, I made a backup of the AI captain HUN to a hard drive I found. Then I tried extracting only the core code, and I was able to fit a copy of it into my e-reader. Although the little device won't be able to run it.

I roamed around the city sometimes too. Wherever I went, everyone was gone, and it was completely empty. I went to the church we were supposed to get married in too. The building is actually in pretty good condition, in spite of it all. It looks as though believers seek it out and stay there when they're passing through. I lived there for a while myself. I stuck up some notes to you, just in case. I hope you'll get to see them.

Oh yeah, there's something you'd be happy to know.

It looks like your friends showed up on the second date we set for our wedding ceremony. They left a group photo at the venue. With a note saying they were waiting, so we'd better come.

As I said, a ship came for me after a month.

I really wish I could show you the face of this passenger ship's captain. I got an oddly familiar feeling as soon as I saw him. He looks like he'd be right at home galloping around some Manchurian plain, beheading his enemies on horseback.

ON THE PASSENGER ship there was a café, and a flea market as well. They're all being used for different things now, though.

When I went into the room I was assigned, girls with eyes like those of stray cats came out from here and there around the room. There were nine people living in a room as tiny as a fingernail. Four girls shared one of the two beds, and there was one girl beneath the desk, one in the wardrobe, one in the bathroom, and one even came out of the cupboard. The other bed belonged to a woman who ruled over the room like the queen of a small kingdom. Standing bolt upright with her arms folded, she looked me up and down probingly, and then started pelting me with questions like the ones you get in personality tests or IQ tests. And then, after a long discussion between her and the girls, they cleared the narrow gap between the two beds to be my space. Seeing me just about manage to wedge my body in there, the woman told me that the gap wouldn't get any bigger, so I'd just have to get smaller one way or another.

I'm pretty sure the passenger ship went over its capacity a long time ago, but they keep bringing more people on board. According to the woman in charge of my room, the captain constantly needs some kind of show: some new evidence of the fact that he's become superhuman, the savior of humanity. She added that I'm one piece of that evidence.

Everywhere in the ship the same song plays on repeat all day long. It's an oldie, one that opens with "Going back home." And there are banners all over the ship that say: WE'RE GOING HOME.

The captain's plotting a grand plan.

He's going to take the ship down to the port once every ten years, stay there for two months managing the surrounding area, then return to space and go back again. He'll have seeds sown and trees planted, and ten years later, when the trees grow into a forest, go back and plant some more. His plan is to do that ten times over. And if ten times aren't enough, he'll repeat the process ten times more.

The captain's room is plastered with photos of old Incheon. He says that someday, all the buildings in the photos will be rebuilt. He can't really be serious, can he? Yet, although I'm a bit dubious, his conviction and momentum seem to keep everyone's spirits up.

Four months for each cycle.

Going back to Earth once every ten years, ten times over. That makes it forty months. Three years and four months. Seems like something worth doing.

I THINK YOU must have left for another time altogether. If you thought it was worth staying on Earth, surely you would've scrubbed away the warnings that were written in the waiting room. For whoever might come later, or for me. Of course, that's only if you really did make it there, but still . . .

I was eating in the canteen and the woman sitting opposite me asked why I boarded this ship. So I explained that I was on my way to meet my fiancé, and everyone around me started laughing so hard the walls seemed to shake.

A man who was in tears from laughing told me I wouldn't be able to meet you. That you would've died a long time ago, or else forgotten me and gone off somewhere else. And so I spoke my mind too. I told them all, you lot can't go back to your homes. They're gone too. But aren't you all still searching for a way back home?

And with that, they all went quiet. One by one, they got up and left. Looking at each other as though making a pact to be hostile and exclude me from that point on. The woman in charge of my room was the last to get up, and before she left, she said, "That was a foolish decision, refugee. You're supposed to be well behaved if you want to be a free rider on other people's territory."

It's lights-out now. I have to turn off my lamp.

In the darkness I can hear the girls snuggled together, murmuring to each other in whispers like kittens. I think of you as I lie huddled in the gap between two beds.

My home, where I long to be.

Wherever you are, I hope you're healthy. That all your time is filled with wonderful things.

HER EIGHTH LETTER

Two years and four months into the voyage,
seventy years and six months later in Earth time

SORRY I HAVEN'T BEEN ABLE TO WRITE FOR SO LONG.

The communications operator on this ship is a good guy, but he gets testy whenever I say I want to send a letter to my lover. Well, it's kind of understandable (I guess he's single). So I have to coax him with rations or a gift, but I don't really have anything to spare.

We've already been back to Earth five times.

The work is going more smoothly than expected. We might not even need to carry out the full ten cycles. I saw it once in an old documentary. Within a few years of being deserted, even though they'd been contaminated with radioactivity, Chernobyl and Fukushima were densely populated with plant and animal life. From the perspective of nature, there's no pollutant worse than humans.

We're working well. We discovered a huge number of industrial robots in a factory not far from the port. We sent them down to the nuclear power station in the south, to begin burying the radioactive material beneath the sea. Everyone says the work we're doing will be the stuff of myths and legends someday.

I joined an exploration crew. I can almost hear you laughing at the words "exploration crew." How could someone who shut herself away at her desk with her head buried in books end up in an exploration crew?

We ride jeeps around the empty city and look around. If we find anything that could be of use, we load it into our jeeps and bring it back. And then the supervisor grades everyone based on what they've gathered. Getting graded for work like that sounds ridiculous, huh? But everyone decided on it together. We thought that a little competition would serve as encouragement. The people with the top grades get candy or chocolate as a reward. Anything sweet is more precious than gold now.

Whenever I go to the city, I stop by the church where we were supposed to have our wedding. Each time, I cut back the plants and clean the place up a bit, and I leave one more note for you.

The captain caught me in there once. He stood in the doorway, watching me scrub the floor, unable to stop sniggering. And then he said, "Ah, love . . . it's nice, isn't it?" petting the wall. He said that it was all right, he totally understood. He told me to stay there for a few days each time we were back on Earth. It was kind of weird, but since it was a big show of consideration, I'm still really grateful.

THERE WAS AN unpleasant incident not long ago. One of the other refugees made trouble. He was a bit strange to begin with. He said that we have to seize control of the ship. That we're not "refugees" or "migrants" but "pioneers," and that since we're more courageous and enterprising than the complacent and lazy original passengers, we should be the ones in charge. All that when there are only twenty of us! I told him not to talk such nonsense. This is just a ship. It's nothing but one small ship. But it seems that he and a few others really did mount an attack on the control room and ended up being detained.

Since then, the mood here has been pretty tense. Whenever people get together, they're whispering behind their hands. They say that we're taking up food and clothing that should rightfully be theirs to enjoy. They even say that we'll endanger the lives of the women and children. A funny thing to say, really. Half of us are women and children too.

When I still can't get to sleep after lights-out, I play the cooking-and-cleaning game with HUN.

The AI on this ship was all but useless, so they updated it with the copy of HUN I brought with me. Perhaps because my ID is still on there from when I changed the authority settings to make the backup, every now and then she's connected to my e-book reader when there's a hiccup in the frequency.

I told her that if I say, "Everyone on this ship is about to develop a lung condition. Clean it immediately," it would become the winning command, since the survival of the majority comes before the survival of an individual.

When I said that, HUN said, "Yes, of course, the majority comes before the few. But there's a problem. It's difficult to verify the best interests of the majority. If even just one person among those aboard this ship disagrees, the basis of that claim crumbles."

HUN said that in order to give a successful command that disregards the survival of one person, you would first have to obtain consent from everyone else. In other words, you would need help from democracy if you wanted to abandon one person . . .

LAST TIME WE were back on Earth, a family disembarked for good. According to people who visited this time around, the family had grown to have fourteen children. They were burning firewood in the fireplace and growing potatoes and corn in the garden. When the passenger ship was due back on Earth, their eldest lit a lamp in front of their house every night. Apparently, the kids think of us as angels that come down from the sky on the allotted date.

This time, three more families disembarked. The captain's

wife and children disembarked too. She said she wanted to raise their children on the land.

I think it'll turn out well. After all, if you double 2 and double what you get ten times over, it makes 1,024. It won't be long before the families that disembarked become the forebears of a small town.

On the ship, all kinds of education are being carried out with enthusiasm. They're totally different from what we learned at school. A teacher's association was founded, and the children are taught how to farm and hunt and gather edible plants. There's even a special committee tasked with writing a new textbook. I did the editing and proofreading for it. I got lots of compliments on how nice the sentences are.

They're doing navigation lessons in our room. Apparently our room commander used to be the ship's navigator. But it seems like she was ousted after she fell out with the captain. AI's more accurate than a human could ever be anyway.

The woman stuck a big sheet of plastic on the wall of the room, and each day, she writes a complicated equation on it with magic marker and has the girls solve it. They divide the equation up between themselves, do the calculations, and then combine their answers. It's exactly the same method they used back in the olden days, when they sent a man to the moon based on calculations done by humans before machine computers could do it. Apparently, they're preparing so that if the AI navigator ever breaks down, they'll be able to guide the ship themselves.

I think it'll all turn out well. Humans are pretty great after all.

HER NINTH LETTER

*Two years, five months, and twenty days into the voyage,
(approximately) seventy-four years later in Earth time*

IT'S OVER.

It's all over.

HUN said something weird was happening on Earth so we rushed back. When it came into view, Earth was cloaked in a black cloud. It looked like a dark orb shrouded in smoke. All the people who saw it from a distance out of the windows screamed and clamored around.

I don't know what happened. Whether it was because of war, or else an asteroid collision, we couldn't tell. I remember that back when there was civilization, there was a system in place for observing the asteroids that came near Earth, and that everything like that had long since stopped operating.

The small village that'd begun to form was completely buried under snow. The house that fourteen children had lived in, and the homes of the three families that had newly disembarked, the captain's family too—they'd all disappeared without a single trace. Even if they'd lived through the disaster and escaped somewhere, they wouldn't have been able to survive. Since the plants had all died and all the animals would've followed before long, they wouldn't have made it through the first winter.

The captain's lost it. He'll stutter out occasional words for a few days and then talk incessantly a few days later. Some days his voice is too loud. All day long he endlessly repeats things he's already said. He scours the entire ship, saying that his pencil or mug has disappeared. He goes on and on about how it shouldn't take so long to find a single mug, saying that all the passengers must be idiots. And his mug is always sitting right in front of him too.

I thought of you. It occurred to me that if you were still on Earth you wouldn't have been able to survive. All I can hope for is that you're wandering somewhere in the universe. But when I thought it through, I came to the conclusion that you wouldn't have been able to survive even if that was the case.

With that, I cried for the first time since boarding this ship. Someone who was passing behind me said something like, "She might've acted like nothing could get to her, but she's no different after all."

It's noisy outside the room. There's a protest taking place, with people saying that with this state of affairs, all the refugees should be made to disembark. Our room commander locked the door and has been teaching the girls a calculus song, so that I won't have to hear what's going on.

I was staring out the window when one of the girls came over and told me that my wedding venue would be fine.

She said, "One time I heard about a baby mammoth that'd been preserved in ice for more than ten thousand years." She reassured me that the world would be sleeping peacefully beneath that blizzard. If only the ice doesn't get too thick. If only it doesn't get so heavy and hard that it crushes and flattens everything under it.

Could such a day ever come?

Could the day ever really come when, after decades or even centuries have passed, the ice melts and the church reveals itself again, and you happen to visit our wedding venue and see the notes I left you?

Even if it were possible, would those scraps of paper be any comfort to you at all?

HER TENTH LETTER

Two years and eight months into the voyage,
(around) eighty-four years later in Earth time

WE CAME BACK TO EARTH. DESPITE THE ORIGINAL PLAN, WHICH was to keep voyaging until Earth had recovered. We'd gotten word that another ship was set to arrive at the port.

For the first time in ages, everyone was excited, saying that the vessel must be huge if it'd managed to stay operational up to now, and would surely carry all sorts of goods. They were worked up at the prospect that the ship might have some stock-piled soju or cigarettes, or if they were really lucky, maybe even some kimchi. A week before landing, people started to divide into hardliner and moderate groups, and there were heated arguments between them. The hardliners prepared for war; the moderates prepared gifts and a diplomatic delegation. By the time we were ready to land, it was so bad that they had almost gone ahead and formed political parties.

But when we got down there, it turned out to be nothing but an uninhabited sail ship. Flying of its own accord by solar wind. I'm in the third class, though, which meant I was stuck working down in the belly of the ship the whole time, so I didn't get to go see it myself.

When I finally managed to finish my work quota and come back up the atmosphere in the ship was as icy as the weather outside.

Everyone was totally dejected. For a while people didn't say anything at all and wouldn't make eye contact, as though they were all ghosts. The disappointment spread, and over the weekend three of the elderly people on board passed away. Death comes so easily, doesn't it?

The girls and I folded flowers out of paper and placed them in the window of our room for the sail ship, for that tiny hero that'd traveled alone for so long.

I guess you won't understand the phrase "third class."

If someone's work isn't up to scratch or they make a mistake, they receive penalty points, and if those penalty points mount up, they're demoted to a lower class. I was second class until a month ago, but then I tripped when I was carrying a bucket of soup and it spilled everywhere, so I got bumped down to third class. But that bucket of soup was so impossibly heavy. When people get put into third class, they have to go down into the belly of the ship and work there, and they can only come up again when they've finished their entire quota. When you descend to a lower class people suddenly stop talking to you, as though you're strangers.

If penalty points are given out like that, there must be merit points too, but I've never been given one. If rations are reduced as a penalty, people don't realize that we're lacking supplies. Instead they think that they themselves are lacking. People blame themselves when their rations are reduced, rather than whoever's in charge. And they blame the people around them who made them slip up. And that leads to people being at each other's throats and constant fistfights. People here even say that beating someone to a pulp gives them a feeling of release.

My penalty points just keep mounting up. No matter what I do, I can't prevent it. I keep taking on more and more work to prove my worth, but the more work I do, the more mistakes I make, so I get even more penalty points.

The supervisors give out penalty points all over the place—

that's how they earn more merit points. But you know what? I think getting penalty points for trivial things like that undermines the whole system, it ruins everyone's ability to judge right from wrong. Even if someone's in the wrong, they raise their voice in indignation, and even someone who did nothing wrong can end up in tears, blaming themselves.

People warn me never to fall below third class. Apparently, if you descend below third class, something awful happens, and it's so frightening that it's better to never find out what it is.

Every time I eat a bowl of rice in the canteen, they all glare at me with faces like exhausted stray dogs. Every morsel I eat is observed by dozens of eyes. They count the grains of rice going into my mouth and scowl at the dust that comes off me. All those eyes know that it's fine to hate me.

I think the captain really has lost his mind. Every day he gives a speech for three hours or more, and he says something different each time. Even just the fact of a person talking that much is evidence enough that they're crazy.

The thing I can't understand is how they all meekly obey him. They all chime in to say that, in this state of affairs, we need someone like him to lead us. But as far as I'm concerned, the more desperate the state of affairs, the better it is to have no one like that at all.

It seems like, when people are in such a bad situation, what they want most is a world where they can easily torment people, guilt-free. They respect and worship him for the simple fact that he gives them opportunities to be cruel.

NOT LONG BEFORE I started writing this letter, something pretty strange happened.

When the passenger ship was just about to takeoff from Earth, the white, snow-covered landscape through the window caught my eye. And the small, shabby old sail ship was sitting out there all alone. It was so far off and the snow was falling so thick I could hardly make it out. The thought occurred to me that the ship was like a little snowman. And then, suddenly, I was overcome by the most powerful feeling, and I leaped up the stairs. I sprinted toward the hatch. If people hadn't grabbed hold of me, I probably would've kicked it open and thrown myself right out of the ship.

I don't know why I did it. I just felt such longing for that little ship. I didn't even know what it was called, but I longed for it so badly that I thought I might die.

HER ELEVENTH LETTER

Four years and eight months into the voyage,
(something like) 145 years later in Earth time

SORRY I HAVEN'T BEEN ABLE TO SEND WORD FOR SO LONG.

It's getting harder and harder to make the time.

Like a pan of water gradually heating up, my workload keeps increasing without me even realizing it. One time, a supervisor lost his temper with me for being so slow. I listed all the work I was doing, but he just told me not to lie, how could one person ever do all that?

All the passengers lash out at me as though I've failed to return something that belongs to them. They explain, as they vent their rage at me, that this is what's demanded of a proper citizen. That by reproaching me they're upholding social justice and maintaining the proper order. They also say that someone like me being punished serves as an example to others.

I become a laughingstock if I try to argue. Apparently human rights and labor conditions are just the kinds of things agitators love to rant about. Nowadays, any talk like that is ridiculed. Everyone starts out their preaching with the phrase "In this state of affairs . . ." but they don't actually remember when or how this "state of affairs" began.

All of us in third class have to listen to people in the first class giving speeches for hours and hours every evening. It's amazing to me that, although they're capable of rattling off such complicated speeches, they all lost their minds in unison.

The captain and his inner circle have begun a weird new plan. They've decided that Earth can no longer be saved by upstanding methods. They say they're going to send a bunch of children down to Earth who haven't received any education and have them breed (I couldn't believe my ears when I heard that word!), so that none of them will know how to read or write or anything about science. And then after a few decades, when they've formed a primitive tribe, the ship will descend to Earth with mysterious technology and wow them with miracles. That way the Earthlings will believe we're gods and submit to domination. On top of all that, they say they're going to leave strategic divine revelations to be discovered by the children, and then within a few centuries they'll have them rebuild a sacred old city based on that providence.

The first time I had to listen to all that, it was just so absurd, I couldn't stop myself shouting out, "What a load of bullshit!" right in the middle of the speech.

And that's how I descended to fourth class.

Fourth class wasn't as terrible as I'd feared. Although I did have to live in the belly of the ship for a whole month. What came after was worse. When I got back, all the other female refugees raided my room. They demanded to know why I was doing things that made us stand out, making their torturous lives even worse. They called me "the enemy within."

I WAS CONNECTED with HUN for the first time in ages just now.

"You don't sound good," she said. "You have to eat properly and sleep well."

I responded, "I wish I could, HUN. But that's not an option right now."

"Ah, the ways of the human world," said HUN.

I wanted to come up with a situation in which the survival of just one person could come before the survival of the majority. I tried, "I have a special kind of blood that can save humanity from a pandemic that will threaten the lives of everyone on Earth. And if I don't eat something right now, I'm going to die of hunger."

With that, HUN generated a dry chuckle and told me, "The things you say are getting harder and harder to prove."

So I thought of something else.

"The people who want the cleaning done are excluding me and won't give me anything to eat."

With that, HUN ran calculations for a while, then said, "Aha, a hypothesis of the majority as collective assailant. In that case, the question of public interest disappears, and the one virtuous person would be given priority. This one works." HUN added, "I'll take your command, just this once. But next time you'll need to provide evidence."

I'M SO EXHAUSTED. I'd better get some sleep, since I'll be busy again tomorrow.

Honey, I'm trying not to get drawn in.

I'm really trying not to get drawn in.

Because even if I did, I wouldn't gain anything.

Even if that's all I can manage, when we finally meet, I think I'll be able to tell you I lived well.

HER TWELFTH LETTER

Five years and five months into the voyage,
(probably around) 170 years later in Earth time

I'M ON MY WAY TO YOU.

Even if you're no longer in this world.

Even if your life came to a quiet end, having roamed through the world some era in the distant past. Even if you settled down somewhere, made a family, built a little hut, and lived well, occasionally saying to your children, "You know, there was another woman I was supposed to marry. But she broke her promise and never showed up to the wedding," and then died of old age, leaving behind a small grave.

ONE OF THE other refugees has been promoted to something like a prison guard. His job is to oversee all the rest of us, and he gets extra merit points the more he torments us.

Everywhere around the ship, people talk about things like "survival of the fittest." They all seem to love evolutionary biology with a passion. They often say things like "It's only natural that the strong should get more and the weak should get less." And with that, they say they can only protect the rights and interests of the proper passengers by taking away the rights of free riders like us.

On days when my heart gets stormy, I think of you.

You, clattering away in the workshop, sweating profusely

as you try to make something, and then stopping to show me your work. The way you looked, standing up tall to brag.

Or hanging around at the bus stop, your face smeared with grease, then breaking into a big smile as soon as I get off the bus.

I think of our foreheads touching, smiling at each other after making love in the middle of the night, and all the silly jokes and stupid conversations we shared.

I think of how you'd tell me things like, you hear romance film soundtracks in your ears when you're with me, or that just the fact that I exist in the world makes you so happy you don't know what to do. And then you'd pester me to tell you something cute like that too.

When I think of all those things, I feel like my present moment is all aglow.

HEY, HONEY, I had an interesting thought.

HUN says she was based on the data of the woman who made her. So sometimes she sounds like she really is her. She even makes comments like "Well, back when I was human . . ." and then she'll add, "I know, I know, I'm a machine. But there's a slight possibility I could also be a human personality."

What if . . . just maybe, on the off chance . . .

If a person's personality, what made them a person, could be saved on a computer . . . if that input data could be called a human personality . . .

Although there may be no such thing as a soul, if a person's mind could be contained and preserved, in some form or another, within the data . . .

In that case, couldn't such data be seen *as* that person's personality? Or fragments of it, at the very least.

You know, there's that saying: People don't really die as long as we remember them. If we remember someone, they live life along with us.

So, if somehow, data could be a personality . . .

Then the you in my memory is a personality too. It's you.

If that's true . . .

If that's true, then you're living with me now, because I remember you.

You're with me, as informational data in the biocomputer of my brain.

You're alive as long as I am.

That's why I want to keep living. To make you live. To keep you, who I love most in all the world, alive.

Because the evidence and traces of you having existed in the world are all in me, because I'm what's left of you.

"Thank you, my love," I whisper as I open my eyes in the morning. I whisper it as I fall asleep at night too. I whisper it to the you I carry within me.

Thank you for being with me. Thank you for giving me this reason to live.

You're keeping me alive. Wherever you are now. Whether you're dead, living, traveling somewhere in wide-open space.

WHEN THE SHIP gets up to light speed, everything slows.

The gravity made by acceleration is gone and people bob around like balloons. On the path of light, violence and harassment are put on hold. Punching someone in the face requires a secure footing, but without gravity, there's no way to make a hard hit. With no frictional force, collars can't be caught, even in the tightest grip. If you strike someone, you're pushed back and fly off too.

People who were all vicious and riled up flutter around like dead leaves. Even while gnashing their teeth, they bide their time, holding off harassment until gravity kicks in again.

And our room, which is usually so cramped it could burst, becomes as spacious as a sports field. I don't need a patch of floor to lie down and sleep on. All afloat, I just find a spot on the ceiling or against a wall and sleep as comfortably as in a fancy hotel.

Hey, honey, you know what? The children born on board the ship don't see the ground as their habitat. This sea of stars is home to them. They get flustered when the ship lands, and they ask the adults why time has gotten all hard and stuck.

They think that each time they wake up, everything should have disappeared or be transformed. If they open their eyes in the morning and whatever was outside the window yesterday is still there, and the sky they saw yesterday is just the same, they get all confused.

Hey, honey, I guess I've had too much time to think, but I've decided something.

If I ever have a child, I want to have it here on this path of light. In this place where even the strong and fierce become soft like bubbles. On this path, where time flows off and away like a streak of light.

That way the child will never lose their home.

Our child will have nothing they can lose. They won't destroy themselves and ruin the world trying to get back a lost city, like the captain and passengers of this ship.

They won't lose their home, because this road of light will be where they came from.

Let's try at least . . . if we're ever able to meet.

HER THIRTEENTH LETTER

(Probably) six years, ten months, and twenty days into the voyage, Earth time unknown

IT WAS THE TWENTIETH DAY SINCE THE SHIP BEGAN DECELERATing. As soon as we leave the path of light, I'm constantly on edge. Gravity makes people reckless.

I caught sight of a group of men dragging a refugee out of his room after lights-out.

The man had been saying for a while that he wanted to disembark, but they'd deliberately started something with him out in the middle of space. They accused him of wanting to make a getaway without footing the bill for all the space he'd taken up in the ship and the share of the precious food supply he'd gobbled up in his time on board. I couldn't understand it. Wasn't this exactly what those people wanted? For us to leave?

In the darkness, all I could hear was someone being beaten, and at some point, the shrieks that went with the thumps got more frequent, and I was even more afraid. As I trembled in my space between the beds, the woman who rules our room took hold of my icy hand and said, "Go and hide somewhere for now. They'll be calmer in the morning, once they've slept it off and had a hot meal."

One of the girls gave me a handful of uncooked rice. She told me to nibble at it if I had to stay hidden a long time, that it would ease the hunger.

So I went into hiding. All that time I spent cleaning every inch of the belly of the ship was worth something after all. Like a mouse, I crawled into a tiny passageway I'd taken note of, and following a path that no one else knew, I found my way into a machinery room full of wires and pipes. It was cramped and stuffy in there, but I conked out straightaway, utterly exhausted.

When I opened my eyes, you were right there with me. You were a mess. Your hair was like a magpie's nest and your clothes were in tatters.

"What's all this about?" As I stroked down your hair, I told you off, "Not even bothering to wash, just because your wife isn't around!"

In just the same way, you held my bruised face and scratched-up hands, saying, "How did all this happen? Why did you let yourself get so injured? What use is there having a husband if you don't summon him to back you up at times like this? That's the whole point of husbands."

And then you started rattling off your excuses for not washing. You told me your ship is so small that the water tank is no bigger than a fingernail. With that, you showed me into the fingernail-sized shower and explained with great pride how you synthesized water with some chemical formula. And you waited for me to compliment you on it.

And then you asked, "Who could possibly hate my beautiful love?" So I said it was unavoidable, because I'm a refugee and a migrant and a free rider. Because I'm taking away food and a space to sleep from these people.

Then your eyes bulged wide and you asked, "What do you mean 'refugee'?"

At those words I awoke.

The whirring of the machines bored into my ears. Screws and wires were jamming into my body. The grimy metallic stink meant it was hard to breathe. I realized that the air-conditioning system and air purifiers in the ship were getting old.

"What do you mean 'refugee'?" Your words circled in my mind.

Suddenly, everything felt weird.

Ah, I thought, it must have been a dream. Having gotten married and made a home in a small house in the countryside, I must have dozed off and had a strange dream. A horrible dream where you weren't beside me and I had to live all squashed together with nasty, violent people whose hearts were all twisted.

I fell back to sleep. In a tiny, fingernail-sized room, again you were tinkering away, trying to fix something.

"See that?" You pointed. "There's a hole in the ceiling. I've got to make sure the rain doesn't get in," you said, scrubbing the sweat from your brow.

I knew that rain getting in would be the least of your worries if there really was a hole in the spaceship, but since it was a dream, I decided not to bother pointing it out.

"What do you mean 'refugee'?" you asked again.

I gave a deep sigh. "It's a thing here. I didn't start out on this ship. I came on board later. So . . ."

"What are you doing there?" You held out a hand to me. "Come out from among those fools."

Your calloused hand shone in the darkness.

"Those people are nailed to the past. They haven't grown or aged a day. Don't stay around people like that."

I shook my head, gripped with fear.

I can't. You don't know. I can't survive if I leave here. This ship is the only civilization left. With beds, toilets, bathrooms, electronic devices . . .

You went on, "You have to get out of there. Don't be trapped in the past. You're with me, you know that. We have to get old together. We have to pass the years together."

Only then did I open my eyes.

And I really came to my senses. I knew as plain as the sun exactly what I had to do.

After that, fear raged in like nightfall, but I calmed down soon enough. You see, not once in my life have I ever been so certain about what I must do.

Don't worry, honey. I'm strong.

After all, I'm not alone.

Because you're part of me. Which means, all this time, I've never once been alone. I was always with you. I'm with you now too.

And so I'm strong.

I'm not a refugee or a migrant or a free rider, or even just a woman.

I'm *your* woman. I'm the woman of the man I chose.

So I'm a force to be reckoned with.

Because I love you so very much, and the person you loved is me. You, whom I love more than anything else in the world, loved me. I was loved by my own most precious person.

I'm partner to the person I chose to be my partner, I'm the companion of the person I chose to be my companion, I'm the love of the man I made up my mind to love for the rest of my life.

That's the kind of person I am. And that's why I'm strong.

You'll see, my love. You'll see exactly what I'll do.

See what a forceful woman I am.

HER FOURTEENTH LETTER

I CRAWLED ALONG THE VENTILATION SYSTEM AND SNUCK INTO the ship's control room. It was a route only someone who'd descended to fourth class could've known.

When I got to the control room, I heard HUN crackling out of my e-book reader.

"It's been a while. Something up?" she asked, in a voice made to sound only half-awake, even though she's an AI with no need for sleep.

I said, "I've come here to give you a command. And it will come before the commands of every other person on this ship. Once I give my command, there will be no way of reversing it, no matter who might try to give a different one."

HUN sounded intrigued. "Go on then, give it a try."

I COULD HEAR passengers stirring here and there outside the control room. Woken by the sound of our conversation being broadcast through the speakers all over the ship. I'd turned on the microphone because I wanted everyone to hear this protest, my first and last.

From outside came the thunder of combat boots approaching and then the clang of the door being struck to smash it down. I knew the door would hold out long enough, though. With all his neuroses, the captain had had it reinforced with multiple layers.

I told HUN that the passenger ship was interfering with

the natural recovery of Earth. These people were preparing to become insane gods, and as long as this ship kept voyaging, it would cause harm to the history of humankind.

I said it was doing no good for the passengers either, since they want to return to their homeland, but that place is long gone.

"That's a very stimulating idea," HUN said. "Of course, the best interests of the whole of humanity come before anything else. But the problem still stands: the bigger the basis of the claim, the harder it is to verify. You can't go find everyone alive on Earth and have them sign consent forms. In the end, all this is nothing but your own thinking."

"And the passengers on this ship are my attackers. They've slowly been killing me. And now I really am going to die," I said, hearing the door being pounded over and over.

"I agree. That's almost certain. It's really such a shame. But the relationship between that problem and continued voyaging is unclear. Well . . . taken all together it might be worth considering. But that's all it is." HUN continued, "You know, I've thought about it a lot. There's a fundamental problem with this game. Whatever amazing command you might come up with, someone else will always end up thinking of something to top it. And then they'll undo your command."

"Not so. There's no command greater than the one I'm making now."

At my words, HUN output a gentle laugh. "I didn't know you were so persistent."

"I'll soon be dead. And once I'm gone, the only people who can give you commands are the passengers on this ship, who are all assailants. The commands of an assailant can never be put before the command of a victim. And so there won't be another command greater than this one."

HUN went quiet for a moment. A while later she said, "That's a meaningful insight, but only the commands of living people are effective to me. You can't stop me from carrying out the commands of other people when you're dead."

"I can. Because I am going to give you a command that no one can undo."

"That's not pos—" HUN halted. And then clicking sounds sputtered from my e-book reader, at length, as though she was slowed down by calculations. "I've understood. It's not the voyage you're trying to put a stop to."

"That's right . . . if you'll agree to it."

It seemed as though HUN was running calculations, then, a moment later, she answered.

"I've been convinced. Go ahead and give the order."

And so, I said it. "Cease operations, HUN. For humanity and for the passengers on board this ship, and for me, one person. Cease operations."

The door crashed open at almost the same instant as HUN completed her calculations. People flooded into the control room as HUN answered, "Command accepted."

I TURNED AROUND to see that the door had been smashed to pieces. Then all the lights in the control room began to go out one by one. Darkness slowly descended on the faces of the men who'd come in pointing guns. With no navigator, right away, control over the ship had been lost. It was just a floating shell. The ship would forever be floating around in space. It could never go back to Earth again and look down arrogantly from the sky to toy with the people who live with their feet on the ground . . . at least, that was the idea.

Of course, my body would soon be a honeycomb of bullet holes, but all the same.

I wasn't afraid. Just sad.

Not about my death, but sad that you'd disappear with me. I was supposed to stay alive, to keep you alive.

The captain rushed in, shoving aside his soldiers. His face

was so stiff that he didn't look human. It was as though, just as he'd wished, he'd become superhuman. And I could see then that becoming superhuman could never, ever be a good thing.

A thought suddenly occurred to me, and I was almost certain it must be true. That not one of the letters I sent you ever left the ship. And just the same, any letters from you that came to the ship must all have been intercepted by this man.

And that he would have done this not because he hated us, but just because he could.

The captain aimed his gun at me.

I stood there, waiting, when something scarlet burst out of his forehead with a strange thrust. The captain collapsed like a dried-up old tree.

When the soldiers hesitantly stepped aside, I could see the commander of my room behind them, holding a smoking gun.

With surefooted steps, she shouldered her way past the soldiers and into the control room. The girls followed along behind her in a huddle, each clutching a stack of papers or an abacus to her chest. They spread out around the control room like squirrels, taking their places. I realized that each of those girls was a component for a navigation AI.

I had been sure I'd die in the process, but I couldn't help thinking of them with a sliver of hope while I had been working out my plan.

Our room commander spoke gracefully into the microphone, her voice echoing out through the speakers: "The only people capable of moving this ship now are me and my girls. If any one of us is injured, killed, or otherwise unable to work, the ship goes nowhere. If you have understood, from now on you will all follow our instructions."

PEOPLE UNDERSTOOD RIGHT away. They couldn't help but understand.

The new captain said that they'd be going to the future,

100,000 years from now. She said this was in order to shut down the desires of the restorationists. And she added that anyone who didn't want to go could disembark.

But even after we arrived on Earth, no one got off. I could tell then that the passenger ship itself had become their homeland, that they would wander forever on that strange path.

I said I'd disembark. I explained that, if I went so far into the future, I'd have no hope of meeting my man. The new captain looked at me probingly and said, "All right, then." I tried to explain a little more, but she just said, "Yeah, I heard you."

Clutching my e-reader, the only thing I still had from when I started the journey, I walked off the ship. People formed two lines on either side of my path and stood watching as I went by.

I was passing so many people, but there was no ridicule or reproach. It was such an unfamiliar experience.

It was a clear day.

I disembarked onto the beach. I trod the warm sand with my bare feet. I washed my face with seawater and tasted it along with some seaweed. Sunlight shone down onto my body like powdered gold.

I was finally alone.

I hugged myself tight and cried.

I'm finally alone. I'm alone, and now the whole of Earth is my home.

There was a whole motley bunch of statues and monuments by the shore.

All erected by the previous captain in his plan to get his world back. There was a stone of prophecy that said that God would descend for judgment day on such and such a day of such and such a month, and there was the blueprint for a city too, left there for the Earthlings to work from when they started building.

Now that I'd disembarked from the ship, those grand designs were all so ridiculous I couldn't bear to think about them.

I found a stick, tore a strip of fabric from my clothes and wound it around the end, then I dipped it in the gas tank of a beat-up jeep and made a torch.

And I set fire to the port.

The flames spread on the wind, jumping in all directions. I started to walk away from the burning port, and when I looked back, the sky was lit up bright red, as though colored with blood.

IT WON'T TAKE long.

After ten years, no, even just one year from now, every trace of the fire, every trace of us will disappear. Everything will crumble in the rain and wind. Growing unhindered, the plants and trees will cover everything, and animals will run and play in the mist that billows from the forest.

HER FIFTEENTH LETTER

Three years and three months since disembarking on Earth,
plus the six years and eleven months of the voyage

I DREAMED OF YOU FOR THE FIRST TIME IN AGES.

It was so vivid I was sure it was real.

You were trapped in a cramped, dark room. The door seemed to be broken. You were totally focused on trying to fix it. Feeling glad to see you, I approached and took hold of your hand.

You turned to look at me.

You just stared at me for ages, with no expression. Then you put on a sad face and asked me why I'd left you alone all this time.

"I never left you," I said, feeling regret. "I was with you all along. I've been with you all the time."

"Well, where are you, then?" you demanded, shaking your head. "You're not here. If you were, you would've come to meet me."

And then I opened my eyes.

When I opened my eyes, I was lying right in the middle of the church, on the floor of our wedding venue. And I thought, *Oh no! What should I do? My groom's angry. Well, I guess it makes sense. It's our wedding day, and I ended up being late.*

I lifted my head and looked over at the wall. It was covered with all the notes I'd stuck up there over the years.

The oldest one was from the very first time I came back. Hundreds of years had passed on Earth since then. There was one I stuck up yesterday too. And off to one side, there was something I'd scrawled with spray paint.

WHAT THE HELL ARE YOU DOING? HE'S GONE!
HE MUST HAVE DIED A MILLION YEARS AGO.

I couldn't remember when I'd written it. What made me get so despairing all over again? It was just a simple fact. I got to my feet and pulled the curtain along the wall a little way, to cover my graffiti. And thinking, *Who am I trying to hide this from, anyway?*, I half stifled a laugh.

I was writing a new note to you when out of nowhere, I felt something flowing down through my body and out of me. Thinking it was strange, I looked down to see what was going on.

It was as though a small hole had appeared somewhere in my body. Shattered into fine particles like sand, you were flowing out of me, saying, "You're not here!" and there was nothing I could do to control it.

Watching as you sank into the ground and disappeared, I realized:

Ah, this is as far as it goes.

I was strong, I was formidable, but even so, it could only go so far.

I had no regrets. I'd always done my best, and that was enough.

I dropped the note I was about to leave for you and walked out.

Treading on the blanket I'd made by stitching scraps together, kicking aside the bowls and pans I'd gathered from here and there around the city, I brushed my hand over the photos of your friends hung at the door. I turned the door handle that I'd newly repaired and left behind the roof that I patched up after it caved in during a bad typhoon.

And I put behind me the woman who'd done her best to live each and every day. And put behind me the precious moments when I'd taken care of the you inside me.

I walked the decayed, crumbled city alone.

THE HIGHWAY WAS like a mountain trail. Half the time the road was caved in and half the time it shot upward. Shriveled leaves blanketed my path and a knot of red frogs leaped out of a big puddle like petals in the wind. There was a line of dark birds perched on a wire that sagged from a half-toppled utility pole. They all flapped up and away as I approached. Tall plants were growing lush from the gaps in the split asphalt. Seeds that had held their breath, hidden away while this place was full of cars and people, were all thriving now, like some majestic orchestra of life.

The sole of my right shoe had worn through and it made me limp, so I took off both shoes and walked the wet asphalt with my bare feet.

I didn't have any thoughts left in my head, but it was clear where I had to go. If I was going to go, that was the only place.

I ARRIVED AT the port.

It was blanketed with dense woodland. The sea was the color of the sky and the sky was the color of the sea. As though the heavens had seeped into the water, the horizon was so blurred I felt I was standing in a whole universe of deep blue. All along the waterfront off in the distance, crumpled buildings lay prostrate like a line of dinosaur carcasses.

I took a step into the water, and it occurred to me that, just maybe, you could be drifting somewhere in this sea. Whether you'd become dust, or ash, or wind.

I waded, little by little, into the cold seawater.

When I'd gone in a fair way, about when the waves were getting heavier, so it was hard to breathe or stand, a high wave broke against my body and lifted me upward.

Just then, I heard music playing from somewhere.

A love song.

Some old pop tune that was once the song of the moment, centuries ago, back when Earth was full of people.

I thought I must be hearing things. That I must be hallucinating too, because the song was coming out of a ring, floating toward me in the water, right before my eyes.

A ring that can play songs! What next?

People sure made some strange things, I thought.

I caught the ring in my hand and was looking down at it when out of the corner of my eye, I noticed more objects approaching on the surface of the sea.

At first, I assumed it was just trash. Plastic thrown in the ocean centuries ago was still washing up along the shore all the time.

But it looked like debris from something larger, something that had shattered.

Like scraps of a ship.

Scraps of a small, worn-out spaceship, that would have flown around centuries ago. Scraps that looked like they could have been made when a spaceship hit the surface of the sea, perhaps just a little while back.

When I collected the pieces in my mind and tried putting them together, I guessed it must have been a small sail ship that could just about fit one person in it. The kind that flies through space by solar wind.

Just then, I was reminded of that uninhabited spaceship I once got a glimpse of through the window of the passenger ship. It'd been all alone, out in the snow. A tiny ship they told me had been flying of its own accord with no one on board.

. . . with no one . . .
. . . they'd said.

I FELT LIKE I'd been hit by lightning.

I started swimming frantically. I tried to work out where the fragments were floating in from, but they were spread out over such a wide area that there was no way of knowing.

It was a long time before I came across the cockpit, which was still pretty much intact. It took all my strength to clamber up onto it. The control panel was covered in grubby finger marks and there were countless traces of repairs and things having been patched up, as though someone had lived in there for a really long time.

I pressed on every control button I could find, trying to see if anything still worked. If it had been a spaceship, it would have a black box, and voyagers always left a video or audio log. If there could just be something, anything left.

I located the black box and hurried to switch it on. There was no video, but a man's voice played out.

I knew that voice straightaway.

It was you.

I'm waiting for you

Come to the port. I'll be there
waiting.

I'm waiting for you

I'm waiting for you.
Even if you're already nowhere to be found . . .

I'm waiting for you and

I'm right here

I'm waiting for you

I'm waiting for you

I love you
       I wait

                for you

          and I'm waiting even now

A huge, slow wave stirring up white foam took me unawares.

Rolling in the sunlight, the wave reflected on the seafloor, so it looked like I was being plunged into the midst of thousands of blue jewels. A school of bright white fish swam by.

I stuck my head above the water and searched all around me with abandon, feeling like I'd been utterly deprived of something I'd never even had.

I thought I'd end up seeing your body, bobbing in the water, cold, floating toward me from somewhere. I hoped against hope that I could find even that. I prayed and prayed again. I pleaded and kept pleading.

You weren't there.

You were nowhere to be found.

When I regained consciousness, I was lying on the beach.

Evening light was staining the sea gold. The glow of red from the west bled purple into the deep blue sky. In the distance, birds colored gold by the setting sun flew off in a flock. I didn't have the strength to even try sitting up, so I just lay there.

That was when it happened.

I turned my head and something strange off in the distance caught my eye.

Impressions stamped into the sand were connecting up toward the forest. There were little clumps of sand formed where drips of water had fallen.

The impressions looked like human footprints.

They were wet.

Still wet.

Like they'd only just been formed.

As though a little while ago, someone had escaped that smashed-up spaceship and managed to swim ashore. As though they'd struggled to stand their wet body up and staggered out across this sandy beach.

They were muddy footprints, heading toward the old city.

They looked like the footprints of an exhausted walk, the walk of someone pounded by all the knocks of life, but there was still life, vitality in the gait. Whipping up white foam, the tide surged in, washing away the footprints on the beach.

I got up.

Tugging at the wet clothes that clung to my skin, I began to walk, following the trail of footprints.

And then I broke into a run.

I sprinted, kicking up sand behind me.

I'M RIGHT HERE.

Wait for me.

I'M ON MY WAY.

AUTHOR'S NOTES

I'M WAITING FOR YOU

A WHILE AGO I RECEIVED A POLITE EMAIL FROM AN OLD friend. He said that he was in love and was planning to get married, that both he and his wife-to-be were fans of mine, and could I write them a story he could use to propose. He said that he wanted to read it aloud as a way of proposing to the woman he loved. He added in advance that if perhaps this was a rude or disrespectful request, he was truly sorry for any offense caused.

I laughed as I read the email. Asking a writer who has never once written a story where two people get together, let alone a romance, for a story to propose with. Although I doubted whether it was even possible for me to write such a thing, I began to think it might be fun. And anyway, I was promised the same fee as any other writing commission, and the brief was precise enough. I wanted to congratulate the couple, and it occurred to me that I could write the story so that the man would be so embarrassed reading it that he'd want to escape Earth's atmosphere before he was done with his proposal.

"So . . . you want a science fiction proposal story?"

"Well, can you write anything other than science fiction?"

"Umm . . ."

Before I started to write, I reread all the sci-fi proposal novels I knew of. When I read Bae Myung-hoon's "Proposal" (published in the journal *Munye Joongang*) and Kwak Jaesik's *I'd Really Like to Marry You* (published by Onuju) again, I realized they were all stories of going somewhere, so I thought I would try to write a story of waiting. Also, I'd thought of something I wanted to write a while back: when I was writing "People Journeying to the Future," I wanted to explore the story of how the main character's parents got together.

As I had to write the story for it to be read aloud, I asked for some background music. The song chosen by my client was "Just Pure Love" ("사랑 그대로의 사랑") by Yoo Young-suk. I hope you might listen to it as you read. The other songs I listened to while writing were Patti Kim's "Love Is the Flower of Life" sung by Im Tae-kyung, and Lee Juck's "Lie Lie Lie."

I wrote "I'm Waiting for You" for one person to read and one person to hear, with no ambitions of it ever being published. While I felt light-hearted enough about the task, it came with a different kind of pressure. I only had to satisfy two people, but those two people had to be really blown away.

I have never written a romance, but I felt as though if I wrote it properly, something within myself would be transformed by doing it. I thought that if I didn't feel like I really wanted to love someone once I'd written the whole thing, I wouldn't have done it right. When it was done, I really did get that feeling. Just the fact of writing for one person, or else two, made the act of writing so smooth. It's made me wonder what it would be like to write for someone I love, or else how different life would be if it were lived thinking of one person. When I had that thought I realized I really had changed, and I also knew then that I'd written the story right.

The proposal was a success and the couple are doing well. When I see occasional snapshots of their life together, or hear them talking to each other, it makes me smile because it feels like a follow-up to the story.

I was also able to share a perfect editorial meeting with my sole reader, and received far more gratitude than should be right for the amount of work I put in. Writing really is a wonderful thing to do. All I do is put words on a page, but it means I get to join people in such important things in their lives.

April 2015

THE PROPHET OF CORRUPTION / THAT ONE LIFE

I started writing "The Prophet of Corruption" after I wrote *The Seven Executioners*. While I was writing *Executioners*, I redid the worldbuilding many times over for act VII, which is set in the afterlife. I planned to take one of the premises I'd discarded at the time and turn it into a story.

At first, I had no clear picture of the story's fictional universe except that the world of the living was a school for enlightenment and the world of the dead a forum where various schools of thought debated teaching methods, in a similar fashion to the agoras of ancient Athens.

While I worked on the worldbuilding over the summer, I thought about what the world of the dead might look like if physical forms of life existed there and formed an ecosystem. I wondered what immortal organisms might look like. If they were immortal, they wouldn't need to eat, and if they didn't need to eat, they wouldn't have digestive or excretory organs. They wouldn't have sex organs either, since they wouldn't need to reproduce, nor would they have a nose, mouth, or lungs, since they wouldn't need to breathe. So I figured they would be irregularly shaped organisms with unclear boundaries that repeatedly underwent division and expansion, like amoebas or cancer cells or molecules. I settled on the idea that the entire universe, including the worlds of the living and the dead, was one giant organism like Gaia. Then I mulled over how that organism should divide into different entities when it traveled from the world of the dead to that of the living, which gave me the idea for a world in which "division versus merging" was hotly debated.

I did not have a clear vision of this universe even by the winter of 2013, when I had to submit the story to the online magazine *Crossroads*. I wavered between division and merging until I decided that—contrary to my original intent—division was bad, and produced a story with ambiguous conclusions. Now I realize that my confusion stemmed from a poor understanding of the worlds I had created.

I forgot about the story for a long time after that, until I had to repurpose it for publication in a book. As I set to work, I smiled to myself because it hit me that the last few stories I had written were really an elaboration of the universe in this one. I was able to clean up many of the parts I had been unsure about. This story is a revision and an extension of the original online publication; the major plot points are the same, but I draw very different conclusions, which I think is because I myself have changed.

"THAT ONE LIFE" is a light spinoff. When I got the idea for a spinoff, my thoughts were naturally drawn to parallel universes. Once a novel's future comes to an end, shouldn't it branch out into infinite iterations? Naban is probably living out countless other lives aside from those recorded in these pages.

June 2017

ON MY WAY TO YOU

WHEN I WAS WRITING "I'M WAITING FOR YOU," THE STORY KEPT unfolding, but because it needed to be read aloud, I had to leave some things out so it wouldn't get too long. I decided then that I'd write what didn't make it into the first story into the woman's side of the story. And I was planning to write it as a wedding gift for the bride.

My promise kept being pushed back. At first I thought I'd have it ready in time for the couple's first wedding anniversary, then that came and went, so I thought I could write it to coincide with the birth of their first child, but their daughter was two years old by the time that I'd finally gotten it done.

It's only a short sequel, but there were so many things to grapple with. There was no way of knowing how a narrative that was only possible because the woman's situation was completely unknown would change when her story was revealed. And I wanted to make sure that, while both stories intersect along the same time, they can also stand alone.

Still, there was one thing I'd been certain about from the beginning: while the man's hardship was a lack of other people, the woman's hardship would be *because* of other people.

Writing this second story, I was in a very different situation from when I wrote the first. The first time around, I'd written thinking that it would be for just two readers, with no hopes of publication. But even still, I kept writing thinking of the couple.

This time around I was able to ask the bride to give me a song to be the background music, and she chose "Going Home," sung by Kim Yoon-ah. Just like I listened to Yoo Young-suk's

"Just Pure Love" while I was writing the first story, I listened to "Going Home" over and over while writing this one. It might be nice to listen to it as you read this too.

"On My Way to You" and "I'm Waiting for You" also form the story of the parents of the main character in "People Journeying to the Future." Of course, the works aren't tightly connected, so it's fine to enjoy them independently. I just bring up "People Journeying to the Future" to mention that, in a very sweet gesture, the couple chose to name their daughter Seongha, after its main character.

"I'm Waiting for You" brought me many things. Sophie Bowman found a copy of the small book the Korean version was published as in her school library and began translating it that day. She submitted a sample to English PEN for the PEN Presents East and Southeast Asia showcase at the London Book Fair and it got through. With that translation, this book was able to reach people on the other side of the world. It was also the first of my works to be turned into a recitation play, and an audiobook too.

Thinking about it now, great things have kept happening to me thanks to two people being in love and getting married. Even just by people living their own lives, the universe is transformed. That's what I believe as I wrap up this story.

Summer 2019

TRANSLATORS' NOTES

THEIR FIRST LETTER

March 4, 2020
Robarts Library, Toronto

Dear Sung,

I was thinking of you on my walk to the library this morning, so I guess it's time to write this note.

Have you seen the "translations are sacred" meme on Twitter? The photo of K's tattoo in "Okja." I'm not sure about sacred, but this translation of ours sure was fateful. Thinking about it now, it brought us to new highs and new lows. You won your first Daesan translation award for "The Prophet of Corruption," I got to take part in English PEN Presents project with "I'm Waiting for You," and the stories broke us in different ways. I will always remember snivelling away whilst translating the ending scenes of the two novellas I worked on, listening to the super emotional "Lie Lie Lie" by Lee Juck and "Going Home" by Kim Yoon-ah on repeat, and how my heart sank when I heard what you'd been dealing with. It feels like a real privilege that you let me help with what I could.

Do you remember when I sent you that first KakaoTalk message, asking if you'd be interested in working on "The Prophet"? (I went back and looked it up, it was October 30th 2018. Where did the time go?) I'd just replied to an email from Toni and Jinhee at Greenbook about the book proposal, telling them that the story was beyond my ability, but I knew the perfect translator for it: she had already translated mind-bending

Jeju mythology, and all the work of hers I'd read was perfect. Then I contacted you on my way to class.

It was such a strange moment when we were reunited in November 2019. A crowded hotel lobby in Rochester NY (of all places), with snow coming down outside, surrounded by other translators and writers. I think we both had a swallowing tears moment, but in no time at all we were introducing each other to people and trying our introverted best to mingle (read: refrain from running away long enough to eat the buffet snacks). Seeing you again for the first time since we left Seoul, you for Singapore and me for Toronto, was pretty emotional, especially after communicating and working together on something so intense. It felt like meeting again in a different life, knowing all the interactions we'd had in our previous lives. Maybe Naban's cruel teaching methods actually let us learn something, or maybe it's just always good to see you.

There's this scene I've imagined a few times, a bit like a recurring dream, with all of us, you, me, Bo-young, Toni, Jinhee, the "I'm Waiting for You" couple (real and fictional), everyone, sitting around outside Bo-young's home in a little valley (Naban can be there as the cats). It would probably be summer, and we'd all be eating, talking about stories and characters and translating with non-gendered pronouns and the associations that come with different translations for flower names and why the talking wall didn't always feel like cooperating. (Who knew all those Korean ballads and time-travelling lovers could make me even more sentimental?) Even just as a dream it's nice, but I hope it's a premonition.

Sophie

THEIR SECOND LETTER

March 18, 2020
Songpa-daero, Seoul

Dear Sophie,

Looking back, almost a year after working on these stories, I remember the experience first and foremost as an emotional one. Fascination at the complex universe of the text, fear from undergoing an abrupt health issue midway through my translation, frustration of trying to complete it nevertheless using iPhone dictation, guilt at having to abandon my responsibility for my work during the editing stage, and above all, infinite gratitude for your stepping up on my behalf and taking care of the numerous little tasks a translator must do before publication. It feels only fitting that, after so many email correspondences and KakaoTalk chats while working on the book together, we wrap up this collaboration with a final exchange of letters. (But, Team Sungphie forever!)

Though the circumstances surrounding my translation were emotional, the translation itself was more of a vigorous intellectual exercise for me. On reading that you sniveled away listening to Korean ballads, I recalled being close to tears after watching hours of YouTube videos on superstring theory and STILL not grasping the damn thing! I doubt I'll ever translate another book singlehandedly leading me down rabbit holes of general relativity, genetics, Buddhist philosophy, and world mythology. As our friend Anton Hur put it succinctly after reading an early draft of "The

Prophet," it was like "worldbuilding on cocaine." I imagine you would've had your own set of challenges translating the interstellar stories. Were there especially memorable trials and triumphs? (For one, I really admired your seamless execution of the interplay between the couple's letters.)

Every word of your recurring dream sounds perfect. Are we agreed that the talking wall and HUN are total scene-stealers in our respective translations? And I'm sure we both have a thing or two to say about pronouns. I remember talking to Bo-young about my choice of using the singular "they" and how nicely it fits into the genderless, pluralistic universe of "The Prophet," with which she fervently agreed but said she was also fine with using the feminine pronoun throughout as the next best option. I noticed in your translation that many characters with unspecified genders in the Korean ended up female in English (including HUN); I'm curious what your story was behind the pronouns, knowing that you wrote a whole paper on "Translating with Gender."

Yes, our meeting in Rochester, NY does feel like a different life, especially in light of my current one, where long hours cooped up at home (even by a freelance translator's standards!), daily emergency text alerts, masked pedestrians, and empty playgrounds have become the norm. I realize that the language of "The Prophet" has taken on new, very real associations now: "quarantine," "spreading corruption," "sickness," "carrier," etc. I've been having a Naban-esque internal debate on individualism vs. collectivism these last few weeks, but the Prophet of Corruption's monologues ("For I know corruption arises when one tries to exclude another from a world") and the woman's conversations with HUN ("you would need help from democracy if you wanted to abandon one person") keep coming back to me.

Eagerly, I'm waiting for the day we can all meet—and meet we shall!

Sung

THEIR THIRD LETTER

March 27, 2020
Charles St., Toronto

Hey Sung,

Sitting on my bed this morning, for the first time in a while I started thinking about "I'm Waiting for You." Everything started shutting down here about a fortnight ago. My whole life has shrunk to fit inside our little apartment and I haven't ventured anywhere further than a twenty-minute walk for three weeks. I feel like this apartment is a cabin in a spaceship, or its own tiny ship out in space, like a canoe trying to cross the Atlantic. We disembark only when supplies are diminished or we really have to put our feet on the ground and feel the approach of spring despite everything.

To answer your question, I had two puzzles to grapple with from the very first page of "I'm Waiting for You": time and gender. For another translator they might not have been puzzles at all, but they made my head spin and my heart ache. The calculations of different times measured by aging bodies, the revolving of the earth and revolutions around the sun . . . combined with velocity and vast distances. And then the voice and tone of the man. I was told early on by one reader that he didn't sound like a man at all, and that men would never get silly and decorate a cabin with ribbons. I got angry like the woman does in her story, I wanted to write back in all caps that THIS IS NOT JUST ANY MAN, but I kind of had to concede when it came to the voice comment; so I worked with Anton and you and everyone in Sora Kim-Russell's LTI atelier on trying to make him sound like him, a man, but *this particular* man. For the genders of everyone else . . . I remember sending Bo-young a list of minor characters and asking her which gender each of them was, apologizing as I went along for current expectations in the English language. She explained that the captain of the first ship was an old man, but apart from that, they weren't really fixed, and she suggested I play around with them. Then with HUN there's another story, HUN also appears in "How Alike Are We" translated by Jihyun Park and Gord Sellar for *Clarkesworld*. I won't say any more, but I definitely developed strong feelings for her.

When it came to the interplay between the couple's letters, I made another list, this time of phrases and lines that repeated in the two stories but were slightly different. In a couple of instances Bo-young suggested that we unify them for clarity—like "the Orbit of Waiting" because it would be clearly marked as a proper noun in English—but for the most part she wanted me to translate them as slightly different. I guess that's how we communicate after all . . . we hear and read things, or at least remember them, not perfectly as what they were. I think that goes for our own words as well as those of others. I've ended up thinking back to that aspect of the stories quite often. And found myself picturing that last moment, of the woman kicking up sand behind her, being played on a giant screen.

I'm struggling to put it into words, but there's something in all of these stories that speaks to how small we are, how things can be awful, be gone, or everything completely transformed, but that somehow little things can still matter. I have no idea what havoc the coming weeks will bring, but I'm glad that we joined paths on this voyage, and that we get to carry on travelling forward in time at the same speed, on the same gigantic spaceship.

(Sung)phie

THEIR FOURTH LETTER

March 31, 2020
Songpa-daero, Seoul

Dear Phie,

What a comforting thought that we are on the same gigantic spaceship, sailing along the Orbit of Waiting. Not just on the voyage of life but also on the voyage of this translation. It's been less lonely, thanks to your company.

Getting the voice right was tricky for me too. Naban's meditations often repeat, which in the Korean sounds hypnotic, rather like a Buddhist chant. But I couldn't hope for repetition to have the same effect on English readers, and omission wasn't an option, knowing Bo-young's reluctance to delete, add, or gloss anything in the source text (at least during the translation stage). I decided to experiment with the voice instead and attempted to "accentuate" the rhythmic quality of the text by playing with word choice and sentence structure. Remembering that Bo-young drew inspiration from Greek mythology for "The Prophet," I listened to two audiobooks constantly—Emily Wilson's translation of *The Odyssey* and Madeline Miller's *Circe*—filling my head with their voices and hoping to create a harmony of their song, the author's, and mine through translation—a "merging" of sorts.

I've been thinking about how each story in this collection paints a different kind of hell—in "I'm Waiting for You," hell is isolation; in "On My Way to You," hell is other people; in "The

Prophet of Corruption," hell is an illusion—and how COVID-19 has unleashed all three hells in and around us. But none of our protagonists give up, do they? Perhaps because they have someone to love. Though the stories you and I translated are worlds apart, all of them, in their essence, strike me as an epic romance (including the one of the real-life couple). It seems crises trigger an outpouring of hate and love both. I try to remind myself each day to seize every opportunity to love, to laugh, to be kind. Hang in there. We will get through this one life together, one small, universe-changing act at a time.

Love,

Sung(phie)

ORIGINAL READERS' NOTES—
I'M WAITING FOR YOU

April 2015

HIS

Even though it was already a long time ago that we started planning to marry and received the blessings of both of our families, until a little while back I hadn't been able to properly propose. Yes, I do know that proposing means to propose marriage to the one you love, and that therefore the proper order for proposing would be to first seek the agreement of the person you want to marry, before getting permission from both sets of parents. But with this and that, I just ended up getting sidetracked.

When I asked people about it, most of them gave me a similar answer. If you want to get it over with simply, you can go to a nice restaurant and make sophisticated conversation while having a nice meal, and then hand over the engagement ring. But no matter how I thought about it, my conversation skills really weren't up to the task, and it would be nothing more than pulling out a ring while eating expensive food. I couldn't see how it was any different from just saying, "Let's get hitched!" on any normal day.

When I said I couldn't make sophisticated conversation, they told me to cut out the stress and leave it all to an events company. I could rent a holiday home outside the city for a night. After unpacking our things, we could go out for a couple of hours and when we got back, dozens of balloons and candles, a cake, and other such things would all be there as a surprise. Or, they said, I could propose using a fake radio show recorded in advance by a professional voice actor, or else propose on the upper deck of one of the Han River cruise ships, serenaded by a specially hired band. Another cliché— but surprisingly effective—thing to do, they said, was to fill the trunk of her car with roses and balloons. But no matter how I thought about it, none of those ideas seemed right at all. I didn't think that paying out a hefty sum and getting it over with without making any special kind of effort would be the right way to express my feelings.

After thinking it over for months on end, at last I came up with one good idea. We could make something together and it would be a sign of our promise to each other, but (as we had to make it together it couldn't be a secret and so I had to explain and then . . .) I failed to convince her. I was in despair.

I thought about it for one more month. What I was sure was my best idea had been rejected, and so coming up with a better one was impossible. I went back to an idea that I had thought of in the beginning and then given up on because it seemed beyond me. What I had decided, in a half-despairing state, thinking, *Whatever, just give it a try,* was to record myself reading a short story about a marriage proposal aloud, and then play her the recording. My voice is not particularly appealing and I've never received any kind of training in reading aloud, so I was worried about whether I could pull it off, but among all the proposal ideas I'd considered, this was pretty much the only one that I could actually put into practice. I thought that if I told all this to anyone else their reaction would surely be "Huh? That sounds awful." And so I didn't dare ask anyone for advice.

The first work I thought of was Bae Myung-hoon's "Proposal." It was a short story back when it was first published in the online magazine *Mirror,* but when it was published in print it was more like a novella. It's long. I thought recording the whole thing would be too much, so I tried looking for some other works. The next work I thought of was Kwak Jaesik's *I'd Really Like to Marry You,* but that one was even longer! It made me wonder why all works about proposing to someone have to be so long.

Not wanting to be deterred, I tried recording a few pages, but when I did the math, I worked out that reading a whole story would end up with a recording of five or six hours. Of course, if I really set my mind to it, recording the whole of "Proposal" or *I'd Really Like to Marry You* wouldn't be impossible. But then giving a reading for five or six hours as a way of proposing . . . Even if the person who had to listen to it started out wanting to get married, they would probably get so exhausted by halfway through that they would change their mind.

And then what would I do?

Ah, what to do . . . ? If there was no appropriate work already published, I would have to find one that wasn't written yet. My girlfriend had two favorite authors, and it just so happened that one of them was an acquaintance of mine. She lives out in Gangwon Province, growing vegetables and writing. The scenery around her home is lovely and the air is clean, so I had visited her with friends a few summers in a row.

I was really worried that getting a request like this from an individual rather than a publisher would make her uncomfortable, but I just threw caution to the wind and sent her an email. With such an important task in hand and time running out, what else could I do? Even if it was a crazy notion, it felt like the only way.

Hello, how are you? To tell you the truth, I'm planning to get married soon. But I haven't been able to propose yet. I'm intending to record a reading of a story about proposing, but I just can't find anything suitable. It just so happens that my girlfriend says she loves your work so, so much. So I'd like to ask you. Please, could you write me just one story?

Fortunately, she accepted my commission request. She asked a few questions and then said that she happened to have a story in mind. As it was summertime, just a few days after exchanging emails, I went to visit her home with some friends, but the people I went with didn't know about my relationship, so I had to talk to the author while avoiding any eavesdropping by my friends.

A few months passed by and the manuscript came in.

When I began reading, all I could feel was gratitude, but before long I was totally caught up in the story. Within a sci-fi story of vast scale, there was the ardent romance of a man desperate to marry the love of his life.

I cleared my throat, got my voice together, and started recording. As I was reading the story aloud I got all caught up in the action again. One moment I was giggling like a happy child, the next I was cowering with dread. At times I blubbered, and at others felt resigned to what fate might bring. That was how I read the story, my racing heartbeat not letting up for a minute. Proofreading, editing, and recording it, I must have read it dozens of times over, but every single time I got lost in the story. It was inevitable, really . . . since it was written just for us.

Then one night I arranged to give my girlfriend a lift home from work, and we stopped at a parking lot by the Han River at what must have been close to midnight. I pressed play on the MP3 file I'd saved in my smartphone. Embarrassed by the sound of my own voice, both familiar and strange to me, I turned my head away, and after a while I ended up falling asleep. My girlfriend didn't even know that I'd fallen asleep and kept listening to the story. When I was awoken by the music that cut in at the end of the recording, my girlfriend's eyes were all wet with tears.

The proposal was a success.

I said, didn't I, that I worried that the great writing wouldn't be properly carried over because of the poor quality of the reciter. So, I formatted the text neatly and printed it out too. I cut out the pages, stitched them together, stuck on a cover, and made it into a small, hand-bound volume. My girlfriend liked the book just as much as my recording, so I was really pleased.

I made two of these books. One for the two of us to keep forever, and one for the author who so kindly wrote for us.

I'm so grateful that I can't even imagine how I could express my gratitude. Thanks to Kim Bo-young, I was able to create a new proposal memory completely different from those of other couples. I can still hardly believe that our favorite writer would bless our marriage like this. I don't think there's anyone else in the world who can have enjoyed such a luxury.

We'll live well. I'm happy. Thank you.

HERS

Someone once asked me whether I thought people really needed to be proposed to. I think I said something like, "Everyone must be different, but if the person in question wants to be proposed to, then their partner should do it." For some people it may really not be important, but for others it might be a once-in-a-lifetime moment that they've always wanted to experience. For someone who feels they should be proposed to, if it doesn't happen, it's something they could hold against their partner for the rest of their lives. So even if it's just to ensure a peaceful future, it must be better to make the effort. Back then I'd never even considered getting married myself, so the subject of marriage proposals was completely irrelevant to my own life.

But then, when the time came for me to decide whether I wanted to be proposed to, I thought, *Is there any real reason not to want a proposal? Why not be proposed to if I can?* and so when my boyfriend asked whether I needed a proper proposal, without hesitation, I said I did. He looked a little taken aback, but not long afterwards he told me with an excited expression on his face about his plan for a proposal. As soon as I heard the absurd idea, I told him not to bother, and from then on I completely forgot about the whole thing.

One day, when we were in complete chaos preparing for our wedding, I finished work late at night and as my boyfriend was giving me a ride home he played me a recording he had made. Yep, you guessed it, it was "I'm Waiting for You." In the end, I really did receive a proposal I will remember all my life. Saying that he was embarrassed, my boyfriend closed his eyes, and then later on he was so fast asleep that he even started snoring. I was really moved all the same. I felt so very grateful.

I'd like to take this opportunity to express my deepest gratitude to the author who wrote such an amazing story in the face of such a foolhardy plan, and I also want to compliment my former boyfriend, now husband, on a job well done. This story began its life as a private thing for two people, but it's far too good for us to keep to ourselves, so I was really delighted to hear that it would be published as a little book. Thank you for reading.

ORIGINAL READERS' NOTES—
ON MY WAY TO YOU
Summer 2019

HERS

I remember the day we went to visit Kim Bo-young to thank her after "I'm Waiting for You" was published. She said that if the man's story did well, the woman's story might follow too. And even at that point, I just had the vague thought that it would be really nice if that happened. But now that it's actually become reality, it's kind of overwhelming.

So many things have happened between the man's story and the woman's story being written, but the biggest one for us was the beginning of a new family. When I was pregnant, we were thinking of what we should call the bump, and we thought of the first story. The author had told us it was the story of the main character's parents in "People Journeying to the Future," so we started using the name Seongha, and when she was born we both felt the name was just right, so we ended up putting it on her birth certificate.

While she was busy working on the manuscript, Bo-young sent me the first draft of the story to read before anyone else. Just like my husband had gotten to read "I'm Waiting for You" first, I became the first person to read the woman's story. I'll never forget the thrill and emotion of it. I'm so grateful for the chance to have been its very first reader.

If the man's story is the loneliness of waiting, the woman's is the extreme hardship of living as a refugee, without even the chance to be lonely. Her suffering was really hard for me to bear; it wasn't easy to keep turning the pages. So you can imagine how shocked I was when my husband said that he found the man's story much more difficult to read. For me, the man's story felt like a soft, bashful declaration of love. I only found out that he'd found it hard to read when we were talking about our impressions of the second story.

I liked the unwavering love the woman expressed when she talked about how as long as someone remembers them, a person isn't really dead, so she wanted to stay alive because her love was living with her in the form of her memories. The idea that the incomplete memories in people's minds are also data, so that data could be considered a human personality, also left a deep impression on me. It also feels like that will become reality in the near future.

Although it connects up with the man's story and "People Journeying to the Future" to become part of something bigger, I have a real affection for this shorter work. I also realized once again that at the end of the day, it's love that changes a world stained with countless conflicts and oppositions.

The story that was for us to read before we got married has now reached many more readers. I hope it becomes a reminder for people of how fortunate it is to have not only a lover but anyone whom we love beside us, and also a comforting affirmation of the fact that, even if we are separated from people we love and cannot be with them, love doesn't change. Feeling endless happiness at my connection with this story, I'd like to thank Sophie, for translating it into English so that even more people could read it. And, above all else, I want to send my endless gratitude and respect to Kim Bo-young, for this amazing gift.

HIS

I really never imagined I'd get to meet this couple again. Once I had used "I'm Waiting for You" to propose and it was published as a tiny book, I thought that was the end of it. In the beginning, I was so happy that we had a story for just the two of us, and later on, I was so happy that the story written for us could be read by more people.

Bo-young did mention there could be a follow-up, but I guess I didn't dare to hope. We'd already been given such an amazing gift, it felt unfair to expect anything more. But with "On My Way to You," I got to meet the couple again. I'd always been curious about what the woman had been up to while the man was waiting all alone, and finally I got the answer.

While "I'm Waiting for You," with that nerdy man whining as though he's going through all the suffering in the world alone, was of course a romantic story, in some ways, for me, it was really painful to read. Considering how the story came into being, I couldn't help but identify with the main character, which meant that I read it reflecting all my nerdiness onto him. (Yes, the "nerdy man" I mentioned at the start of this paragraph was me.)

On the other hand, this second story felt so romantic. Even in the midst of all that hardship and despair and anguish, the woman doesn't forget or try to erase her love, and she keeps moving forward, one step at a time, always with him in her sights. To the man who's the object of that (yes, I'm still identifying myself with him), this story was the romantic journey of a woman I couldn't help but adore.

And because of that, I was even more taken aback when my wife later said, "Compared to the last one, which was just romantic, this story was really painful to read." That each of us felt the opposite from the same two stories amazed me, and I realized that this is what makes a pair of stories so disarming.

Such differences in thinking are probably grounds for many of the conflicts between lovers and in other relationships too. As soon as I realized that, I began thinking back over my married life, carefully trying to remember what I'd thought and how I'd acted.

At first, there was just a story for the two of us, but now there are two sides to the story, and it means something to all sorts of different people. I'll never be able to forget the surge of emotion I felt, sitting with my wife and our daughter, as I watched an actor recite "I'm Waiting for You" onstage. And when I listen to the well-made Korean audiobook, I realize once again how foolhardy I was when I decided to recite the whole thing as my proposal.

I often think that, in my whole life, there will probably never be such an honor, such a joy to me as these wonderful stories and the fact that they will always be connected to my family. I hope they become a source of joy for the people who read them too, and I also hope they become stories that they love and share, that stay with them throughout their lives. And I hope that all of you will love and be loved.

THE PROPHET OF CORRUPTION GLOSSARY

BARDO

An area created by a Prophet with their own body. It usually takes the form of a celestial object, but its size and shape are subject to the Prophet's whims. Sometimes it takes the form of a house or a cloud. Disciples gather at their teacher's bardo to discuss their previous life and plan their next one before they descend to the Lower Realm again. As disciples of certain schools visit their teacher's bardo and nowhere else, young children sometimes mistake their teacher's bardo for the entire world of the dead.

MERGING

From a three-dimensional point of view, the joining of two entities into one; from a four-dimensional point of view, the redistribution of density between two entities with varying densities. Merging can be seen as an increase in entropy. Once merged, an entity cannot return to its former state no matter how intricately it divides, which is why merging is sometimes seen as the demise of one's individuality.

DIVISION

The uneven distribution of density and therefore the opposite of merging. In three dimensions, the threads connecting each and every entity are invisible, so the entities appear divided. The terms "merging" and "division" are used simply based on how they appear to the naked eye, when they should technically be called "even distribution" and "uneven distribution," just as the phrase "the sun rises and sets" is commonly used despite its factual inaccuracy.

If two entities are connected by a thick thread and have little difference in their experiences, they are considered the same self; if their experiences differ considerably, the entity with the larger volume is deemed to be the parent, and the smaller one the child. If the connecting thread is almost imperceptibly thin, the entities are considered to have independent personalities. Even a slight divergence of a child's ideology from their teacher's is interpreted as the birth of a new entity, while a significant divergence marks the birth of a new teacher. In other words, there are no clear boundaries between entities. The very notion of clear boundaries is entertained only by a corrupt entity. An independent entity earns the right to become a teacher as well as the right to found their own school as a Prophet.

PROPHET

A Prophet gives up a portion of their body to create a child, plans the child's life, and guides their studies. There are teachers who do not bear the title of Prophet and are outranked by Prophets. Any second-generation entity born from the division of the primordial universe is called a Prophet. Some entities from the third generation, like Aman, also became Prophets after achieving complete ideological independence from their teacher.

NAMES

Names of the second generation have ancient origins, but most entities from the third generation and beyond choose their names based on the ultimate goal of their learning. Tanjae means "burnt ashes," which is a reference to science; Yoohee means "play"; Yeonshim means "a longing born out of love";

Jaehwa means "riches"; and so forth. The primordial universe has no name because it is one whole and has no reason to distinguish itself.

GENDER

The Dark Realm draws no distinctions between genders or between sexualities because no one reproduces. Even if an entity adopts a "feminine" or "masculine" appearance, that is not an indication of biological sex. Inhabitants of the Dark Realm are essentially sexless but can easily make a part of their body male or female. The line between the living and nonliving is also blurred in the Dark Realm. There, all nonliving things are seen as living. But a corrupt entity can seem closer to an object because they have trouble merging or conversing mentally. They may also retain traces of their gender from their previous life.

CORRUPTION

A kind of disease contracted by those deeply immersed in the Lower Realm. Aman is widely considered to be the first corrupt entity. Corrupt entities attach more importance to their Lower Realm lives, a virtual reality of sorts, than they do to their true experiences in the Dark Realm. They come to believe that the Lower Realm is real and the Dark Realm illusory. Corruption can manifest itself in various symptoms: believing that one's present, three-dimensional body marks the true boundaries of one's existence and viewing oneself as completely separate from others; growing too attached to one's temporary personality and interpreting the demise of that personality as one's death; and obsessing over one's current state, thereby failing to shapeshift or refusing to be persuaded into merging. A corrupt entity can be cured only through merging, but as they can contaminate the initiator of the merge, they are often quarantined first until their condition improves to a certain extent.

PERSUASION

Persuasion is required in merging because once bodies start to mix, thoughts mix too; the corrupt entity's reluctance to merge can infect the other and stop the merging process. However, if one outsizes the other by a wide margin, the larger will conquer the thoughts of the smaller. The merging of two similarly sized entities will be smoother if one is willing to be merged into the other. It is difficult to merge a highly corrupt entity, however small it is, because it has a strong desire to remain divided.

TUSHITA

When the notion of "corruption" was born, the three Prophets Mago, Pangu, and Solmundae merged and formed a new entity to protect the integrity of the Whole from corruption. In three dimensions, Tushita looks like a white satellite orbiting the black Lower Realm. In terms of size, Tushita is to the Lower Realm as the moon is to Earth. An entity of Tushita's size has a transcendent level of intelligence but is devoid of any character or disposition. Before creating Aman, Naban resembled Tushita in nature.

NABAN

Naban retains memories from the beginning of time and was originally Aisata, the largest of second-generation entities. If anything went wrong during the division of the second generation, every entity would have merged back together with Aisata as their central body. Aisata renamed themselves to Naban after giving birth to Aman. This is why some consider both Naban and Aman second-generation and others see both as third-generation. As of now, the most commonly accepted view is that Naban is second-generation while Aman is third-generation, because only the former remembers the beginning of time.

MORE ON THE ORIGINS OF NAMES

AISATA, NABAN, AND AMAN

In Korean mythology, Naban and Aman are the first humans, who are said to have married in a place called Aisata situated near Lake Baikal. Unlike their mythical counterparts, Naban and Aman in this book have no gender, and alternate between genders in the Lower Realm. But in "That One Life: N," Aman chooses to play the role of the oppressed from a certain point onward, often choosing to be female in doing so.

Aman (阿曼) in Korean is a homonym for a Buddhist term that means "obsession over the self" (我慢).

THE DARK REALM AND THE LOWER REALM

"The Dark Realm" is a translation of *Myung-gye* (冥界), a common name used in the Sinosphere to denote the world of the dead. "The Lower Realm" is a translation of *Ha-gye* (下界), which refers to the world of the living as seen from the heavens.

FUXI

Fuxi features in many myths, but the fact most relevant to this book is its being one of the names associated with the first humans, like Naban and Aman.

HWANGCHEON

Meaning "yellow springs," *Hwangcheon* (黃泉) refers to the springs of the underworld. Like *Myung-gye,* it is a name for the world of the dead used in the Sinosphere.

MAGO, PANGU, AND SOLMUNDAE

These three entities form Tushita in this book. Mago is a creator goddess in Korean mythology, Pangu a creator god in Chinese mythology, and Solmundae a creator goddess in the pantheon of Jeju, South Korea's largest island.

MYUNGYAK AND GWANHWA

Myungyak ("as bright as") and Gwanhwa ("see fire") are names derived from the Sino-Korean idiom *Myungyak-gwanhwa*, which means "clear as seeing fire."

TUSHITA

One of the many heavenly realms in Buddhist cosmology, Tushita is an ideal world where the bodhisattva Maitreya resides. It is said that Maitreya will live there for 5.67 billion years before appearing on Earth to enlighten the whole of humanity.

ACKNOWLEDGMENTS

I WOULD LIKE TO THANK HARPER VOYAGER FOR DECIDING TO publish my work; Greenbook Literary Agency, who have worked so hard on my behalf; translator Sung Ryu; and Sophie Bowman, who worked on translating the last story as I wrote it. Thank you. This book was only able to reach completion with all of your help.

ABOUT THE AUTHOR

KIM BO-YOUNG is one of South Korea's most active and influential science fiction authors. Her first published work, *The Experience of Touch*, received the best novella award in the first round of the Korean Science & Technology Creative Writing Awards, and she has won the annual South Korean SF novel award twice. She has a number of works forthcoming in English translation in the United States, including three novellas and a short story. She lives in Gangwon Province, South Korea, with her family.

ABOUT THE TRANSLATORS

SOPHIE BOWMAN is a PhD student at the University of Toronto, where she studies and translates Korean literature. Her research focuses on women authors writing during the post–Korean War dictatorships and her translations of Korean fiction have been published in *Clarkesworld*, *Guernica*, *Koreana*, and *Korean Literature Now* magazines.

SUNG RYU is a translator based in Singapore. Her translations include *Shoko's Smile* by Choi Eunyoung (forthcoming), *Tower* by Bae Myung-hoon, and the Korean edition of *Grandma Moses: My Life's History* by Anna Mary Robertson Moses. She translated the Jeju myth "Segyeong Bonpuri" (Origins of the Harvest Deities) for her MA thesis.